PATCHWORK

Society

The Bread and Roses Series

Matrons and Madams
Patchwork Society

The Bread and Roses Series

PATCHWORK
Society

Sharon Johnston

DUNDURN
TORONTO

Publisher: Scott Fraser | Editor: Michael Carroll
Cover designer: Laura Boyle
Cover image: Otto Wilhelm Thome, 1885
Printer: Marquis Book Printing Inc.

Library and Archives Canada Cataloguing in Publication

Title: Patchwork society / Sharon Johnston.
Names: Johnston, Sharon, 1943- author.
Description: Series statement: The bread and roses series
Identifiers: Canadiana (print) 20190231084 | Canadiana (ebook) 20190231092 | ISBN 9781459737051 (softcover) | ISBN 9781459737068 (PDF) | ISBN 9781459737075 (EPUB)
Classification: LCC PS8619.O4875 P38 2020 | DDC C813/.6—dc23

We acknowledge the support of the Canada Council for the Arts and the Ontario Arts Council for our publishing program. We also acknowledge the financial support of the Government of Ontario, through the Ontario Book Publishing Tax Credit and Ontario Creates, and the Government of Canada.

Care has been taken to trace the ownership of copyright material used in this book. The author and the publisher welcome any information enabling them to rectify any references or credits in subsequent editions.

The publisher is not responsible for websites or their content unless they are owned by the publisher.

Printed and bound in Canada.

VISIT US AT

 dundurn.com | @dundurnpress | dundurnpress | dundurnpress

Dundurn
3 Church Street, Suite 500
Toronto, Ontario, Canada
M5E 1M2

To my five daughters, who have worked for a stronger society through justice, equality of opportunity, healthcare, environmental protection, and inclusive education throughout their professional lives.

AUTHOR'S NOTE

I grew up in Sault Ste. Marie in Northern Ontario. The Soo, as its citizens call it, is situated on the St. Marys River, which separates two countries and connects Lake Superior with Lake Huron. Bordering on the Canadian Shield, the area has spectacular geography. It is surrounded by many Indigenous reserves of the Ojibwa and Cree Nations. In the 1930s and 1940s, well-educated professionals from Southern Ontario moved to the Soo for the adventurous lifestyle, while entrepreneurs arrived to tap the natural resources. Italians seeking a better life for their families settled near the industries that employed them. Seventy-five Indigenous children lived in a rundown residential school that had been condemned by the fire department for more than a decade. *Patchwork Society* describes the intersecting lives of these disparate groups.

In this complex social mix, my grandmother, a British-trained nurse, began working as the head nurse of the residential school. I discovered what she did while researching this novel. As an honorary witness at Canada's Truth and Reconciliation Commission, I found this knowledge unsettling. I adored my grandmother.

I remember many happy occasions with Indigenous children. I never asked if they missed their parents or their community. The history I recount in *Patchwork Society* is taken from many government, medical, and public documents. Personal interviews of those still alive were a treasure trove of information, and I have drawn on my own experiences.

When I was growing up, the Soo was a cosmopolitan place with rich and poor, Indigenous people and white people, living in the same space. The values I learned from the people and situations of my childhood were what allowed me to just be myself, despite living an extraordinary life as the wife of a governor general. The nicest thing any of the thousands of visitors could say when they came to the grand official residence of Rideau Hall was "You're just like us."

CAST OF CHARACTERS

DURLING, BARNABY, AND DONNELLY FAMILIES

Clara Ives Durling: Nurse-matron at Shingwauk School in Sault Ste. Marie (the Soo), Ontario, and former superintendent at the Galt Hospital in Lethbridge, Alberta.

William "Billy" Durling: Clara's late son.

George Durling: Clara's late husband and Ivy's father.

Ivy Durling Donnelly: Daughter of Clara and George Durling.

Red Donnelly: Ivy's husband and son of Ellen and Ed Donnelly.

Alice Donnelly: Ivy's daughter.

Nora Donnelly: Ivy's daughter.

Lily Barnaby: Clara's niece.

Edward Parsons, Sr.: Lily's first husband.

James Barnaby (called just Barnaby): Lily's second husband.

Edward "Teddy" Parsons, Jr.: Lily's son with her first husband, Edward Parsons, Sr.

Jane Barnaby: Lily's daughter with her second husband, James Barnaby.

Amelia Ives White: Lily's mother and Clara's sister.

Robert White: Lily's father.

Beth White: Lily's sister.

Ed Donnelly: President of I.J. Donnelly and Sons (later Donnelly Building Materials).

Ellen Donnelly: Wife of Ed Donnelly.

Jean Donnelly Nesbitt: Daughter of Ed and Ellen Donnelly.

Rupert Nesbitt: Fiancé and later husband of Jean Donnelly Nesbitt.

Jack Donnelly: Son of Ed and Ellen Donnelly.

Ian Donnelly: Son of Ed and Ellen Donnelly.

I.J. Donnelly: Father of Ed Donnelly and founder of I.J. Donnelly and Sons.

Geordie Plaxon: Brother of Ellen Donnelly.

Annabel Nurser: Young woman onboard Clara's ship from England to Canada.

Florence Nurser Sampson: Annabel's daughter.

Mary Sampson: Florence's adoptive mother.

Percy Sampson: Florence's adoptive father.

SHINGWAUK SCHOOL STUDENTS

Lila Martin

William Martin: Lila's brother.

Abe Martin: Lila's brother.

Albert Martin: Lila's grandfather.

Doris Canoe

Aka Round Stone

Jimmy Sagebrush

Denis Plain

Ada Kusugak: Inuit student at Shingwauk and later Clara Durling's live-in helper.

Dudley Shilling: Shingwauk student who drowned.

Nellie Big Smoke

Chief Big Smoke: Nellie's father.

Mrs. Big Smoke: Nellie's mother.

Tina Courtney

Bobby Courtney: Tina's brother.

Little Feather: Tina's daughter.

SHINGWAUK SCHOOL STAFF

Reverend Charles Hives: Headmaster.

Jean Hives: Reverend Hives's wife.

Violette Dumont: Native girl living with the Hiveses.

Dr. Andrew McCaig: Medical officer of health for Northern Ontario and Shingwauk doctor.

Veera Aalto: Laundress.

Noel Thomas: Farm manager.

Beatrice Crossly: Custodian in charge of the senior girls' dormitory.

Agnes Boniface: Teacher.

Kay Loucks: Teacher.

Mable Morrison: Custodian in charge of the junior boys' dormitory.

DURLING, BARNABY, AND DONNELLY FAMILIES' FRIENDS

Sergeant Robert Stuart: Clara's RCMP friend from Lethbridge, now living in the Soo.

Etta Iverson: Clara and Ivy's friend in Lethbridge.

Katherine Iverson: Etta's daughter and friend of Ivy.

Alistair Harwood: Clara's late friend and former mayor of Lethbridge.

Maggie Stone: Clara's real-estate agent in the Soo.

Sal D'Agostina: Italian friend of Lily in the Soo.

Gino D'Agostina: Sal's late husband.

Dominic D'Agostina: Sal's son.

Irma D'Agostina: Sal's daughter.

Julio Valenti: Sal's defence attorney.

K.G. Rossiter: Clara's Hilltop neighbour in the Soo.

Jessie Rossiter: Wife of K.G. Rossiter.

Anne Rossiter Blake: Daughter of K.G. and Jessie Rossiter.

Tom Blake: Anne's husband.

Daniel Blake: Anne's son.

Arnold Clement: Financial officer for Algoma Steel.

Jocelyn Clement: Wife of Arnold Clement.

James Francis: Head of St. Marys Pulp and Paper Mill in the Soo.

Dorothy Francis: Wife of James Francis.

Roberta McCarthy: Clara's bridge partner at the Rossiters'.

Louis Derrer: Senior engineer at Algoma Steel.

Kathryn Derrer: Wife of Louis Derrer.

Harry Derrer: Son of Louis and Kathryn Derrer.

Audrey Derrer: Daughter of Louis and Kathryn Derrer.

Harriet Burns: Derrers' cottage neighbour on Gawas Bay.

James Crowder: Owner of *Sault Star* newspaper.

Adam Crowder: Son of James Crowder and editor of the *Sault Star*.

Phyllis Crowder: Wife of Adam Crowder.

Grant Howland: Radio broadcaster in the Soo.

Eileen Howland: Wife of Grant Howland.

Beau Greensted: Friend of Red Donnelly.

Betty Kingston Greensted: Wife of Beau Greensted.

Temple Kingston: Brother of Betty Greensted.

George Frederick Kingston: Father of Betty Greensted and dean of the University of Toronto's Trinity College.

Jeff Wilkes: Friend of Red Donnelly.

Ruth Cohen Wilkes: Wife of Jeff Wilkes.

Nancy Stratichuk: Secretary and mistress of Red Donnelly.

Dr. Chas Greer: Friend of Red and Ivy Donnelly.

Dot Walker Greer: Wife of Dr. Chas Greer.

D.T. Walker: Father of Dot Walker and Soo school inspector.

Dave Brewster: CEO of Algoma Steel.

Patsy Brewster: Wife of Dave Brewster.

Carl Grey: Owner of the Tea and Talk Café in the Soo.

Mildred Grey: Wife of Carl Grey.

Marc Russo: Fellow social worker and friend of Ivy.

Dan MacIntyre: Artist, First World War veteran, and friend of Clara.

Gerda MacIntyre: Wife of Dan MacIntyre.

Dr. Francis Newbury: Late friend of Clara and former doctor at the Galt Hospital in Lethbridge.

Max Laird: Friend of Red Donnelly.

ROYAL VICTORIA HOSPITAL (RVH) AND MONTREAL CHARACTERS

Cecily "Sass" Mitchell: Ivy's friend at Royal Victoria Hospital (RVH) in Montreal.

Robert Mason: Cecily "Sass" Mitchell's fiancé and later husband.

Pamela Hobbs: Director of nurses at RVH.

Marta Pelletier: Mailroom manager at RVH.

Monique Seguin: Patient at RVH.

Dr. Pierre Lavoie: Doctor at RVH.

Deirdre MacKay: Patient at RVH.

Hugh Carsley: Montreal friend of Ivy.

MISCELLANEOUS CHARACTERS

Gordon Sims: Department of Indian Affairs agent in Soo area.

Dan Roswell: Chief of police in the Soo.

Bob Glimp: American union organizer in Lethbridge.

Sam McClintock: Clara's real-estate agent in Lethbridge.

Percy Paris: Dean of St. Luke's Anglican Church in the Soo.

Francis Clergue: American founder of Algoma Steel.

James Scutter: American businessman.

Philemon Riel: Lighthouse keeper at Corbeil Point near the Soo.

Leila Shell: Neighbour of Clara in the Soo.

Father Maurice: Retired headmaster of Catholic residential school in Spanish, Ontario.

William Plummer: Late Soo civic booster.

Sir James Dunn: President of Algoma Steel.

Marcia Dunn: Third wife of Sir James Dunn.

Henry Hamilton: Member of Parliament for the Soo.

Ivan Slater: Cost estimator at Donnelly Building Materials.

Clem Giovanni: Foreman at Donnelly Building Materials.

Bob Snelling: Employee at Donnelly Building Materials.

Sister Marie Claire: Director-general of female staff at Sault Ste. Marie's General Hospital.

Anna McCrea: Principal of McFadden Public School in the Soo.

Joe Mancini: Foundry foreman at Algoma Steel in the Soo.

Maud Irving: Red Donnelly's math teacher.

Fanny Pace: Nora Donnelly's teacher.

Milton Redman: Clara and Ivy's Hilltop neighbour.

Marvin Redman: Son of Milton Redman.

Keith Messenger: Pilot who takes Ivy to Wawa, Ontario.

Stan Nahdee: Wawa Cree guide for Ivy in Wawa.

Stella Brownlee: Cree welfare client of Ivy in Wawa.

Cindy Brownlee: Daughter of Stella Brownlee.

Sylvie Brownlee: Granddaughter of Stella Brownlee.

Betty Sanchez: Lethbridge prostitute and friend of Dan MacIntyre.

Reginald Monteith: Bank of Montreal manager in the Soo.

Adam Wright: Lawyer for Ivy.

Russ Thompson: Algoma District regional welfare officer.

Bill Langdon: Magistrate in the Soo.

PART ONE

New Beginnings – Rough Start

CHAPTER 1

It was Clara Durling's job as the Shingwauk School nurse to check the heads of incoming children for lice. She had joined the staff in late August 1932, just as Indian agents, or sometimes the police, were hauling Native children into the dilapidated building, some from as far away as Baffin Island. Despite being August, a fire was lit in the gymnasium to offset the damp interior cold. The room was in such a state from water damage that it served only as the inspection station at the beginning of the year. So much plaster had fallen down that Clara could see the darkened ceiling joists, still wet from a leaked pipe, evidence that the toilets had overflowed into the gymnasium.

William, Lila, and Abe Martin from the nearby Batchewana Reserve were the first to be shoved into the room.

Clara smiled. "Batchewana is an interesting name." She had moss-green eyes and a wholesome, straightforward English face that, while serious, appeared kind. "What does the word mean?"

William glanced at the nearby custodian, who gripped a large pair of scissors, and remained silent.

"We have all day," Clara said. "There's no school until tomorrow."

"Great Waters," Lila piped in, afraid Clara might hit her if the question wasn't answered.

"Thank you for telling me," Clara said. "I'm a newcomer to Northern Ontario."

Lila relaxed her small shoulders.

"Stand by the stove," the custodian barked, as though not approving of idle conversation. She raised her scissors in one hand and pointed with the other to where William should stand for the clipping. "Nits are easier to find in short hair," she added. It took three snips to remove the long braid that William had tied with deer gut. The custodian tossed the shiny black braid into the fire and then nodded at Lila to come forward.

William shuffled toward Clara and bowed his head.

"Your hair will grow back," she whispered as she swabbed him gingerly with kerosene.

"Ouch," Lila uttered when the lady custodian nicked her earlobe.

Clara's face mirrored little Abe Martin's woeful look as he reached back to find his ponytail gone. Lila took Abe's hand and walked him to the door of the gymnasium. Recently, Clara had cut her wiry pepper-grey hair into a short bob for expedience. She missed her long hair, which for most of her adult life she had wound into a chignon each morning to fit it under her nurse's cap.

The Department of Indian Affairs had decreed that children must receive an education in English despite their diverse cultures and languages. There were few schools on reserves, which meant Native children were sent to residential establishments often hundreds of miles from their homes. Life skills learned in the bush weren't considered important by the government. Clara had been horrified when she first stepped into her small office to find an official document referring to the children as savages.

A British nurse, Clara had arrived in Canada in 1920 to become the superintendent of the Galt Hospital in Lethbridge, Alberta. That was the same year Arthur Meighen was elected prime minister of Canada. He had been the superintendent general of Indian Affairs before entering politics. At the time, Clara hadn't understood the power of Indian Affairs. Twelve years later, as the Shingwauk nurse, she was acutely conscious of the influence an Indian agent had over the functioning of the school. The headmaster would have to comply with the Indian Affairs Department or lose his job.

"It will be important for me to learn how the system functions," Clara had said to the headmaster, Reverend Charles Hives, on her first day at Shingwauk. Standing at the school entrance, she watched the older boys mill around the grounds until their names were called. They seemed downright dangerous, so filled with rage. These were healthy-looking children who had spent the summer in the bush with their parents.

Clara knew she would never forget that first week on the job: boys and girls lined up in the dark, musty, windowless corridor outside the gymnasium, each child waiting to be inspected for lice. Ojibwa, Cree, and other Native languages filled the halls, since Reverend Hives was giving the children a few days to adjust to school life before applying the "speak English" rule.

The lopping off of pigtails, ponytails, and shoulder-length hair continued until all the children were admitted to the school. No one got past the gymnasium without being shorn and deloused. By early September, there were fifty-five boys and twenty girls registered in Shingwauk. The smell of kerosene and burnt hair lingered in Clara's nostrils.

One evening, she returned home and searched for the blank address book she'd been given by a friend as a going-away gift. At the time of leaving Lethbridge, there hadn't been many addresses she wished to record. Now she sat at her desk, wondering what to write that would reflect the past few days at Shingwauk. The kid-leather notebook wasn't a diary, but it did have space to write. However, her thoughts about what to put on paper were interrupted by Lily Barnaby, her thirty-five-year-old niece.

Clara was staying with Lily and her husband, James, who had been a psychiatrist at the Galt Hospital before accepting the position of city coroner in Sault Ste. Marie. Barnaby, as James liked to be called, had written to Clara that an opening for a nurse at Shingwauk had been advertised in the *Anglican Bulletin*. He had been Clara's loyal advocate, witnessing the toxic atmosphere in which she tried to run the hospital. Falling on the wrong side of hospital politics, she'd been fired, though the hospital board hadn't used that word.

Now Lily was holding two ice-filled glasses of Scotch whisky and handed one to Clara. "I thought you might like to chat," she said, settling on the bed beside Clara's desk.

Clara put down the address book and smiled wanly. "I still feel discarded."

"You couldn't have seen what was happening. Even Barnaby was dismayed at the dishonesty."

"I certainly knew I was heading for a clash with the hospital establishment. I was the frugal British war widow against the newly rich."

"Well, they got their comeuppance. There won't be a new hospital because of the financial crash."

Clara shook her head. "That's true. But I won't forget Dr. Loring's sarcastic tone when he suggested Shingwauk might be my *schadenfreude*. The directors have had the last laugh."

"I'm sure no one's laughing, Clara."

"Then why did the board believe the trumped-up charge that I'd gone off on a caper without leaving proper instructions for the covering nurse? My dismissal felt like a physical push, though the directors didn't actually shove me but made accusations that would require a lawyer I couldn't afford."

"I did hear that the nurse who made the accusation replaced you as superintendent. The Depression has clouded everyone's good judgment. You'll feel more settled when Ivy arrives and you find a house."

Clara had been hired at Shingwauk without an interview. Reverend Hives hadn't asked for references or her reason for leaving Lethbridge. That avoided explanations as to why she'd left, but it also suggested that the headmaster was desperate to fill the post. Jobs in Lethbridge were being lost daily as the economic crisis raged on. Clara knew she couldn't be picky; her widow's pension from the Great War was hardly enough to pay for food, and Ivy was still in school.

"Giving Ivy more time in Lethbridge was the compromise I needed to get her to the Soo," Clara told Lily. Three weeks at Bow Lake near Calgary with Katherine Iverson, Ivy's friend, and her parents was the deal she'd made with Ivy. Clara was sure Etta, Katherine's mother, could keep track of two high-spirited seventeen-year-olds.

"I know Ivy wanted to complete her last year of high school in Lethbridge," Lily said kindly. She and Barnaby had acted as surrogate parents while Clara had fought to keep her job as superintendent of the Galt Hospital. Glancing at the address book, Lily added, "A light Scotch will help you put your thoughts on paper."

September 9, 1932
Does hair have a ceremonial meaning for Indian boys? Is a ponytail a rite of passage to Indians as baptism is to Christians or circumcision to Jewish boys? I didn't relinquish my culture when I came to Canada, and I'm sure these children don't wish to relinquish theirs. They are outdoors children. They don't want to lose their language any more than I want to lose my British accent. Culture is the way we face hardship and loss as well as happiness and celebration.

CHAPTER 2

Two weeks after the hair-shearing and delousing were accomplished for all incoming students, Dr. Andrew McCaig, the medical officer of health for Northern Ontario, bustled into the infirmary, apologizing for being late. He was a man of about sixty whose blue eyes smiled. Dressed in a navy-blue-striped linen suit, bowtie, and well-polished oxfords, he looked incongruous in the rundown school. Dr. McCaig was slighter in build than the muscled Native boys and not much taller. Clara soon discovered the doctor had a simple manner of speaking that invoked trust. She also noticed he didn't use big words that the children couldn't understand.

Being a British-trained nurse, Clara stood at attention in her starched white uniform.

Dr. McCaig slipped into the white coat she offered him and placed some instruments on a tray, rubbing his hands with a jovial air. "Are we ready?"

Clara nodded and opened the door. A custodian stood in the hallway to control the flow. First, the teenage boys were led into the infirmary two at a time. One sat while the other was being examined.

Dr. McCaig put the otoscope in the first boy's ear, saying something that caused the child to laugh and show a mouthful of bad teeth. Then the doctor repeated the procedure on the second boy.

"It took Indian Affairs six months to send us toothbrushes," he said, handing one to each of the boys. "Now you must use it or the dentist from Ottawa who comes once a year will pull out your teeth."

The boys shrugged and stuck the toothbrushes in their back pockets.

"Use it," he called after them, and the next pair was ushered in.

This examination was more complicated because the boys needed eyeglasses. They squinted at even medium-sized letters on the chart.

"Eyes, like teeth, are another problem with the government," Dr. McCaig said. "By the time the prescription is filled in Ottawa, the child needs a new pair. It can take as long as a year. We're asking Indian Affairs to pay a local optometrist, but until that happens I'll pay for him myself."

"Is Shingwauk your missionary work?" Clara asked after the last examination.

Dr. McCaig smiled. "I've been doing this for many years."

"And you speak their languages," Clara said admiringly.

"Caring for these children over time, I've learned enough Oji-Cree to be understood," he said with a self-deprecating smile.

Other than the headmaster, there's no one else in the school speaking the Native tongues, Clara thought. "It's nice that you address the children by their Christian names," she said. "Most of the custodians identify a child by his number."

"I make a point of remembering their names. Christian is a misnomer, however. Most of these children aren't baptized. The unfortunate reality of keeping track of a residential school population is that a number is easier than a name. The more students enrolled, the bigger the government grant to a residential school."

"I see," Clara said doubtfully. "Numbers, not needs, determine the grants."

"It's complicated. Last year the Indian school in Spanish had more than thirty children escape. The government threatened to reduce funding unless the children were returned. A number rather than a name makes it easier to track a runaway, especially if a family name can be spelled several different ways. Sadly, this led to severe corporal punishment for those runaways who were returned. They were blamed for lowering the subsidies to the school." The doctor put his hand on Clara's shoulder. "Welcome aboard, Matron. I'll need your help to keep these children healthy." He was about to leave the gymnasium when he turned back to her. "I almost forgot. Reverend Hives asked to speak with me when I finished my examinations."

"Follow me," Clara said. "Headmaster Hives and his wife, Jean, are living in the staff lounge."

"There's nowhere in the school that's safe to walk," Dr. McCaig said. "The school structure is crumbling as we speak."

Clara glanced at the cracked walls and nodded. "The school directors are looking for a nearby house they can rent. In the meantime, *home* is the staff lounge."

Dr. McCaig knocked on the lounge door, and Mrs. Hives responded with a finger on her lips. The doctor slipped into the room, followed by Clara. The headmaster was rocking in a chair. The spindly brown legs of a child asleep on his lap could be seen beneath the girl's thin cotton dress.

"She has a fever," Reverend Hives whispered, pushing the child's matted black hair off her damp forehead.

Dr. McCaig opened his medical bag and pulled out a stethoscope, warming it with his hands. "How old is she?"

The reverend held up four fingers.

The doctor frowned. "Too young for residential school, I'd say."

"Jean and I both agree." Reverend Hives smiled affectionately at his wife. "Gordon Sims, the Indian agent for our area, brought this little girl by train from Chapleau. Sims is normally a crusty man, but this time he returned from the reserve quite shaken. We learned he arrived to find a police officer trying to get to the bottom of a fight that killed the girl's parents."

Dr. McCaig winced, thinking the child understood the cruel words.

As if reading his mind, Reverend Hives said, "She understands only French and Cree."

"She's ours for the moment," Mrs. Hives added. "Her name's Violette Dumont."

CHAPTER 3

Clara had been separated from her daughter for a few weeks, but it seemed much longer. Ivy was to arrive on the four o'clock train. Initially, she had fought Clara's decision to move to Sault Ste. Marie, arguing that she had one more year to graduate in Alberta whereas in Ontario it would take two because that province had five years of high school instead of four. However, the argument didn't hold up, especially after the principal of Ivy's new school in the Soo, who had come from the Alberta system, assured her that she could do two years in one. He offered to personally oversee her accelerated program.

Since Clara didn't own a car, Lily offered to drive her to the train station to meet Ivy.

"She's in the third car!" Lily said, waving energetically.

Ivy pushed back her long blond hair as she pressed her face against the window.

"*And* she's smiling," Clara added, not disguising her relief. The battle with Ivy over their move to Northern Ontario was still raw in her mind.

The moment the train ground to a halt, Ivy, ignoring the porter's extended hand, jumped onto the platform and embraced Lily first.

"I'm glad you've arrived," Clara said, not letting her daughter's slight spoil her own joy that she was finally in the Soo.

Several family friends had offered Ivy a place to stay while she finished the last year of high school in Alberta. In a moment of hurtful candour, Ivy had said to Clara, "Moving to the Soo will be less humiliating than facing my friends whose fathers are doctors at the hospital."

Clara put the rancour behind her and enjoyed the moment of greeting her daughter. Families wandered around searching for loved ones getting off the train. An elderly black man pulled the baggage cart to the end of the platform, helping passengers identify their luggage. He smiled broadly and offered a cheery comment as he removed a bag.

"That's quite a load for you," Clara observed.

"Doing this for thirty years," the man said. Ivy identified her suitcase, and the old man smiled. "Home for a holiday?"

"I'm not sure I have a home," she retorted. These words ripped at Clara's heart. Home had been elusive for Ivy. Living in the nurses' residence at the Galt Hospital had made it difficult to make friends. Leaving England had been an economic decision because the Galt Hospital had offered room and board for herself and Ivy. Ivy was five at the time and too young to appreciate Clara's sacrifice. Clara had sold her wedding ring to pay for their passage.

"I'm about to make an offer on a duplex close to your school and far from my work," Clara said as soon as they settled in Lily's blue Rambler. She raised her finger to make a positive comment. "But the headmaster of Shingwauk has offered me the use of the school car."

Ivy leaned forward, draping her arms over Clara's shoulders as she laughed. "Mum, you don't know how to drive."

"Then I'll have to learn," Clara offered with a chuckle, warmed by the hug. "We're going to see the duplex now!"

"Does James like being a coroner?" Ivy asked as they headed north on Pim Hill. "It was a big decision you made last year to move to the Soo."

Lily shook her head. "Only the good Lord knows why my blessed husband finds working with the deceased less depressing than counselling unhappy veterans who wish they were. We both enjoy living in the Soo," she added, taking her hand off the steering wheel to wag her finger at Ivy. "You will, too."

Turning left at the top of the hill, Lily stopped in front of a white stucco house with green shutters on the west side of the street. A black car was parked across from the duplex.

The realtor, a woman named Maggie Stone, bounced out, smiling broadly. "*You* must be Ivy," she said, extending her hand. "This is a perfect location to bring friends home. Sault Collegiate is just a block away." The realtor pointed in the direction of the intersecting street.

Ivy glared at her mother. Clara knew her daughter believed she had spoken to the realtor about Ivy's difficulty making friends in Lethbridge. Then her daughter followed the agent reluctantly into the vestibule leading to the duplexes.

"The single front door with a common foyer makes the duplex look like a one-family home," Maggie offered as an added feature.

"We'll have the lower duplex if you like the house," Clara said. "If I buy, Sergeant Robert Stuart would love to rent the upstairs."

"Mum, you're not telling the truth," Ivy said.

"She is," Maggie interjected. "I understand he was your riding instructor in Lethbridge. The city has hired two RCMP officers to stop liquor smuggling across the St. Marys River to the Americans."

"And why did Sergeant Stuart apply?" Ivy asked, tossing a cheeky glance at Clara.

Maggie hastily opened the door to the lower duplex and let her clients step in.

Clara felt a wave of sadness at the sight of the overstuffed dark blue furniture the owners had left. The pieces reminded her of the matron's apartment she'd inhabited at the Galt Hospital where Mayor Alistair Harwood, chairman of the hospital board, would come for a drink and sometimes a round of two-handed bridge at the end of a long day. The mayor had been changing the way Lethbridge was run, while Clara had been transforming the culture in the hospital. They were both battlers and had often commiserated during their card games. Alistair appeared to have healed from a stomach ulcer when Clara left for England in 1929 to visit her family. Before she returned, she received a message that he was admitted to hospital during her absence. Alistair was found dead in Clara's apartment. She only learned once she was back in Lethbridge that he had scribbled a note on a bridge-scoring pad: "You were my oasis."

Maggie broke Clara's sombre reminiscence to discuss financing. "The Bank of Montreal would be amenable to a loan for an income-producing house."

"I don't wish to be hasty," Clara said. "Perhaps I should see more houses."

"This one is the most reasonable price and best location of any I can show you," Maggie said." "It will be snapped up in no time," she added, peering out the front window at a large vacant lot on the other side of Hilltop. "One of my clients has already bought the land opposite and has plans to build. I can't give details because the buyer has asked for confidentiality."

Ivy wanted to see the upstairs where Sergeant Stuart would live. Lily climbed the carpeted stairs behind her.

Ivy chuckled. "Sergeant Stuart can be Mum's personal chauffeur if he moves in."

She and Lily grinned, conscious that Clara had rebuffed the poor officer's advances.

"I'm sure it's coincidence that the officer moved from Lethbridge to the Soo," Lily said.

Ivy yawned and rubbed her eyes.

"You must be tired after your travels," Clara said.

"Why don't I take Ivy home and you can tour the neighbourhood with Maggie?" Lily offered.

"A sensible idea," Maggie declared, wanting to improve her chance of a sale.

"Does that suit you, Ivy?" Clara asked.

Ivy nodded and followed Lily.

"I like the house," Clara said, standing by Maggie's car and gazing across the street at the duplex. "What can you tell me about the neighbours?"

Maggie headed north on Hilltop. A few houses beyond the intersection the appearance of poverty was noticeable in the jalopies under repair littering front yards. "Many of these folks have lost their jobs at the paper and steel mills. They can't afford the gas to drive those cars." She made a U-turn and crossed Pim to the eastern block of Hilltop to where manor-like residences overlooked the city, the river, and the border with the United States.

"These are the homes of the managers of the plants," Maggie said. "They have chauffeurs to drive their cars."

"Goodness!" Clara exclaimed. "Hilltop Crescent is a paradox of income disparity."

"It's a mirror of our city," Maggie said. "The duplex is somewhere in between the social extremes. Just where you should be, Mrs. Durling."

Clara mulled it over. She knew it was a good house. The fact that it was furnished was a definite asset. And she wanted a home for her and Ivy. "I'll buy it."

Maggie grinned. "I knew you would. I know my clients."

CHAPTER 4

The Sault Ste. Marie Royal Canadian Legion planned a wreath-laying ceremony on November 11, Remembrance Day, to commemorate those from the Soo who perished in the First World War. The cenotaph, having been designed by an architect from Southern Ontario, was cause for local pride. Barnaby's lost arm was a visible testament to the horrors of war, and he was asked to lay the wreath. Normally a calm man, Barnaby became agitated in his sleep a few days before fulfilling the Legion's request. Lily recounted her husband's mumblings to Clara, who had nursed hundreds of wounded soldiers during the war. Clara suggested a nightcap — *two ounces of rye in eight ounces of sweetened warm milk*. The nightly libation worked well until Lily discovered that there was no more rye in the liquor cabinet. It was a Sunday, so she called Clara.

"We've run out of rye, Clara. Can you lend me a bottle?"

"I'm out myself. I'll never understand why liquor stores have such restricted hours. There's a wine merchant on every corner in Britain. An Englishman never runs out!"

"If I come by in an hour, will you go with me to Singapore Sal's?"

"What has an Asian woman got to do with rye?" Clara asked. "I didn't know rye was popular in Asia."

"Sal D'Agostina's Italian. She bootlegs out of her house."

Clara hung up, intrigued that she would be in the part of town where the bootleggers lived.

A brisk wind outside had blown away the last leaves from the trees on the property across the street. While she waited for Lily's honk, she imagined a house on the lot that would block her view of the ferries crossing back and forth between the Canadian and American Soos. She had placed her writing desk at the window for that view and hoped she would like the family who would eventually become her neighbours. Her thoughts were broken by the anticipated blast of Lily's horn. Clara considered this rude but threw on her coat and hustled to the car before Sergeant Stuart could descend the stairs to say "Good morning."

"I don't need the rye until evening," Lily said as Clara got into the car. "Would you like a quick tour?"

Clara nodded and clutched the dashboard as Lily sped down the hill behind Sault Collegiate Institute. They crossed Wellington Street and headed to the river's edge where they parked. As they picked their way to the shoreline along a muddy path, Clara was glad she had put on old shoes. Turbulent water jigged and swirled above the rocks, frothing and then rushing forward to dance on another rock.

Clara put her hand to her chest. "I can feel the energy in these rapids."

Lily chuckled as Clara relaxed after the car ride. *I know what she's thinking*, Clara thought. *I have an unfortunate history with cars.* Her niece was no doubt recalling the legendary story of how she had driven Alistair's fancy car into the Oldman River while he was teaching her to drive.

A man was casting from the foot of an iron bridge, and when he saw the ladies, he sauntered over. "I've fished here since I was a boy," the brown-skinned man told them.

"I hope we're not intruding," Clara said.

"What can you tell us about these rapids?" Lily asked.

"Are you from the area?" the man queried.

"My husband's the new city coroner," Lily said.

The man grinned. "Hope I don't meet him too soon." He nodded at Clara. "And you?"

"I'm the new nurse at Shingwauk School."

The man laughed. "I'm half-Indian. My Scottish father wouldn't let me attend the residential school. He worked for Francis Clergue as a bookkeeper. My mother moved off the Garden River Reserve when she married my father, and we lived in that building over there." He pointed to a strange structure that looked as though it had been constructed upside down with a wide log cabin set on a much narrower stone base.

"I've never heard of Clergue," Lily said.

"Clergue was an American industrialist backed by financiers from Philadelphia who saw the energy potential in the rapids. They turned this sleepy hamlet into an industrial powerhouse. Until then, Indians had fished here thousands of years and traded with the white men when they arrived. Whitefish jumped out of these rapids by the thousands, making them easy to catch. The Sault Rapids was the site of the largest summer gathering of Indians to catch and dry whitefish until white men came to build their factories. You might say I'm a throwback from the past."

"It looks like some of these buildings are abandoned," Lily noted.

"The Philadelphia group pulled out after investing $30 million, leaving Clergue bankrupt. When he couldn't pay his men, they trashed his office and the buildings around it."

"And then?" Clara asked.

"Reserve troops arrived from Toronto, and the rioting stopped."

"I guess, like many visionaries, Clergue never saw the obstacles," Clara offered. *Nor did I in Lethbridge*, she thought.

The man finished talking and then wandered back to the bridge, waving as the ladies moved away.

"I think I'm going to enjoy living in the Soo," Clara said.

They got in the car and headed west. "Italians and a few Finns for variety inhabit this part of the city," Lily said. As the Rambler neared the intersection of Queen and Gore Streets, Lily slowed down. Several rough-looking, pale-skinned youths were idling on the road. "This is the geographic divide between foreigners and Anglo-Saxons." She had stopped to let the boys get off the road when a big fellow put his face to the window.

"Get out of the car!" he demanded. His eyes were sharp and mean.

Lily hopped out with her hands on her hips. Then she pushed her fingers through her thick, curly blond hair as though she meant business, narrowing her eyes — green, like Clara's. "When were *you* selected as border control?"

"Bitch!" he sneered as the others moved in.

Lily pushed the boy so hard in the chest that he tumbled backward while the others moved away, fearful Lily might run them over.

She was shaking when she got back in the car. "It was a bully who killed Ed." Her voice was taut with emotion.

Lily rarely spoke about her first husband, Edward Parsons. His tragic accident had occurred before Clara had arrived in Lethbridge. However, she knew the story. Ed had died as a result of a mining accident while picketing during a strike. Lily had been standing on the rail line with Ed's birthday lunch, hoping to surprise him. A militant union organizer, Bob Glimp, uncoupled a coal cart, and as it sped down the line toward Lily, Ed lurched forward to push her out of the way. His kidney was badly damaged, and after a long hospital stay, he died. Lily had stood up to Glimp's bullying, and he hated her.

"Good for you, giving those boys a piece of your mind," Clara said.

Lily drove past the teenagers, eyes straight ahead. "Sal lives on Cathcart Street," she said, as though nothing had happened. Once they arrived at Sal's place, they sat in front of it until Lily was breathing normally.

When Clara finally met Sal at the door, she saw that unlike most Italian women in the neighbourhood, the woman was tall and thin. Her deep-set brown eyes were wary until Lily identified herself. Chattering in the background stopped until Sal shouted, "It's okay!"

"At the inquest into my husband's death, Dr. Barnaby recommended that all doctors speak some Italian," Sal said. "He attended Gino's funeral."

"Mrs. D'Agostina, my husband is full of surprises!" Lily said.

Sal smiled and asked Lily and Clara to come in while she fetched the requested bottles. The children seemed shy and followed their mother upstairs.

"I speak English all the time," Sal said when she returned with the bottles. But Gino — he worked at the plant with Italians. His English wasn't too good."

Lily herself is full of surprises, Clara thought when she got back in the Rambler. As they passed the border-patrolled area, she reflected on the twists of her niece's life. Lily had stood first in her class at Truro normal school in Nova Scotia. Yet she had been unable to find a teaching job when she moved to Lethbridge with Ed. Western schools preferred the American curriculum to the British methods that Lily had learned. After Ed's death, her economic circumstances forced her to take on the management of a brothel to support her young son.

It didn't surprise Clara that Lily was teaching English soon after moving to the Soo. She had taught proper diction and language while managing the brothel so that the girls might find better jobs than being prostitutes. That was how the same teaching instinct was brought to the Italian community in the west end of the Soo.

Mothers and grandmothers had problems communicating with their children once they started school. English was the language they were taught in. Anna McCrea, the principal of McFadden Public School, had sent home a note that every pupil must obtain a library card and bring a book to school. Within weeks, dozens of McFadden pupils had borrowed a book. Two months after Miss McCrea's ultimatum, Lily started a Saturday afternoon reading hour. She had expected the mothers to drop off their children, but they stayed in the background. Instead, they gawked as their children mysteriously disappeared into the stacks to choose a book. Barely understanding what Lily was saying, they nodded that they wanted to learn English, as well. Lily offered them English classes after the reading hour. Occasionally, the tough economic circumstances showed on the women's faces. Sometimes it was a bruise on the cheek or a mother and her children just stopped coming. Lily had to exercise diplomacy when a disgruntled husband marched in to take home his wife.

The English classes were held at the West End Library, a functional, two-storey building with thick vinyl flooring normally seen in battleships. Formerly, it had been the Steelton Post Office. Its high windows let in plenty of light, creating a warm atmosphere. Although Italian women rarely left home except on Sundays for Mass or to shop along James Street, they did bring their children to the library. Lily established another attraction to ensure the mothers, despite pressure from their husbands to stay home, would still come. She solicited discarded clothes from her well-off east end neighbours and received plenty of donations. These elaborate dresses and suits and the occasional long gown were unsuitable for the heavy-set Italian women. The cast-offs were deposited in a large bin at the entrance to the West End Library, and the Italian mothers cleverly modified them to fit their daughters.

Lemons to lemonade, Clara thought. She smiled as Lily drove past Gore Street, still indignant from the young ruffian's challenge. The teens were no longer in sight, though.

CHAPTER 5

Clara witnessed many obstacles during her first three months as the nurse at Shingwauk. Optometrists, dentists, and even school desks were problematic. As Christmas approached, she discovered yet another hardship. Children from distant communities couldn't spend the holidays with their families. The students who could return to their families for Christmas were dubbed the "Lucky Ones." Before the exodus, Reverend Hives arranged a party so that all the children at the school could give and receive presents, as had been the case with the three Wise Men and Jesus in the Bible, learning about Christmas in the process.

"Jesus gives us everlasting life," Reverend Hives said, reiterating in his Sunday sermon the importance of the birth of Jesus.

He spoke of the gifts of gold, frankincense, and myrrh. Since the children had nothing to give, the ladies' guild of the Anglican Church collected second-hand clothing, wrapped it, and organized a gift exchange. An evergreen tree cut from the woods behind the school was erected in the dining room and the tables pushed aside. The younger children sat cross-legged in a circle, watching wide-eyed as girls from the home economics class placed trays of decorated cookies on the table. Cookies were completely out of the ordinary. No one fidgeted, fearful that even at a party the custodians would crack down. Four-year-old Violette Dumont, who was living with the Hiveses, wore a red dress that stood out from the drab garments of the boarders. The normally placid faces of the children were all smiles as they passed Violette around to play.

Ivy had come reluctantly to the Christmas celebration, saying that Shingwauk reminded her of the Galt Hospital. When the gift-giving began, however, she displayed her usual good manners and helped distribute the gifts. Toques, scarves, mittens, socks, hockey pucks, skipping ropes, and baseballs for the warmer season emerged from the brightly wrapped packages. The children immediately began to barter, and items passed back and forth. Reverend Hives lifted his hand to stop Beatrice Crossly, the custodian of the senior girls' dormitory, from stepping forward to cease the trading.

Clara had seen the custodian's disapproval in the autumn when the children were sharing their tools as they closed down the garden before winter. Rakes, hoes, pitchforks, and spades were traded, as the task at hand required. She thought Mrs. Crossly had been afraid of Native children holding lethal instruments in their hands. Having another perspective Clara had marvelled at the efficiency of the young gardeners switching tools to suit the task.

"This is their custom," the reverend now said with an eye on Mrs. Crossly. "Indians have bartered and traded for hundreds of years. White men wouldn't have survived in our harsh climate if they hadn't learned to do this. Why, furs were an essential part of their winter dress!"

When the trading ended, the reverend announced a surprise. The clicks of Sergeant Stuart's metal spurs could be heard as he marched into the dining room in his red serge uniform. It had been Clara's suggestion to liven up the Christmas party by inviting the sergeant. In the absence of a Santa Claus, she hoped his colourful outfit would brighten up the dreary surroundings, but she wasn't prepared for the children's immediate reaction. Their faces filled with fear, some with loathing.

Clara didn't know that RCMP officers had wreaked havoc in Native communities. Some of the children at the Christmas party had seen their parents arrested by the Mounties. Others had watched their siblings dragged off, screaming the whole while. Hiding under the cabin was the most common escape. Reverend Hives and Dr. McCaig were the only white people in the school the children trusted. Now they stared at the headmaster with piercing brown eyes as though he had betrayed them. On every child's mind was: *Why did you invite an RCMP officer to our Christmas party?*

The children didn't consider Clara, as the nurse, to be part of the school. When they visited her, she didn't care *what* language they spoke as long as she understood their problems. To them, she was the lady who removed slivers, bandaged scraped knees, and called Dr. McCaig for anything serious.

There was a drop in tension when Clara spoke. "Sergeant Stuart is a riding instructor. How many of you have ever been on a horse?" Clara had been a devotee of Buffalo Bill Cody when he visited London during her nurse's training at St. George's Hospital across from Hyde Park, where the American had put on his show. She had followed his performances for years. Clara had assumed all Natives rode horses, but not a single hand went up in answer to her question.

In an effort to make friends at her school when she was living in Lethbridge, Ivy had learned that being funny could break the ice. Surprised by the dilemma created by Sergeant Stuart, Ivy hoped hijinks might do the same in a residential school. She grabbed one of the traded woollen hats and placed it on her head. The cap had a dangling fringe that looked like a horse's mane. She walked, trotted, and cantered around the room, nickering and neighing. The staff looked mortified. Now Ivy felt challenged. Mrs. Crossly resembled the senior nurse at the Galt who had regularly scolded her.

"Let's all be horses!" she said, pulling a small boy up and putting him on her back piggyback-style. He held on tightly to Ivy's shoulders as she galloped around the room.

A handful of children from the nearby Garden River Reserve, who had arrived at Shingwauk without force, were brave enough to canter behind Ivy.

"*Whoa!* Pull on the reins to slow your horse down," Ivy said, gripping her imaginary pair.

Mrs. Hives began a knee-bobbing trot with Violette. "This is the way the ladies ride!" she cried.

Her husband chuckled at the antics. When Ivy let the little boy slip off her shoulders, the reverend stood up to indicate the party should end, speaking in a language that elicited smiles. Then he repeated in English, "I hope you enjoyed the Christmas party." The children got up to leave the dining room.

Reverend Hives had cancelled classes and workshops the day of the party. Talking above the rustle of students getting into their winter clothes to go outside, he said, "My Christmas present is to let everyone speak his or her own language. No English today." The children filed out silently.

A few days later, Ivy sat on the toilet seat as Clara parted her blond hair, picking at the nits with a fine-toothed comb. "I'm sorry you're missing the party at Sault Collegiate," Clara said. "The hat with the fringe must have contained lice." She tightened the thick cotton cap reeking of kerosene on Ivy's bowed head.

CHAPTER 6

Ivy knew there was no point in arguing with Clara, so she lied to her mother. "I'll stay at Lily's after my New Year's Party."

Clara assumed the party was in the east end where the Barnabys lived. She was unaware that Ivy had accepted an invitation from Irma D'Agostina, a classmate who lived west of Gore Street. The party would be held at Marconi Hall, the social hub for Italians located a few blocks from Irma's.

"My mother bootlegs in our basement, and the kids sleep on the top floor," Irma had said upon issuing the invitation. Ivy had understood the admission of Mrs. D'Agostina's work as a friendship test.

"I know a bit about bootlegging," Ivy had replied. "I grew up in the Galt Hospital in Lethbridge three blocks from the brothels where men went to drink during prohibition."

"I thought your mother was strict," Irma had said.

"She was, but she couldn't stop me from seeing what was going on. I used to look at patients' charts when the nurses were busy elsewhere. It surprised me how many upright citizens had drinking problems."

"On New Year's Eve, the liquor stores will be closed and business will be brisk. Mama sells to anyone. She lets the wife deal with the drinking problem!"

Both girls had giggled at their mutual revelations.

"Why are you taking a suitcase?" Clara asked, interrupting Ivy's recollections of her conversation with Irma. "I thought you had an entire wardrobe at the Barnabys.'"

"I'm going to change it," Ivy lied, not looking at Clara. "That's why I packed my suitcase." She hated deception with her mother who was truthful to a fault. "I hope you win your bridge tournament," she said to change the conversation, giving Clara a peck on the cheek and rushing out the door, grateful that Lily wasn't late.

Clara stood on the porch, which had been cleared of snow by Sergeant Stuart. "It bothers the neighbours when you honk," she called to Lily.

Lily waved cheerily. She, too, knew better than to argue with Clara. As soon as Ivy jumped in the car, Lily sped away. "Did you tell Clara what I'm doing?"

"Of course not," Ivy answered. "We're not bandits."

"I know, but your mother won't appreciate the deceit."

"Mum has misgivings about Italians because she believes they waffled before joining England in the war. She is fiercely loyal to her homeland."

"Those weren't Soo Italians," Lily retorted, driving faster.

Ivy pulled her sleeve as they rushed down Bruce Hill. "Slow down!"

The hoodlums policing Gore Street jumped to the side when they spotted Lily's car. She passed them without a glance and pulled up in front of Marconi Hall where Irma stood beside her brother, Dominic. Having quit Sault Technical College after his father died, Dominic had applied for a job at Algoma Steel. The company had laid off younger labourers, keeping jobs for men with families. Dominic, a single man of nineteen, was lucky to be hired as a railway maintenance man. A family friend had apparently used pull to get him the job because he was now supporting the family. Dominic's goal was to be promoted to a job inside the plant before spring.

Lily opened her window, and Irma stuck her head in, landing a kiss on each cheek. "We'll look after her," Irma promised.

"How do you know my aunt?" Ivy asked after she got out of the car and said goodbye to Lily.

"I see her at the library on Saturdays." Ivy's eyebrows showed her surprise at this revelation. *What does Lily do there?* Ivy wondered, but there wasn't a moment to ask.

Dominic put his hand on the girls' backs, hustling them inside. "Cops are driving around looking for Italians they can arrest."

The hall was thick with cigar smoke. A stout man inside the door took their coats and Ivy's suitcase. "You should leave around ten," Dominic told them, heading farther into the room where the men had congregated around the bar. A short, broad-shouldered fellow whose belly strained the buttons of his suit came forward to greet him. He raised his glass of wine in salutation. Dominic beamed. Joe Mancini was the foundry foreman at Algoma Steel and was considered very important.

"Are you twenty-one?" the bartender asked Dominic. He was wary that on New Year's Eve the police might raid Marconi Hall. The new chief of police, Dan Roswell, had boasted he would clean up the Soo. It was understood that meant Italians. The previous chief had distinguished between the amateurs selling to the locals and professionals peddling liquor to the United States. Roswell was a three-hundred-pound moralist who used his bulk to intimidate. The bartender passed Dominic a glass of wine with a warning. "Be ready to dump your drink if the cops arrive."

Dominic moved around the room, thanking men who had been at his father's funeral. Irma pushed Ivy through an observation gallery of stout matrons seated against a wall. They pinched Ivy's cheek as if testing a piece of fruit at the market on James Street.

"Ivy's a relative of Lily Barnaby," Irma said, not exactly certain of the relationship.

The ladies responded chorus-like. "She learn us English to speak with our grandchildren."

"Lily gives English classes at the West End Library on Saturdays," Irma said.

"But you already speak English," Ivy said, surprised. "Why would *you* go to Lily's classes?"

"I don't, but I can borrow books from the library, and sometimes if things are chaotic at home, I do my homework there."

"Are they *all* widows?" Ivy asked once they had passed the seated ladies.

"An Italian dies every week, so black is convenient." Irma raised her arms with palms up in resignation. "There's only one ladies' dress shop on James Street. It sells white for confirmations and black for funerals. The fashionable dress shops are downtown. Italians don't buy from Jews. They won't set foot in Friedman's Department Store."

"I guess everyone needs someone to hate. In Lethbridge, it was the Chinese. They made them live in a separate area."

"Like the Italians," Irma said with a note of sarcasm.

The conversation changed when a lady asked, "How's your mama doing, Irma?"

"The liquor stores are closed tonight. Otherwise she'd be here."

The "elder ladies" appeared collectively downcast when Irma led her friend to the other side of the room where a parade of younger women placed dishes of Italian cuisine on a thirty-foot table. It was covered with a white tablecloth and decorated its entire length with plastic flowers. Any nearby matron scolded young children trying to snatch goodies. The men lined up, plates in hand, and the ladies on the other side of the grand table heaped food on the extended plates, listening carefully for requests.

Men with their plates in one hand and cutlery in the other wandered the hall, searching for tables with friends. The tables had been set with crystal glasses and hand-embroidered tablecloths worthy of a banquet. Dominic sat with a group of men who had been friends with his father. Once the men were seated, the ladies liberally replenished the glasses, carefully tipping up the wine jug to avoid spills on the fancy tablecloth.

Ivy was astonished that none of the men seemed drunk. "Don't the women eat?"

"They eat while they're cooking the meal," Irma replied. "The real pleasure is seeing the men enjoy the food."

The eating portion of the evening lasted until nine o'clock, the men demanding seconds and complimenting the ladies who served them. Then a band of dark-haired, tawny-faced men played music and couples danced. Children with arms outstretched whirled around in their own orbits. Tables were cleared and set up for cards. A few cigar smokers lit up, and wine continued to flow. The girls helped in the kitchen, donning white cotton aprons to protect their dresses.

"Is your mama still running the restaurant?" a lady at the sink asked.

"She's a great cook," Irma replied tersely. Speaking behind her hand, she explained, "That woman's husband runs a rival establishment, but *she* can't boil an egg. I think we should leave now." They fetched their coats, and Dominic joined them.

Fog had drifted in from the river, and Ivy gripped her suitcase, ready to wallop anyone who stepped in her way. Despite Dominic's presence, she was nervous and wondered if coming to the west end was a bad idea. He flicked his cigarette onto the ground as two young women, arms linked and purses hung off their shoulders, walked past. They were scantily dressed despite the freezing cold.

"Have any cigarettes?" they asked.

Dominic removed a package from under his coat and handed each of the girls a cigarette.

"It's dangerous for them to be out on the street," Ivy remarked. "In Lethbridge, there was an area segregated where prostitutes could work without violence. The intent was to keep the girls off the street."

"How do you know so much?" Dominic asked.

"The segregated area was next to the hospital where my mother worked." The conversation ended when a man, obviously tipsy, grabbed the arm of one of the girls who had passed by. Her companion slid the purse off her shoulder and began whacking the man. He hit back.

"You don't have a right to hit that girl!" Ivy shouted.

"Shut up, or he'll hit *you*," Dominic hissed, holding Ivy's and Irma's sleeves until they reached the D'Agostina house. He knocked an irregular pattern, and his mother opened the door upon hearing the secret knock.

Sal smiled at her son, who had taken the place of her husband. "Now that the girls are home, *you* can go back to the party," she told him.

CHAPTER 7

Irma's home was different than Ivy had imagined. She had expected it to be more like a bar salon. The living room had nice furniture, some covered in plastic. The kitchen appeared unused.

"My mother has a small kitchen in the basement," Irma said.

"Where does Dominic sleep?"

"There are two bedrooms down there. Sometimes my mother rents them out. If that happens, Dominic and my mother sleep on the living room sofas."

"Does she rent if someone has too much to drink?"

"Not necessarily. Sometimes it's an American who's missed the last ferry looking for a place to stay overnight." Irma shrugged. "It all works."

They tiptoed upstairs to the children's bedrooms. Once there, Irma put a finger to her lips and lifted the corner of one of the mattresses to show where the extra liquor bottles were kept.

Ivy smiled. "That's a marvellous trick, hiding the bottles in the kids' room."

Laughing, Irma said, "My mother has another trick. She knows men like to drink when they're eating, so she feeds them."

Ivy admired Mrs. D'Agostina's cleverness.

"Our plan to move to a bigger house ended when my papa died. The girls are in this room and the boys are crowded across the hall."

Ivy slipped into a set of clown pajamas covered in balloons.

Perched on the side of the bed, Irma snorted. "I just sleep in my underwear. You're the first WASP I've invited home."

"A wasp is like a hornet. That doesn't make me sound very nice," Ivy added, uncertain if she was being insulted.

"It means White Anglo-Saxon Protestant. Italians are *wops*."

"And that means?"

"Some people say it means 'without papers' or 'without passport,' suggesting that every Italian is an illegal immigrant. My father actually told me the word came from our own language — *guappo* or *guappu* — something many Italians new to this country called themselves. It means 'dandy' or 'swaggerer,' but it got shortened to *guap* by non-Italians and became a bad word for us. Papa was still called a *wop*, even though he did have papers." Irma made a funny face. "We're *wops* until a WASP comes to buy our alcohol. Then we're *EYE*-talians."

Ivy laughed, though she wasn't sure it was a joke.

"Some people are hypocrites," Ivy offered. "You don't want them as friends."

Dan Roswell and two armed constables leaned against a paddy wagon waiting for the Nicolet Hotel to close. Just past midnight, two of the hotel's customers stumbled out the back door, crossing the laneway to Sal's to continue their revelry. Roswell had to catch Sal red-handed to lay a charge. He believed arresting the most successful bootlegger in town would be a demonstration of his authority. The guns in the constables' holsters were meant to intimidate.

The chief of police raised his hand, and the constables leaped from the wagon, ready to bash down the steel door with a discarded telephone pole if Sal failed to answer. The men thrust forward, not waiting for Sal, and the door flew open.

Sal stood at the bottom of the stairs, arms outstretched. "You wouldn't!"

Roswell shoved her aside and did what no other police officer had done — he rushed up the stairs two at a time and entered a child's bedroom. Ivy in her clown pajamas and Irma in her underclothes stood agape as he ripped back the mattress, kicking the liquor bottles to the floor. The sound of breaking glass brought the little boys to the doorway. The smell of liquor was overpowering. There was a scuffle as the two inebriated men from the Nicolet Hotel scrambled up from the basement so they wouldn't be caught in the pandemonium.

"Ignore them!" Roswell shouted. "It's the woman we want."

Sal didn't resist, and Dominic arrived home to see his mother in handcuffs. They hadn't even given her time to put on a coat or galoshes.

CHAPTER 8

Clara first met her neighbour, K.G. Rossiter, when he arrived at Shingwauk for a meeting of the school trustees. He popped into her office while he waited for the other gentlemen to arrive. The Rossiters owned the grandest house on the wealthier part of Hilltop. K.G. was a paradox, a man who mastered Ojibwa to communicate with his Native crew and yet had patrician manners.

"I understand your husband was a Royal Engineer in the communications division," K.G. said. "It was a rough job crawling through those muddy trenches laying down lines, but it kept thousands of us alive. I was sorry to learn your husband didn't survive the gassing."

"He did return to the front, but it wasn't long before he was on his way home with intractable pneumonia. Unfortunately, he didn't reach England before he died."

K.G. nodded sympathetically. "You've carried on well, Mrs. Durling. My wife, Jessie, tells me you've earned your master points at several bridge clubs. We'd like to invite you over for a few rounds and maybe dinner to follow."

The thought of playing bridge at her neighbour's posh residence pleased Clara. "Reverend Hives suggested you're a most valuable trustee because of your scholarship around Indian folklore."

"I learned to speak Ojibwa," K.G. replied. "While I surveyed up north for the hydro lines, I was completely dependent on the Indians' knowledge of the inhospitable bush and its inhabitants." He chuckled. "We ate some strange food."

"The children are comfortable with you."

"That's because I laid down the hydro lines vital to mining communities alongside their fathers. It was those summers in the bush that paid for our lovely house. I valued the loyalty that kept the Indians from hopping on the nearest train to go back to the reserve. They could make more money trapping and selling furs than surveying."

The headmaster poked his head into Clara's office to inform K.G. that the other trustees had arrived. Before leaving, K.G. reiterated the possibility of a bridge party. Clara reflected on how cards had brought her into Lethbridge society soon after she arrived. Then another thought popped into her head: *Right after the war, British nurses were held in very high regard and my card-playing prowess might have been less important.*

Hilltop residents knew Clara was British and assumed she would be interested in Jessie Rossiter's experience following the war. "Jessie," a neighbour confided, "resided at Cranston Towers in Great Windsor Park hobnobbing with Royals while K.G. stayed in Paris with postwar deliberations." The "neighbour-informant" smiled. "Perhaps the Rossiters built riding stables to remind them of horses in the park."

It wasn't until December that Clara received the Rossiters' invitation to play bridge. "I've planned a New Year's Eve card party with neighbours and friends," Jessie wrote. "I'd be delighted if you'd join us. Perhaps Ivy can come along and visit with my daughters."

When Clara wrote back, she told Jessie that Ivy was pleased at being included but had accepted a previous engagement. It occurred to Clara that the Rossiter family driver could take the eldest girl, Anne, to Ivy's New Year's party, something she would propose.

Clara was covered in snow when Jessie opened the door with her uniformed maid ready to take Clara's worn fur coat and galoshes.

"First storm of the season," Jessie said. "Our driver will take you home at the end of the night."

"I enjoy walking," Clara said.

"Well, not in this weather," Jessie replied firmly. She escorted Clara into the mahogany-panelled library where the other guests stood close to the fireplace with drinks in their hands. K.G. introduced her as the nurse-matron of Shingwauk School.

Jocelyn, the wife of Arnold Clement, the financial officer for the steel plant, remarked, "It's unusual for women to take work when so many men are unemployed."

"I don't know of any male nurses," Clara said with a smile.

"Of course," Jocelyn said, reddening.

"I was the superintendent of the Galt Hospital in Lethbridge for ten years," Clara said. "I moved to the Soo for health reasons." She accepted a Scotch, "with plenty of water," and turned to strike up a conversation with James and Dorothy Francis. James ran St. Marys Pulp and Paper Mill. He had moved to the Soo from Cleveland to marry Dorothy, the daughter of a doctor at General Hospital.

"Jessie is such an exotic hostess," Dorothy said. "We're going to dine on lobsters that were shipped in ice from a fish market in Toronto."

Clara's bridge partner for the evening was Roberta McCarthy, who was a house guest of the Rossiters. She had recently been widowed and had known Jessie from childhood. Roberta's large diamond wedding ring reminded Clara that she had had to sell hers. *Fortunately, I don't show my hardship*, she thought. Clara was congratulated heartily when she made a grand slam. With an impish grin, she admitted to being a master player at the Sault Ladies' Bridge Club. At the end of the game, Jessie escaped to the kitchen to see if the lobsters were being boiled humanely.

Anne Rossiter, who was Ivy's age, slipped into the library and complained, "I'm bored playing canasta with my sisters. They both cheat."

"Would you like to join my daughter?" Clara asked. "She's at a party with friends."

"My driver can take her if you give me the address," K.G. suggested.

"I'll have to call my niece. She acted as chauffeur this evening."

K.G. led Clara into his study to use the phone.

"Where's Ivy's party?" she asked Lily when her niece answered. "Anne Rossiter would like to meet young people her age."

"I'm not sure," Lily said.

"But you drove her."

"I did."

"Then where is it?" Clara could see Jessie waiting at the study door. She hung up with a clack and apologized. "I'm so sorry. Ivy's taken ill," Clara lied. "She's in bed at Dr. and Mrs. Barnaby's."

"Anne is here for another week. If Ivy recovers, we'll invite her for tea."

"That would be nice," Clara said, smiling but furious. Her daughter had hoodwinked her while she was at her own New Year's Eve party. As Clara dined on the succulent lobster, she contemplated accepting Jessie's offer to be chauffeured and asking to be taken to the Barnabys'. She wanted to chastise Lily right away rather than wait until morning when Ivy returned home. She was sure Barnaby would support her. By the end of the meal, she had cooled down and asked the chauffeur to drop her at the duplex instead. She felt relief as she noted from Sergeant Stuart's darkened window that he had already gone to bed. He had suggested several times that Clara was too controlling of Ivy, and she preferred not to discuss this evening's events.

CHAPTER 9

The constables conducting the New Year's raid on Sal's home had taken down Ivy's name and threatened to speak to her parents. So Lily couldn't hide the truth from Clara, knowing her aunt would tell the officers, "My daughter stayed overnight at Dr. Barnaby's and certainly wouldn't be part of a raid on a bootlegger's establishment." When Clara learned what had happened, she was disappointed that both Lily and Ivy had lied to her.

The next day the *Sault Star* published a photo of Ivy in her clown pajamas huddled with her half-clad friend, holding a pillow for modesty and standing beside an upturned mattress and broken liquor bottles. The article was terse and short, stating only that the police had made an arrest without mentioning the family name. The newspaper was focused on the fifty men let go at Algoma Steel at the beginning of the New Year. The *Sault Star* covered this social calamity with a photograph of despondent men, mostly Italians, lined up at Algoma Steel's pay office for their last cheques.

As Lily read the two articles, she reflected on the paradox that unemployed Italians had to resort to bootlegging to support their families. She had found it painful to hear about the women in her

English classes being forced to rent half their houses to other families despite having large families themselves. *The financial crisis has had much less impact on the wealthier people in town*, she mused.

Sal was kept in the city jail for several days until she came before a judge. Julio Valenti, an articling law student, defended her. His widowed mother bootlegged, as well, but she had none of the ebullience of Sal's establishment. Julio adored Sal and used every argument he could muster, but the judge wouldn't budge. Even the image of young children fending for themselves didn't move him. The owner of the *Sault Star*, James Crowder, published an editorial:

> Sault Ste. Marie is not Chicago. Chief Dan Roswell and his armed constables practised Chicago-style law enforcement by arresting a bootlegger in front of her children. They should be going after Le Mano Nero, an organized crime unit operating out of Hamilton that bootlegs to the Americans. Upright citizens frequent bootleggers to avoid the sniffling little clerks who record our purchases with moralizing comments in the mandatory permit book. The draconian rules that surround the consumption of alcohol make every purchaser feel like a drunk. Bootlegging when men are laid off may be the only way to support their families. Buying illicit liquor when the stores and bars are closed should not be shameful. What is shameful is sending a widowed mother of eight to jail for three months.

Clara was more hurt than angry that Ivy had been in cahoots with Lily, leaving her ignorant of a plan that could have ended badly. The vigilante-style arrest with guns was certainly dangerous. Dominic had begun to argue, and only Sal's quick reaction to go quietly had prevented the situation from escalating.

"Why don't you come this Saturday and meet the Italian women I teach, Clara?" Lily suggested soon after the incident. "Many of them sell liquor from their houses. Until Dan Roswell there had never been a raid. If I had anticipated that, I certainly would have discouraged Ivy from spending the night at the D'Agostina house."

There was a blizzard, but Saturday, the day set for Clara to visit the library, was cold and clear. Lily's blue Rambler pulled into the shovelled parking lot of the West End Library. Several women bundled in black wool coats and headscarves were gathered on the front steps.

"The blonds are Finnish ladies who come to socialize," Lily said. "The rest are Italians."

"Maybe they know Veera Aalto, the laundress at Shingwauk," Clara said. "Her husband owns Aalto's Finnish Baths."

Lily laughed. "They're most likely his competitor."

The ladies greeted Lily with embraces and smiled politely at Clara.

"You come to see Lily's library?" a lady in black asked. "Even my husband take sometime a book."

Clara stepped into the large main room with a long wooden table centrally placed and steel shelves stacked with books lining the walls.

"The books were donated by my neighbours," Lily said proudly. "Barnaby found this unused table in the basement of the hospital. Not the morgue," she added with a chuckle.

Clara perused the stacks that were low enough for children to reach. When she turned, she noticed three girls bent over their books at the table. They glanced up, and Clara recognized Irma D'Agostina, who seemed embarrassed. The girl had the classic chiselled features so often depicted on ancient Roman busts, making her a beautiful young Italian. Clara could understand her light-skinned, green-eyed, blond daughter's attraction to this exotic girl.

Irma stood up and faced Clara. "I'm sorry Ivy was involved in a police raid."

The two girls at the table gathered up their books and left.

"The police have never gone after a home operation before," Irma said, lowering her voice. "My mother has to bootleg to pay for the family. I'm hoping to go to university next year."

"How's your mother doing?" Clara asked. "It was high-handed of the police and the judge."

"My mother has to iron the cotton shirts of the fat jail guard while he sits with his feet on his desk," Irma said bitterly. "He boasted when I last visited, 'Your mama's better at ironing than my missus.' Lily and Miss McCrea have helped my sisters and brothers to keep up with their schooling while Mama's away."

"I'm not worried about the raid. I was offended by the lying. I'm sorry, Irma, that my daughter felt she couldn't tell me the truth. She's seen just about everything growing up in a public hospital. There was no need for deceit."

Irma shot Clara a grateful glance. "My brother, Dominic, and I are in charge until Mama's released. We live in a tightly knit neighbourhood. We have more food than Mama could cook," she added, smiling and noticeably more relaxed.

CHAPTER 10

Because Clara arrived at Shingwauk in August, she hadn't yet experienced many of the school's defects. However, by late January, the temperature dipped below minus four degrees Fahrenheit, causing the external pipes to the girls' bathroom to freeze and requiring them to use the boys' showers and toilets. The rule, "no water after five," was being strictly enforced to avoid night trips to the toilet. Clara was firmly opposed to limiting water.

"Mark my words," she argued, "we'll start seeing bladder infections in the girls."

"What goes in has to come out," a custodian retorted. "We control that so we don't encounter these savages in the dark. You go home in the evening, Matron, but for us who stay, there's always the fear of violence. They hate us."

"*I'd* hate you, too, if I were dying of thirst," Clara countered. "The children will sneak to the toilets to get a drink, but they're *not* savages! Indeed, you are if you limit their water and bathroom use."

"We can cut off the water to the second floor," the custodian challenged.

Clara gasped and marched to the headmaster's office, where Reverend Hives greeted her with a wan smile.

He looks tired from his temporary living arrangement in the staff lounge, and now the toilets, Clara thought. "I hate to bring up the water issue," she said, standing in front of the reverend's desk.

"Matron, I'm worried about the hanky-panky that will go on at night with shared washrooms. The female custodians are afraid of the bigger boys. They don't know how to handle them, especially in the dark."

"Cutting off water to the bathrooms isn't a solution. Better to educate the girls on the risk of sexual misbehaviour."

"That would put ideas in their heads. Why discuss something until it happens?"

"I set up the first venereal disease clinic in Alberta," Clara said. "Soldiers were passing VD to their partners after the Great War. But risky behaviour isn't confined to soldiers."

The headmaster cupped his head as though he didn't want to hear what Clara was about to say.

"A pregnancy would be a black mark on your school," Clara pressed. "There needs to be some education."

"Let's wait and see."

"As the school nurse, I'll have to take care of the consequences if a pregnancy occurs. Let me speak with the older girls."

Reverend Hives reluctantly agreed and asked Clara to report back to him.

According to Veera Aalto, the laundress who washed the bloody sheets, there were only ten girls in the school who could get pregnant. Mrs. Aalto was an amiable, heavy-set blond woman with ruddy arms from too much exposure to detergents. She was proud to announce, "Aalto tubs were selected the best Finnish baths in the Soo this year."

"I'll have to try them," Clara said. She had no intention of sharing her bath, something she'd had to do during the war years to conserve water.

"How's everything up top?" Mrs. Aalto asked. "I rarely see the children unless they work in the laundry. I know them by their sheets — bedwetters, menstruating girls, boys coming into puberty." She burst into an earthy laugh.

"I need your help," Clara said, and then explained the dilemma of the shared washrooms.

"The senior girl in the laundry is Doris Canoe," Mrs. Aalto said. "She's responsible for the mangle. I can trust her not to get her fingers caught in the large wooden rollers as she's expelling water from the sheets."

"She'd need to trust that I have the girls' best interests at heart," Clara said.

"Doris's father came out of residential school with his dukes up. Doris isn't afraid of anyone. She can keep the boys in check while the girls are sharing the washrooms."

"Could Doris supervise late night excursions to the toilet?" Clara asked.

"The girl needs her sleep, but as long as it's not too late, she could take the place of the night custodian."

Clara took Mrs. Aalto's list of numbered students and searched for the matching names in the school registry. The home economics room that was familiar to the older girls seemed a suitable place for an intimate chat. The girls spread out as they entered the room, avoiding the inevitable rebuke if they spoke to a friend in their own language. They hadn't been told why they were congregating, but usually a meeting of this kind was to reiterate the language rules. Mrs. Aalto, like Clara, didn't care what language the girls spoke as long as they understood.

"Good afternoon," Clara said. "Before we start, why don't you tell me where you're from?" Places that Clara had never heard of spilled off the girls' lips, which served as an icebreaker before she began her facts-of-life spiel.

"Mrs. Aalto gave me the names of students who are menstruating," Clara began. "The laundress breaks the rules often to give you ladies at that time of the month a new set of sheets. She doesn't want to invade your privacy. However, you're in charge of your own bodies and must not be coaxed by the boys to fool around. *They* might think it's funny, but *you* won't if you get pregnant."

"How would I get pregnant?" a girl asked.

Clara thought the girl was joking until all eyes were on her, so she gave a simple description of intercourse. Glances and smirks were exchanged. *They know what I'm talking about,* Clara thought. "I don't know how long you'll have to share washrooms, but Doris Canoe will ensure that the boys are respectful," she added.

The girls shuffled out, whispering and giggling, no doubt thinking that Clara was a bit odd but perhaps realizing that at least she wasn't mean like the custodians.

"I was a ten-year-old in Lethbridge when I overheard the student nurses giggling that you'd discussed the facts of life," Ivy said when Clara described what she was doing at Shingwauk. "No one wants to know the yucky details until they have to," her daughter added with a grimace.

Clara shot Ivy a wry smile, thinking about what the school handyman had told her. According to him, the pipes couldn't be repaired until spring, so Reverend Hives had used his Sunday sermon to tell the boys they had to respect the girls' privacy. The headmaster interpreted the passive brown eyes before him as indications of shyness.

CHAPTER 11

Nellie Big Smoke of the Odawa tribe had arrived three years ago as a frail five-year-old from Manitoulin Island. Her three years at the school had been marked by a persistent dry cough, which often kept her in the infirmary. In March, the cough became productive and streaked with dark blood. Suspecting the child had tuberculosis, Clara isolated her in the infirmary. Dr. McCaig examined the girl, tapping her chest and listening through his stethoscope. Nellie's temperature was elevated, and she had developed chills.

As Clara sponged the little girl with cool towels, Dr. McCaig's normally cheerful face looked unhappy. Visibly angry, he said, "We have a problem, Matron. The government's been experimenting with a vaccine for tuberculosis for Indian children. The BCG vaccine is available, but I wouldn't give Nellie an unapproved vaccine. It's completely underhanded that our government is using wards of the state to test the vaccine and other experimentation."

"Could you call a sanatorium and see what's available?" Clara asked.

Dr. McCaig went to Clara's office to use the phone. Connected with a sanatorium director in Southern Ontario, he explained the child's case.

"Where's the girl from?" the director asked.

"Manitoulin Island."

"Aha, that's treaty territory! We're only allowed to accept non-treaty Indians. Treaty Indians must have the consent of the Indian Department and then, if we're lucky, the government pays."

"I'm asking for an eight-year-old child who could be dead by the time the Indian agent gives us an answer!" Dr. McCaig shouted into the phone.

"I would lose my job," the director mumbled. He cited a few bureaucratic platitudes and hung up.

"Nellie can't stay at the school," Dr. McCaig said when he returned to Clara. "Fortunately, her living circumstances are better than most."

"I know. Her father's the band chief."

Nellie stared at the doctor with feverish brown eyes. *"Giiwe?"* she asked tearfully in Ojibwa.

"Yes, you're going home," Dr. McCaig answered.

Clara would accompany the child on the train, and she stood beside the house mother as the woman packed Nellie's cardboard suitcase. The threadbare state of her belongings saddened Clara, but they were spanking clean, thanks to Mrs. Aalto. The little girl had a nightgown and a pair of inherited pajamas from a brother who was no longer at the school. There was one nice dress that reflected her family's better circumstances. The custodian had never let her wear it.

Reverend Hives drove Clara and Nellie to the train station, handing Clara the tickets with moist eyes. *He senses the loneliness of these children now that he has Violette*, she thought.

"Let's sit by the toilets," Clara said. "No one will want those seats."

Passengers did use the washrooms during the three-hour train journey. Nellie sat next to the window with her head on Clara's lap.

Just before Espanola, a queue for the toilets developed, and Clara ignored the worried stares. Passengers could now identify the source of the coughing. They also recognized the poorly cropped black hair as that of an Indian child.

"I'm a nurse," Clara said when a lady inquired what she was doing on the train. "I'm taking this little girl home to her parents." She smiled cordially but felt angry when she recalled Dr. McCaig's conversation with the sanatorium.

As she got off the train, Clara was relieved to see Chief and Mrs. Big Smoke standing on the snow-covered platform. Their sled dogs yipped behind a ten-foot snowbank.

"I'm so sorry," Clara said. "The sanatorium didn't have an available bed," she explained without adding "for a treaty Indian." Her words seemed hollow in the quietness.

Mrs. Big Smoke, a small woman, braids poking out from her fur hat, slid to the back of the sled. The chief placed Nellie on her mother's lap, covering them with a coarse blanket. Yanking the restraining hook out of the frozen ground, he cracked a whip, and the dogs began to run. He neither waved nor looked back.

Clara stood alone on the platform, weeping quietly. The scene brought back the day she waited for a horse-drawn carriage to transport her dead son to the Knockholt Cemetery where he was buried in the same grave as his father. *Had Billy survived, he'd have studied horticultural science*, she thought. *He wanted to be a gardener when he grew up.* Clara watched the sled disappear. *Nellie might not grow up to realize her dream. She's very sick.*

After she warmed her hands at the wood stove in the station house, Clara headed to the home of Father Maurice, the retired headmaster of a Catholic residential school in the town of Spanish. He had offered her the housekeeper's quarters for the night until the return train to the Soo. A little later, at dinnertime at the priest's house, he seemed awkward having a visitor sitting across the table.

To break the ice, she finally said, "Tell me about the bread crisis. I understand from Reverend Hives that some parents hired a lawyer when they believed the bread served at the school had no nutritional value. Didn't the *Indian Act* make it illegal to obtain counsel?"

"That was a different matter," Father Maurice said. "In 1927, the government amended the *Indian Act* to prevent Indians from claiming title to certain lands." He chuckled. "Nothing to do with bread."

"The bread problem must have been serious if the parents took legal action."

"I was in charge of their souls, not their bodies." He raised his hands as if a soul were tangible.

"It's hard to have a soul when you're starving. I understand the investigation found the bread had sufficient nutritional value but tasted like sawdust."

"I'm eating the same sawdust," the priest said, bowing his head as though he intended to end the meal with another prayer. "The government decided to assimilate the Indians, and we Catholics jumped at the chance to Christianize them — as Catholics, of course. None of us thought of the cost."

Later, alone in the housekeeper's room, Clara wrote in her address book:

March 1934
It's quite lonely here. There's little heat from the small gas fireplace. I'm sitting on the edge of the bed with covers pulled over my head to write. I'm beginning to see that governments and churches make terrible partnerships. The Canadian government beats out a way of life, and the churches are bent on filling these empty souls with their ideas of faith. [She crossed out the words *beats out* and replaced them with *removes*.] The tender for a new Shingwauk was cancelled because neither the government nor the Anglican Church could afford it. Is money the root of the problem? No! Money cannot take away the loneliness a child feels without parents.

CHAPTER 12

Spring was a long way off, so to mitigate the washroom crisis, Reverend Hives resurrected the outdoor latrines that hadn't been in operation for thirty years. The boys were told to use the outdoor toilets during the day. Many of the children had never encountered a flush toilet until they came to the school. Some preferred to relieve themselves in the woods. At least until the plumbing was fixed, the latrines were considered a healthier alternative. Noel Thomas, the farm manager, utilized the ashes from the furnaces to cut down the odour.

The latrines soon became a clubhouse where boys and girls could meet, an escape from the confinement of the residential school. A coal delivery hatch no longer in use provided their exit. Although custodians hadn't reported anything out of order in the workshops or classroom, Clara detected cigarette smoke. Mrs. Aalto confirmed she had also smelled smoke in the clothing and noticed the occasional burn hole. They agreed to keep quiet until Clara could do a bit of sleuthing.

"I learned to ferret out the truth about what my nursing students at the Galt Hospital were doing to circumvent the rules,"

Clara told Mrs. Aalto. "I discovered through my young daughter, who was an accidental informer, that students were using a fire escape to get into the hospital after curfew hours."

"Young people will do anything to stay out and have fun," Mrs. Aalto said. "What did you do to stop the sneaking in?"

"I had the maintenance man cut off the lower rung. Unfortunately, an enterprising girl used her boyfriend's shoulders to reach the ladder and fell, breaking her arm." Clara didn't add that the girl's father was on the hospital board and furious when she suspended his daughter for six months.

Mrs. Aalto laughed heartily. "You're quite a Sherlock Holmes!"

Clara marched off, enjoying the conspiracy.

One April evening, Clara decided to check the latrines. The crocuses hadn't poked up yet from the ground, but the sewage stench was a sign that it was thawing. Clara stepped onto the concrete block and into the latrine, hoping she wouldn't intercept anyone. The cubicle doors were covered in a graffiti text that she didn't understand. Angry thoughts in Ojibwa or Cree, she imagined. The cigarette butts and gum wrappers littering the floor didn't surprise her. Ivy had brought Clara into the modern world of gum chewing and smoking. Once a year, Clara smoked a cigarette so unattractively that she hoped Ivy would never take up the bad habit, but the tactic hadn't worked.

The stalls themselves were grubby with human waste, but what caught Clara's eye was a small metal container of condoms. She didn't know whether to laugh or cry at the naïveté of her sex talk. Picking up the container with her gloved hands, she opened it and shook the contents onto the floor, then felt sick. The rubber was in such a bad state that it could no longer be protective against pregnancy or disease.

Later that day, she called for a meeting with Reverend Hives, Dr. McCaig, and Mrs. Aalto. Dr. McCaig, as the medical officer of public health, had an established VD clinic downtown and wasn't shy to talk about sexual behaviour.

The headmaster blamed himself for opening up the latrines and lamented that if they had the new school, such things wouldn't happen.

Clara and Dr. McCaig exchanged amused glances.

"These young people are doing this because they're angry," the reverend added.

"They're doing this because it's fun," Dr. McCaig said with a slight smile. "The young never think of consequences."

"I kept a chart of the girls' times of the month," Mrs. Aalto ventured. She seemed pleased to be conspiring with the headmaster and doctor.

"If there's a pregnancy, the girl might not know who the father is," Dr. McCaig suggested. "It looked a bit like a free-for-all in that bathroom."

Reverend Hives sighed. "This is a disaster."

"It doesn't have to be," Dr. McCaig retorted.

Clara was given the job of extracting the truth because she had given the facts-of-life lecture. However, when she assembled the girls, she didn't expect them to be so tight-lipped. While the girls were from different Native communities, they shared the same hatred for the school and were united in their silence, even Doris Canoe.

The waiting ended a month after the girls' silent treatment when Tina Courtney walked into Clara's office. "My pinafore doesn't fit, Matron."

She said it so matter-of-factly that Clara didn't notice the rounded tummy on the girl's small frame. Tina's nickname was "Tiny." Clara wondered if Tina had a boyfriend in the school or if her condition had happened because of coercion. *Regardless of how she got in the family way,* Clara thought, *I'll try to orchestrate an adoption. I did this several years ago in Lethbridge, and the child and adoptive parents are still happy.*

Tina was from a faraway reserve in Northern Ontario. She and her six-year-old brother, Bobby, had flown from Fort Hope to the Soo on the Consolidated Gold Mines plane. Until then, Fort Hope children had gone to a local school. Mine workers had brought alcohol into the community and violence erupted, causing the teacher to leave. To make amends, the Consolidated management offered to fly children to Shingwauk so they could continue their education.

"I thought my ladies-beware chat would have prevented something like this from happening," Clara said.

"My mother will take the baby so I can stay in school," Tina replied.

"Let's start with a bigger tunic."

Dr. McCaig confirmed that "Miss Tiny," as he called her, would deliver a baby in August. The girl confided to the doctor that *it* had happened in the boys' washroom when he suggested *it* had occurred in the outdoor latrines.

Reverend Hives, in his third year as headmaster, revealed the frustration of running a school condemned by the local health department and fire chief. "I'll have to ask the young girl to leave the school. Alas, I can't ask Consolidated to return a pregnant girl to her parents."

"The home across from General Hospital cares for unwed girls and arranges their adoptions," Dr. McCaig offered. He appeared as hamstrung as the headmaster. "We don't have many options for this young girl."

"Years ago I experienced the high-handedness of the Catholic Church over an adoption," Clara said. "Give me a week and I'll find an alternative to the Catholic Home for Wayward Girls."

That evening, Clara woke from a dream with her heart pounding. She went to the kitchen, poured a small glass of brandy, and sat down.

Likely hearing Clara stirring, Ivy came into the kitchen to find her shaking. "What's the matter, Mum?"

"A nightmare. We were back on the ship crossing the Atlantic with Annabel."

"Do you want to talk about it?"

Clara placed a hand under her left breast. "Maybe that will calm me down. The dream was so real. I could feel Annabel's baby, Florence, in my arms as the child's mother hurled herself into the icy waters. In the dream, I was blaming myself for translating the letter from Florence's Quebec grandparents, saying they'd never accept Annabel as their dead son's wife."

Ivy was five years old at the time of Annabel's suicide. Florence's father had died in the war, just as Clara's husband had. It was the letter in French from the dead soldier's parents, translated by Barnaby at Clara's insistence, that had upset Annabel so terribly.

"That was twelve years ago, Mum. You arranged for Florence's adoption and she's now very happy. Were you thinking about Annabel before you went to sleep?"

"No, I was thinking about what I have to do for a pregnant sixteen-year-old Shingwauk girl so she won't feel abandoned like Annabel."

Ivy looked exasperated. "That's what happens when you bring up the facts of life. The girls want to try it."

"I had hoped for the opposite…. Do you remember, Ivy, when we landed in Montreal, there was a newspaperman who kept pestering me?"

"I was only five, but I could read the paper he kept waving at us. It said 'British Nurse Takes Care of Catholic Baby' or something like that."

"I think it was how the priest tried to take little Florence that made me sour on the Catholic Church," Clara said.

"I do remember how angry you were in the customs office. But you need your sleep. Are you worried this girl at Shingwauk might try to kill herself?"

"No. The girl's happy to have her baby."

Ivy frowned. "So was Annabel until she learned the Catholic parents of the dead soldier would abandon *her* but take the baby. Do you think this girl's parents will do the same?"

"It won't matter because I'll arrange an adoption."

"You did well with Annabel's baby, Florence. She's made Mary and Percy Sampson very happy." Ivy rubbed Clara's shoulder. "Mum, you tackled the Catholic Church and won."

Clara smiled. "I'll never forget that smug priest trying to put Florence in a Catholic orphanage. I'll find a good home for Tina Courtney's baby."

"Have you asked Tina what she wants to do?"

"She's digging in her heels right now, but she'll come around. No sixteen-year-old wants to be burdened with a baby."

"An Indian girl might not see things the same way," Ivy suggested.

"Nor did the Catholic Church."

CHAPTER 13

Even though Ivy knew Clara was busy making arrangements for Tina Courtney, she expected her mother to attend her graduation at Sault Collegiate. "Graduation will be held in our gymnasium at eleven in the morning. I'm banking on you being there, Mum."

"I will if you give me the date. Perhaps Lily and I can bury the hatchet and we'll both go."

"That would make me so happy. The Italian students will come with an entourage of relatives. Grandmas, parents, and siblings will take up all the seats, so you better get to the school early."

Ivy had completed her final year of secondary school with high marks in all subjects except French. To justify Ivy's low mark in class, the French teacher had written in her end-of-year report: "Ivy frequently clowned around."

"You're going to have to speak some French when you get to Montreal," Clara said.

"I'll just have to wing it."

"A wing *and* a prayer." *She'll learn quickly how it matters to speak to patients in their own language*, Clara thought.

At the graduation ceremony, Ivy won the English prize, which didn't surprise Clara, since her daughter had won a literary prize at twelve, receiving a leather-bound edition of Rudyard Kipling's Mowgli stories, which she loved. The irony wasn't lost on Ivy as the principal presented her with the heavy two-volume edition of the *Petit Robert* dictionary.

"We thought this appropriate for a young lady going to Montreal," he said. "Shall I help you carry them?"

Clara chuckled. "She'll have to bring the heavy tomes to the bedside of her French patients."

Lily laughed, too. Clara had rarely spoken to Lily after the New Year's Eve deceit. She had demanded of Lily: "If you could drive Ivy to Marconi Hall, why couldn't you bring her home rather than let her be part of a police raid?"

"Maybe *you* should learn to drive," Lily had retorted. But that was also when she apologized. Ivy's graduation signalled a truce between the two sparring ladies.

Relatives of the graduates streamed out onto the hillside after the ceremony. The south side of the school had a commanding view of the St. Marys River and the American Soo. Parents, many with little education, showed their pride at having a graduate in the family. Bottles of home-brewed wine were handed to embarrassed teachers.

"I'm surprised to see liquor at a graduation exercise," Clara said.

"Wine is the Italian way of saying thank you," Lily said. "It serves as cash in this bad economy."

Clara circulated through the crowd, occasionally asking, "What will you do with your diploma?" She expected the young Italians to say they would look for jobs at the steel plant, but she was surprised that most were going on to higher education. This contrasted with the Anglo-Saxon girls, who hoped to clerk in a ladies' department store.

Ivy had disappeared with other graduates to a beach party, and Lily decided to have a cordial with Clara. They were both proud of Ivy making a nice group of friends and doing well in her school results. In Lethbridge, a few of the girls in Ivy's class had nicknamed her "Ether" until the teacher demanded they stop or she would report it to their parents. Some of the meanness went underground, which was harder for the teacher to control.

"I noticed you had quite a conversation with Irma D'Agostina," Lily said to Clara. "She's a lovely girl."

"An ambitious girl. She was accepted at the University of Toronto."

"And like most second-generation Italians, she'll move to the east end," Lily said. "They'll become lawyers and doctors."

"Marriage is hard enough, Lily, without adding religious or cultural hurdles. Ivy has already had too many complications brought on by the war. I don't want her to have to work as I have. A good marriage will ensure she *doesn't* have to."

Clara and Lily rarely hugged, but they embraced each other with tears.

"We've both had our hardships," Lily said. "And Ivy will, too. We can't prevent that."

CHAPTER 14

Mindful of how hard nursing students work, Clara wanted Ivy to spend at least part of her summer at a cottage before leaving for Montreal. Clara could afford to take three unpaid weeks of her own choosing. Before telling Reverend Hives about her plans to be away from school, she paid a visit to Maggie Stone, her real-estate agent, and told the woman she was looking for a cottage to rent. Cottages on a lake were relatively rare in England.

"I'd like my daughter to have a real Canadian holiday before she leaves," Clara told Maggie.

"I have a cottage — or camp, as we Sooites say — to rent for the month of August at Batchawana Bay, a forty-five-mile train ride from the Soo. It's an enclave of local families just on the edge of an Indian reserve — a beautiful area that's attracted painters from Southern Ontario."

"Ivy will be more interested in people her age than the scenery," Clara said.

"The camp is next door to a family with a daughter Ivy's age."

"I'll take it! You've served us well, Maggie." Outside the agent's office, she chuckled at the memory of the real-estate broker in

Lethbridge. Sam McClintock was a shyster who rented brothels to prostitutes. *No comparison*, she thought.

The two-hour train ride wasn't disappointing. Clara could understand why artists travelled long distances to capture on canvas the cascading rivers that flowed into Lake Superior through thick forests. This romantic notion was accompanied by the thought of the bugs they would encounter. The cottage was a twenty-minute walk from the train station through a well-trod path in the mosquito-ridden woods. But the buzzing mosquitos were completely forgotten the moment she and Ivy spotted Lake Superior beyond the sandy beach.

"It's the size of an ocean!" Ivy exclaimed. Inside the cottage, she remarked on the peculiar odour.

"All cottages smell the same," Clara said. "It's a mixture of old wood, fireplace ashes, and musty mattresses."

"I only remember holidaying at the main lodge at Waterton Park in Alberta," Ivy said, obviously confused by Clara's seeming familiarity with cottaging.

"A few years ago when you were away visiting a friend, I rented a summer cabin at Waterton Park. I remember the fireplace was made of puddingstone, which is local to the Soo but not Alberta." Clara's face grew wistful as she ran her hand over the multi-hued pink puddingstones of the fireplace. "Memories ... we never forget the precious ones."

Clara wondered if Ivy was aware that she hadn't been alone in the Waterton cabin. Perhaps her daughter knew she had been there with her friend, Alistair. Ivy, as far as Clara understood, only knew Alistair as an amateur astrologist who read the lines on her small hand and predicted her future.

Leaving Clara to reflect on her past privately, Ivy went into the smaller bedroom to unpack. When her daughter returned to the living room, she gave Clara a big hug.

*   *   *

Ivy and Clara had arrived at Batchawana on a Monday, and as the days passed, Ivy began to miss her school chums and asked if she could invite a friend to the cottage for a few days. They were discussing what friend when a striking dark-haired girl emerged from the trees and opened the door of the screened-in porch where mother and daughter were shelling peas.

"I'm Jean Donnelly," she said. "My mother would like you to come for a glass of sherry at five today. My brothers arrive tomorrow with my dad, and the house will be chaos. Just the girls tonight."

"That's a welcome invitation," Clara said. "It's been rather quiet this week."

"It's nice to meet someone my age," Ivy said. "Should I bring my bathing suit?"

"If you like swimming in the Arctic."

Clara and the girls laughed.

"I don't swim," Clara added.

"My mother doesn't, either. See you at five," Jean said, disappearing into the woods.

The Donnelly cottage was much bigger than the one Clara had rented. Ed Donnelly had inherited a coal and building supply company from his father, who had been a businessman and chief of police in the area. At his death, it was hard to find a casket big enough to fit his enormous frame. An astute yet jovial man, he had been respected and loved by his constables. He had bought many of the properties for sale along the waterfront when Francis Clergue, the American industrialist, went bankrupt.

Ellen Donnelly had a ceremonial manner about her that seemed strange for a woman who grew up on a farm with a dozen siblings. "I had to adopt city ways when I married Ed," she explained as she served the sherry on a silver tray with linen napkins. "My sisters think I'm putting on airs, but Ed likes the formality."

Jean and Ivy came running up from the lake, shivering under their towels. Dressed in warmer clothes, they sat by the fire with glasses of sherry to discuss nursing school in Toronto. Jean was in her second year and full of gruesome stories.

Ellen didn't know there was a residential school in the Soo. Despite this ignorance, she was intently interested in the health problems that Clara described, particularly those due to the poor nutrition in the food.

"Do they have a farm?" Ellen asked.

"They do, but much of what they grow is sold. The children were drinking milk directly from the cow. The city banned unpasteurized milk, but the school's outside the city limits, so they could get away with it until Ogre Durling arrived."

Ivy and Jean escaped to the outdoor porch leaving the mothers to their own gossip.

"Private conversation," Clara joked as they watched their daughters leave.

"Jean's no doubt telling your daughter about her brothers, none of which will be positive."

Both ladies chuckled.

Later, when Clara and Ivy returned to the rented cottage, Clara had to reignite the wood stove. "It's a simple supper tonight," she said. "Baked ham, bread, and peas. What did Jean have to say?"

Ivy wasn't coy. "Her older brother's called Red. He has thick, wavy brown hair and bronze skin from being outdoors. Jean's story is that Red blushed in elementary school when the teacher remarked that his buttons were open. His classmates teased him, and the name stuck. He's in pre-med at the University of Toronto."

"What about the other brothers?"

"They *do* have red hair. I only remember Jack Donnelly, who's in grade ten. He's a bit of a rascal."

"Too young for you."

"Jean said I wouldn't like any of them."

Clara soon discovered that everyone with a cottage on the bay was related to Ellen. Ed had been the first to build, and some of her relatives followed. They were an outdoors family and spent the weekends fishing, cooking, and then eating their catch of the day. Ivy enjoyed baking with Mrs. Donnelly who, unlike Clara, was a marvellous cook.

The Donnelly boys worked for their father during the summer doing whatever job *he* felt would build character. Ed Donnelly had smoked since he was ten and suffered from emphysema. The construction and coal dust he had breathed through most of his life had further compromised his lungs. He was breathless after a short walk to the beach.

One sunny afternoon, Red returned from fishing and Clara noticed the scar on his side when he went off to get dressed.

"I suppose you're wondering about that ugly scar," Ellen said. "It might not be so noticeable if it wasn't keloid."

"I assumed your son had a kidney operation," Clara said.

"Yes. One of his kidneys was removed at Montreal General Hospital when he was sixteen. The stones were excruciating when they passed." Ellen tossed her head back and laughed. "Maud Irving, a crusty old math teacher, came to the house to tutor him. Maud always liked Red," she added thoughtfully. "Mothers, like teachers, shouldn't have favourites. Miss Irving and I are responsible for Red being a bit spoiled." Turning the subject away from Red, Ellen asked Clara, "What brought you to the Soo?"

"I moved for health reasons. High blood pressure indicated I should get out of the mountains."

"Ed tells me Batchawana is the fourth-highest mountain in Ontario," Ellen said. "But that's nothing like the Rocky Mountains."

Clara realized Ellen was thinking of Calgary, but there was nothing in her tone that suggested she didn't believe Clara. If Ellen had pursued the issue further, Clara would have mentioned losing her job, but Ellen didn't seem curious. If her new friend had been the gossipy sort, she would know that Clara had been the superintendent of a hospital in Lethbridge and was now a nurse at a residential school. Certainly, poor health wouldn't direct Clara to such awful circumstances.

Returning to her cottage through the woods, Clara dispelled her fear by remembering the clash she'd had with the newly wealthy Lethbridge businessmen. *They wanted to build a new hospital, and I argued to expand the existing one. I put up a fight that angered the recent millionaires, and when the crash came and they were no longer so powerful, I was a target of their disappointment. I could have been more diplomatic,* she mused.

The two ladies sought each other's company daily during the remaining weeks Clara rented the nearby cottage. Ellen was as domestic as Clara was professional. She brought over homemade berry pies that Clara and Ivy could never finish. When Ellen learned that Clara had treated hundreds of soldiers with breathing problems, she had questions as to what could be done for Ed.

Clara told Ellen what she could about breathing problems and then said, "After all this chatting, I need some exercise."

"Berry picking will do the trick," Ellen suggested, and drew a map of the paths around the cottage. "Keep your head up because bears are looking for berries, too."

CHAPTER 15

August was the height of the blueberry season. Ellen's inland map led Clara to an explosive patch of blue-grey and green. She listened for any motion that might mean bears were nearby and then clanged the metal bucket she was carrying with a rock, dropping berries into the pail and occasionally into her mouth. A rustle made her jump, and she expected to see a bear. Her heart raced. Two brown-skinned women with braided hair were on their knees filling their own pails. They nodded and stood up to move elsewhere.

Clara raised her hand so they wouldn't walk away. "Do you speak English?"

They shrugged as though Clara had asked a stupid question.

"Can you show me how to get to the Martin family? William Martin?" She lowered her hand so they would understand she was asking about a boy.

Their glances were wary, and Clara decided not to mention that she knew the Martin children from Shingwauk. *These women might well be former students*, she thought. *They'll know what white people do to braids.*

The ladies walked Clara a hundred yards through the trees until they reached the edge of a clearing where children were running, laughing, and trying not to be "it." Then they turned back toward the berry patch without uttering a word.

The game of tag is as old as Methuselah, Clara thought. Rubbish, broken parts of machines, and unidentifiable discarded items provided an obstacle course to avoid getting tagged. The children stopped playing when Clara approached.

"William Martin?" Clara queried, again lowering her hand.

Lila Martin scuffled forward with her chin on her chest. "I'm Lila," she whispered, raising her hand as if she were in a classroom.

Clara couldn't hear what the little girl had said but recognized her as the one whose hair she'd checked for lice. "I've come to say hello."

The children circled Clara, hoping for a treat. She smiled and extended her berry pail. The little hands dug in greedily, and Clara put the risk of getting pinworms from dirty hands to the back of her mind. *The berries will be cooked in a pie*, she hoped. Pinworms were a constant problem at Shingwauk, since children scratched their behinds and had no place to wash their hands.

The tag game resumed, and Lila led Clara to her cabin, which backed onto the woods at the edge of the clearing. Clara waited while Lila informed the family there was a visitor. A tall man limping on a right peg leg, looking anxious and hostile, came out on the stoop. He was darker-skinned than Lila and more square-jawed. His long grey braid rested on his shoulder, and Clara assumed the man was Lila's grandfather.

"I'm the school nurse," Clara said. "I was picking blueberries nearby and came to say hello."

"I'm Albert Martin, Lila's grandfather," the man said, seeming less hostile. "I thought you might be from Children's Aid."

"Just a friendly visit. How are you managing on the wooden leg?"

Albert came down the stairs, holding the railing for support. "I was a non-commissioned lance corporal in the Great War, earning a citation for bravery. 'Follow the braid!' my commander would shout." He flipped his braid. "I had to fight to keep this hair. I had to prove myself by being the best marksman." Albert enjoyed seeing Clara's surprise. "Killed hundreds of Germans."

"I didn't know Indians fought in the war."

"One hundred Indians just from Northern Ontario," Albert said. "We're warriors, naturals on a battlefield. The government don't know what to do with us now we're home."

"I nursed in England during the war."

"But no Indians."

"They were all soldiers. My husband didn't make it. He died when the Germans used gas."

"I'm sorry." His manner softened.

"Is William here?"

"He works with his father at the logging camp when he comes home in the summer. The missus goes along to cook. Lila and me keep the fires burning here and look after the boy."

"Go back with your friends," Clara said, tweaking the girl's ear gently.

Albert was a talker, and Clara stayed for a while before she delivered the pail of berries to Ellen.

August 1934

I picked blueberries today near the Batchewana Reserve, not far from where the Martin children live. Some Native ladies at the blueberry patch led me to the Martins where I met Albert, the children's grandfather hobbling around on the original peg leg he was provided after the war. I discovered that without formal education, he was passed over for commissioned officer even though he was a decorated soldier. Worse still, only commissioned officers get upgraded legs. More government trickery to keep the Indian down. I think it was Duncan Campbell Scott who said take the Indian out of the child. I'm trying not to be part of that.

CHAPTER 16

Returning to the city to pack for Montreal was a letdown for Ivy after a fun-filled summer at Batchawana. Clara had overheard Jean Donnelly's advice on nursing schools. "Royal Victoria Hospital in the heart of Montreal will have stricter rules than Toronto General," she had said. "It's the difference between the mostly Presbyterian society in Toronto and the French Catholics in Montreal."

The three-week holiday provided an opportunity for Clara and Ivy to enjoy each other without the intrusions they'd experienced at the Galt. Living at the hospital had meant Clara was always on call. When they moved into the Hilltop duplex, Clara had ordered a cord of wood despite her usual frugality. *I'll miss our fireside chats*, she thought, sitting on Ivy's bed while her daughter packed.

The next morning, Ivy was off to the train station with Sergeant Stuart and Clara. The police officer, with the help of a platform worker, loaded Ivy's trunk into the baggage car, leaving Ivy with a small overnight suitcase to keep on the train. Clara tried to hold back her tears.

"I'll make you proud," Ivy said.

Clara mouthed "Write often" from the platform, hoping Ivy could read her lips.

Ivy nodded, clutching the first-class ticket Clara had purchased, which included dinner in the dining car. She pressed her face against the window to be funny, but Clara could see the tears. Sergeant Stuart handed her his handkerchief, and Clara realized she was crying, too.

In the days that followed Ivy's departure, Clara performed the lice checks with the stern-faced custodians, dreading the routine. They never asked if a youngster had had a nice holiday or if they had anything important to report like the birth of a sibling or any other major event. This was Clara's second year, and she noted happily that if hair hadn't grown much in the summer, it wasn't lopped off. The newcomers had no such advantage.

Reverend Hives planned a picnic for the boys at Point aux Pins, fourteen miles from the school, to take advantage of the end-of-August weather. It was cooler in the evenings, but the days were hot. The kitchen prepared food the children had never tasted, such as meat sandwiches and fresh fruit. Reverend Hives, who wasn't going on the picnic, hovered over the kitchen staff to make sure everything was done to his order, including the girls being served the same sandwiches at lunch.

Clara was asked to supervise the outing. She gave the idea some serious thought but declined because she couldn't swim. Her holidays as a child in England were at the seaside where she admired the ocean but never dived in. She was, however, on hand the morning of the outing to herd the line of rambunctious boys into the back of the farm truck. The boys pushed one another and jabbered in their own languages until the farm manager, Noel Thomas, told them good-naturedly to "Shut up."

"Boys might wander off the path into a thicket of poison ivy," Clara said, handing a first-aid kit containing anti-itch cream to Kay Loucks, the teacher going on the trip. Mable Morrison, the other lady on the outing, was the custodian in charge of the junior boys' dormitory. The two women were too busy gossiping to notice the jostling.

The engine sputtered several times before engaging. Noel leaned out the window. "I do know something about trucks," he said as he settled into the front cabin. "I was a mechanic during the war and a vehicle broke down every hour."

The older boys exchanged glances, suggesting they didn't believe Noel could fix anything. As the truck rolled forward, Clara admonished herself quietly for not knowing how to swim. *I would have loved an outing on Lake Superior*, she thought.

Around three in the afternoon, she walked toward the river, anticipating the return of the farm truck momentarily. When the boys came back, she expected to be cleaning a number of scrapes and cuts typical of a day in the woods. Small wounds scratched by dirty hands became impetigo, which could spread throughout the school. Reaching the edge of the river, she shivered as the strong current snatched debris and carried it downstream. The temperature had dropped, and she regretted not putting on a sweater. Reverend Hives came running down the driveway, and Clara rushed to meet him. It was now two hours after the expected arrival time, and she suspected the headmaster had bad news. *Perhaps the truck broke down and the children are walking back to the school*, she thought.

The headmaster was out of breath and agitated when he intercepted Clara. "I've just received a telephone call from Dr. McCaig. He's at Point aux Pins with the police. Dudley Shilling drowned. Miss Loucks and Miss Morrison have stayed back to explain what happened."

"Oh, no!" Clara gasped. "This is terrible. How on earth did Dudley drown with three adults supervising?" She shook her head in disbelief and walked quickly with Reverend Hives to intercept the truck rattling up the driveway.

Before Noel could open the back hatch, the boys jumped over the sides of the truck and huddled in a group, bewildered and frightened. Dudley's younger brother was the smallest boy on the trip. He looked overwhelmed. Dudley had been his protector against bullies in the school. The Shilling boys had become wards of the school when their parents died. Dudley was a prankster and very popular with the boys, though he was a headache for the staff. The only thing that kept him from running away was not having a place to go. Little Henry spoke oddly with a severe harelip. The boys imitated him until Dudley stepped in.

Reverend Hives asked the boys to meet him in the dining room. "We need to discuss what happened."

Clara followed him into the school with her arm around Henry. "There *will* be an inquest, then?"

Without answering, Reverend Hives entered the dining hall and closed the door behind him. Clara was hurt and disturbed that he didn't include her, the school nurse, in such a tragic matter. She put on a sweater and went outside.

She could hear digging in the cemetery and walked over to speak with Noel, who was slumped over a shovel and peering down a hole. "Reverend Hives has kept me out of the loop. Tell me what happened, Noel."

"I don't know, Matron."

"What do you mean, you don't know? You drove the boys!"

"I couldn't drive the truck through the soft sand, so I parked it some distance from the picnic area and let the boys walk the rest of the way. There have been reports of vandalism in the Point aux Pins area and I was worried hoodlums might strip my truck, so I stayed back. People are desperate these days."

"So you didn't see Dudley drown?"

"I didn't even hear the commotion. I just don't know what happened."

Clara knew Noel could swim across the St. Marys River to the American side. Had he been present, he likely could have intervened. "Can Miss Morrison and Miss Loucks swim?"

"I'm not sure. I suspect so, or they wouldn't have offered to supervise. I'm ashamed my truck came before the boys' safety."

Noel jammed the shovel into the dirt. "I'm sure this will come out in an inquest."

"An inquest isn't a court of law, Noel. It serves to identify problems and make recommendations."

Noel released the breath he'd been holding while he listened to Clara.

She put her hand on his shoulder. "We all make mistakes, Noel."

Clara walked toward the stone church named after Bishop Fauquier, who had been buried at Shingwauk the same year she was born. She stood on the steps of the chapel and gazed west down Queen Street. Noel's house was adjacent to the school property. His teenage sons were tossing a football on the lawn. The boisterous shouts of his boys contrasted with the sombre conversation inside the school.

CHAPTER 17

Miss Loucks and Miss Morrison didn't appear at the school the week following the drowning. Reverend Hives assured Clara that the police and coroner reports would be available to read as well as his own before they were sent to Indian Affairs. He used the word *accident* to describe the drowning. Clara felt strongly that an inquest should be held to determine what had gone wrong. When she was in charge at the Galt Hospital, there had been inquests that, in her mind, improved the standard of care without blaming the staff or hospital. *The school is* in loco parentis *for these children who are so far away from their homes,* she thought. *An inquest could prevent another drowning and any other accident.* All these thoughts and more whirled in her head as she waited to read the reports.

The interment took place Saturday afternoon in the school graveyard, laying Dudley to rest among many other deceased students who were marked by crude wooden crosses, many of them rotted. After the burial service, Clara wandered through the cemetery, which testified to the history of the school. An eight-year-old girl from Walpole Island had died in 1918 from the flu pandemic. Clara wondered if she, like Dudley, was a ward of the school. A deteriorated headstone with the inscription "Arthur, Son of a Supreme Court Justice" seemed odd and even more unusual in a residential school cemetery.

This burial would be well before Reverend Hives's time, Clara thought. *Perhaps the child was adopted from an Indian family or the father wanted his son, buried in this lonely graveyard, to have status.*

Clara's eye was caught by another inscription describing a deceased who had worked at the school as "devoted." *She would have to be*, Clara thought. What struck her was the separation of Native graves from white ones.

Sergeant Stuart was waiting to drive Clara home. She signalled that she needed to retrieve something in her office. After fifteen minutes, Clara noticed he had entered the doorway, reluctant to disturb her. She was bent over documents spread out on a table, hands on her hips, a matron's posture. Something was wrong. She turned abruptly and said tersely, "How could the Shingwauk employees on the outing to Point aux Pins not be aware six boys had buggered off?" Clara could see the surprise on Sergeant Stuart's face. He had never heard her swear.

"The attempt to rescue and resuscitate the boy would have taken forty minutes," Clara added. "How could they not hear something dreadful was taking place? There are three differing accounts of what happened to the boy and those who tried to save him. The reports don't add up to a truthful explanation."

The sergeant had seen Clara indignant before. She valued the truth. It was a nurse's lies that had led to her dismissal from the Galt Hospital.

"Sergeant Stuart, this is a whitewash," she insisted.

He stepped forward with the patient expression he always offered Clara. Despite a ten-year friendship, she had never called him by his Christian name, Robert.

"The report has already been sent to Indian Affairs," Clara told him. "I'm reading a copy."

"Is that not what you expected, Matron?"

Clara perceived the sarcasm. Sergeant Stuart wasn't an admirer of the Anglican Church.

"No, it wasn't! I expected Reverend Hives to have me read the report before it was sent to Indian Affairs. I'm the school nurse and responsible for the children's well-being. This makes me unwittingly part of a whitewash, but I won't remain silent."

CHAPTER 18

Clara was deeply disturbed by the incompetence cover-up of Miss Loucks and Miss Morrison, so she did something unusual. Knocking on the door of the upper duplex, she asked Sergeant Stuart to come down for a drink to continue the conversation about the drowning report. Clara had reduced the sergeant's rent to reflect the many chores he performed — she felt this avoided the social obligation she would incur if he worked for her as a favour. Tonight, however, she needed to talk about the drowning and thought a police officer would understand her concerns. Lily and Barnaby arrived at Clara's just as the sergeant was descending the stairs.

"Were we invited to chaperon?" Barnaby quipped.

Clara shook her head and laughed. "No need of that," she replied with an impish grin before her face became serious. "As a coroner, Barnaby, can you explain why there wasn't an inquest into the drowning of a Shingwauk student?" She handed him the copies of the accident report. Then, with Lily, she went into the kitchen to prepare drinks.

Lily attached Barnaby's adaptive handle to a cup and poured two ounces of rye. "He rarely uses the prosthetic arm," she said cheerily, "but he wouldn't part with this handle." She topped his drink with ice and placed it at Barnaby's left side. Clara had arranged her living room furniture for his convenience.

"These are quite different accounts," Barnaby said, handing back the written reports. "The American Coast Guard describes their attempt to resuscitate the boy. On the other hand, Reverend Hives obviously reported the boys' conflicting accounts of the accident. It's quite extraordinary that the youngest boys rushed down the beach unnoticed to find a rowboat and then paddled back to where Dudley had gone down. There must have been screaming."

"Exactly!" Clara cried. "Where were Miss Loucks and Miss Morrison when the tragedy was happening?"

"I suspect cowering in fear for their own safety," Lily offered, "otherwise they would have run to get the boat rather than leave two little boys to do this! They absolutely had to hear the shouts."

"The farm manager, Noel Thomas, said the women weren't more than a hundred yards away," Clara said. "In essence, Reverend Hives has protected the reputation of the school and these two spineless ladies, and no one in the school is apologizing."

"It's a conundrum that Reverend Hives concluded the boys were at fault after chronicling their heroic actions," Sergeant Stuart said. "The word *misadventure* in his report should have been replaced by the word *drowning*. He doesn't even mention that adults were on the outing. And the government official reading these reports didn't ask if there were supervisors present when the boy was drowning."

"There could have been more than one drowning in the chaos of the boys trying to save and then recover Dudley's body in such a strong current," Clara said emotionally. "Miss Loucks and Miss Morrison should have attempted to rescue the boy, not let eight-year-olds step into the emergency!"

"The police officer would report what he was told," the sergeant said. "In the absence of seeing what happened, Miss Loucks and Miss Morrison would have to concoct credible stories. Perhaps the Coast Guard needed its own version of events. They are, after all, responsible for safety in those waters."

"Dr. McCaig is devoted to those children," Barnaby said. "His work with them is entirely voluntary."

"Shouldn't he have interviewed the boys?" Clara asked.

"He would have no reason to doubt Miss Loucks's and Miss Morrison's accounts," Barnaby said. "Perhaps he was afraid to stir up controversy with the possibility of a new school being built. All Indian Affairs wants is the number of the deceased student. They aren't concerned with the details."

Clara considered the possibility of quitting and searching for work as a public health nurse. The thought of buying a car and driving daily to see her patients eliminated this thread of thinking. She did, however, ruminate on the recent events that were hard to understand. Until the drowning, Clara had never doubted Reverend Hives's concern for the children in his school. He had learned their language, buried them in their own tongue, and made his own exceptions to the *Indian Act*. Dr. McCaig's affection for the children was obvious. The doctor and headmaster had taken the train to personally petition government leaders in Ottawa for a new school.

Dr. McCaig was in the headmaster's office, and Clara decided this was the time to confront them with her misgivings. They had wittingly or unwittingly been part of the cover-up of Dudley's drowning. Clara was in her second year at the school and didn't want to become a pariah as she had in Lethbridge. Dr. McCaig was reading an official-looking letter over Reverend Hives's shoulder. They glanced up with such triumphant smiles that Clara knew this wasn't the time for accusations.

"We're going to have a new school," Reverend Hives said emotionally.

Clara figured they probably knew from her face that she had come on another matter, despite telling them, "Congratulations to you both."

"I can read your thoughts," Dr. McCaig said. "Reverend Hives told me you felt strongly that an inquest should have been held."

"Miss Morrison and Miss Loucks told you that they had no idea there was a commotion. I don't think you heard the truth, Dr. McCaig. I wish you'd spoken with the boys and not just taken the words of Miss Loucks and Miss Morrison for what happened."

"I'm very sorry that I was misled by the ladies. I had no reason to doubt their accounts of the events."

"The government would use *any excuse* to put off this project," Reverend Hives interjected.

"Inquests into Indian deaths take years," Dr. McCaig offered.

"Our funds are secured," Reverend Hives added, looking at the document on his desk. "Canadian National Railways deposited government bonds in the Bank of Montreal yesterday to be used to build the Shingwauk School. Would you want those funds to be relegated to another building project, Matron? It's a case of David and Goliath."

"A new school won't improve residential life unless the ethos changes," Clara insisted.

That evening, after her meeting with Reverend Hives and Dr. McCaig, Clara noted in her address book a brief thought:

August 15, 1934
Residential schools are bringing out the worst in everyone.

PART TWO

Change of Heart

CHAPTER 19

In her first letter home, Ivy wrote:

> I bought a smart little hat at Ogilvy's Department Store on Mountain Street. Student nurses must wear *un chapeau* when they leave the hospital. Being hatless when I arrived, I borrowed one from Sass to walk the six blocks to Ogilvy's.

A good sign if Ivy's using French, Clara thought. She had to read on to learn that "Sass" was Cecily Mitchell from Senneville, a fancy suburban area west of Montreal. Ivy's letter was brief, but Clara enjoyed the chattiness.

In a second letter, Clara learned more:

> Sass lives in the room next door and has a serious beau that her parents don't know about. He's a second-year resident and five years older. She says her parents wouldn't approve. They took us out for lunch when they dropped her off at the residence. According to Sass, her mother

writes crime novels under another name, but I'm not sure I believe her. If she does, I'll send you one. The Mitchells asked me to come to Senneville when we have a day off, but Sass said that never happens.

A third letter was concerning to Clara because Ivy seemed to be involved in some kind of residence intrigue:

We were too many ladies to be housed in the original nurses' residence, so the overflow, including me, had to share half the medical residents' ward. There's a strict rule that nursing students aren't to socialize with them. The authorities separated us with doubled particleboards. We strung a clothesline between the partitions to send messages. Sass wasn't in the overflow group, so I sent her notes down the clothesline. We have many ways to get around the rules.

Our residence looks like an ancient castle with turrets, gables, and dormer windows that don't let in much light. We have to pass through a narrow, dark corridor to get to the hospital where we have our classrooms. We do have a brightly lit foyer with beautiful antiques to entertain our friends under the watchful eye of a senior nurse. Sadly, poor Sass has to meet her medical resident beau in the utility closet.

Clara gleaned from the letter that Ivy was having fun. She did worry that amusement might turn to contempt for authority as it had with a student at the Galt Hospital.

"Curfews are made to keep your daughter safe," Clara had explained to the director in front of the hospital board. "Your daughter chose to stay out late and tumbled off the ladder, trying to get into the hospital unnoticed."

Clara sat at her writing desk to compose a return letter to Ivy. After conveying the local news that might interest her daughter, she ended with a motherly reminder: "Remember that you went to Montreal to train as a nurse, not a comedian."

In November, Clara received a letter from Ivy indicating she wouldn't be home for Christmas. "I thought out-of-town first-year students were given a week at Christmas to visit their families and to recuperate from the rigours of the first few months," Clara wrote back. She was disappointed and sent a follow-up letter to ask why before waiting for Ivy's answer:

> Sass isn't considered out-of-town but desperately wants to have a few days with her medical student boyfriend, Robert Mason, somewhere other than a utility closet. I've offered to cover for her so she can go home. Pamela Hobbs, our director, is agreeable.

Clara didn't comment further and accepted that Ivy was staying in Montreal for a friend.

Had Clara inquired further about Pamela Hobbs, she would have learned the true story behind Ivy's altruism. In her first few months, Ivy had adjustment difficulties. She fainted while observing her first operation on the surgical ward. The procedure was the amputation of a diabetic patient's leg. It wasn't the surgery itself that overwhelmed her, but the condition of the leg. Until the elderly man arrived in hospital as an emergency patient, he had never seen a doctor. The putrid smell of his ulcerated, infected skin nauseated Ivy. She dropped to the floor. Her last recollection was the doctor giving her a shove with his foot, saying, "Get her out of here!"

But it was Ivy's second disgrace that led Miss Hobbs to take action. Ivy had thrown up on the operating table during a messy bowel operation. That time she didn't pass out and was able to navigate to the washroom. The head nurse was waiting at the door when Ivy came out, ghost-like and embarrassed. She transferred Ivy to the geriatric ward.

It was there during a December cold snap that Ivy began to shine. The hospital heating system had broken down, and the frail patients were shivering under thin bedcovers. The hospital budget had no money for ward supplies due to the economic crisis. Ivy went to Miss Hobbs for permission to collect blankets from the rich families in Montreal's Golden Square Mile.

"Many of these Square Mile mansions are empty," Miss Hobbs said. "The stock market crash wiped out fortunes, and the hospital, alas, lost its major benefactors."

"Miss Hobbs," Ivy began in her most respectful voice, aware she had been a problem for the director, "perhaps being able to lend blankets during an emergency will restore these benefactors' sense of philanthropy without it costing a red cent."

Miss Hobbs laughed. "Miss Durling, you remind me of your mother. She was a master at improvisation."

She knows Clara, Ivy thought. *Why didn't Mum tell me? That must be the reason Miss Hobbs didn't send me home.* Ivy waited for an explanation.

"I was one of five probationers graduating from the Galt Hospital in the class of 1921," Miss Hobbs explained. "Your mother had just arrived from England. I believe you were five or six at the time. We had few medical supplies following the war. Matron Durling would march to the kitchen and retrieve items from the utensil drawer and then place them in the sterilizer. I recall a staff doctor calling your mother a genius."

Ivy felt a deep pride for her mother that she rarely expressed.

"Until the Depression, over half the wealth of Canada was owned by fifty men living in the Square Mile neighbourhood right next door to the hospital," Miss Hobbs continued. "We looked after their health. Who knows, Miss Durling? Maybe one of these entrepreneurs will contribute to new boilers as well as donating a blanket."

With a "Good luck" from Miss Hobbs, Ivy, wearing her obligatory *chapeau*, left the hospital, heading south to Sherbrooke Street through the McGill University campus and yanking a five-seat toboggan behind her. As she passed the greystone McTavish Reservoir, she had the measure of Montreal's grandness. *The reservoir just holds water but is as elegant as the buildings around it,* she thought. According to Miss Hobbs, the money in the Square Mile came from industries such as furs, shipping, timber, mining, railways, and banking. Ivy was thrilled to be on the McGill campus where many of the doctors at the Galt Hospital had trained.

Winter had only begun, but already the snow was deep. A dozen men heaved the heavy white blanket to clear pathways for the students, many having already left for the holidays. She was glad she had purchased fashionable winter boots at Ogilvy's. Since the clothing requirements for nursing students only listed galoshes, she didn't mention the boots in her letters home, certain she could economize on other things to stay within her budget. Clara never mentioned her financial concerns, but Ivy knew about her mother's sacrifices.

Ivy passed through the Roddick Gates onto Sherbrooke Street, the principal east-west corridor. She intended to go door-to-door on the small streets running north or south from the main route. She had been warned and thus wasn't surprised to see two mansions on Sherbrooke with FOR SALE signs. Ivy decided to try both houses. There was no answer at the first. A young man was clearing the sidewalk a few mansions along, and Ivy approached him.

"My family moved to Westmount," he said.

"Would anyone have left anything behind?" Ivy asked. When the man looked surprised, Ivy quickly added, "I'm a student nurse collecting blankets for elderly patients because our heating system is down."

The man continued to stare at Ivy. She was turning to leave, and he grabbed her arm. "Wait! There are boxes left for a charity. I don't know what's inside. I'll have a look."

Ivy stood at the bottom of the steps. Clara had warned her of the dangers of men. "Always carry a hatpin," she had said. "A quick jab and the element of surprise is enough to get away," she had added. Ivy giggled at the recollection of Clara's old-fashioned ideas. The man returned with an armful of blankets. He secured the piles with a rope, slipping it through the cord that ran the length of the toboggan. Then he insisted on pulling the toboggan up the mountain.

Ivy argued to no avail and then thanked the man.

"I'm Hugh Carsley. My parents bought a smaller house in Westmount. No one wants to buy a mansion these days. I keep the walk shovelled for the real-estate agent."

CHAPTER 20

While Ivy was finding her way as a nursing student in Montreal, Clara was in the Soo patrolling the site where the new school was to be built. She was disturbed to discover the Shingwauk children were playing in the excavated muck. They had made a slide into the gaping hole for the foundation. The chasm was filled with rain and melted snow typical for November, reminding Clara of the bomb craters where many soldiers of the Great War had perished. Few of them could swim, and if they could, crawling up the slippery mud slopes was next to impossible.

The new location was high on a hill behind the original Shingwauk. The old school had weathered seventy years, but the fire department and health authorities had condemned the building years ago. The lack of fire escapes in such an outdated structure was a constant worry for Reverend Hives.

Clara stood on the perimeter, watching a ship loaded with steel cargo navigate the St. Marys River, which separated two countries and joined two Great Lakes. *This is where Chief Shingwauk had wanted to establish a teaching wigwam*, she mused, gazing down at the dismal structure, the "teaching wigwam" that would be torn down. *Chief Shingwauk believed Natives had to learn the white man's ways. He didn't want them to abandon their own,* she thought. Clara flinched, recalling an episode she'd witnessed from outside Agnes Boniface's classroom.

Soon after Clara began work as the school nurse, a little girl named Aka Round Stone arrived in the middle of the week when classes had already started. Shoved into the classroom by a custodian, the shy girl repeated her name when asked.

"In this school, we don't use the names of minerals, animals — or plants, for that matter — to identify a student," Miss Boniface replied. "You'll be Number 321 until I can think of something to call you. Now, Number 321, please go to the back of the classroom and sit in the empty seat."

As little Aka walked to the back, Clara could hear giggles, and minutes later Aka was being shepherded into the corridor, her shoes sopping. The girl's legs were chapped from the urine, and Clara wondered if this was a first accident for the little girl.

"You needed to use the toilet," Clara said softly.

Aka stared up blankly.

Clara knelt and embraced the child. "Oh, my, you don't even know the word."

The memory of little Aka depressed Clara until she returned home to find a letter from Ivy. She was overjoyed that her daughter would have three weeks of summer vacation. Ivy's holiday would be a week longer than the other nursing students — a reward from Miss Hobbs for securing a large financial donation to the hospital as a result of her blanket campaign.

"I'm like Hans Christian Andersen's Little Match Girl," Ivy wrote, causing Clara's mood to brighten. Ivy had tucked in a note from her patients addressed to *La Poupée.* Clara chuckled when she recalled Ivy's disdain for learning French. The image of her daughter lugging the heavy *Petit Robert* off the stage at graduation made her smile.

Ivy's letter made Clara look forward to the summer and prompted her to call Maggie, the real-estate agent, to ask if the cottage beside the Donnellys' was still available to rent. It was. Then Clara wrote to Ellen Donnelly with the news that she and Ivy would be at Batchawana in August. Ellen's reply indicated her daughter, Jean, wouldn't arrive at Batchawana until Ivy's final week. She did say her sons, Red, Jack, and Ian, would be at the cottage on weekends.

Clara decided she wouldn't mention that Jean's arrival at the cottage would be delayed until the last week of Ivy's vacation. However, she relayed the good news that the Barnabys would be renting a cottage nearby.

Ivy replied that she already knew, and Clara buried the hurt that she hadn't been able to surprise her own daughter. She wondered how often Lily and Ivy corresponded with each other.

CHAPTER 21

Once Lily got one project on its feet, she quickly looked for something else to initiate. She had established an English-language teaching centre in the west end of the Soo. It was running well and she no longer spent much time at the West End Library. As she was considering what might be an interesting pursuit, she recalled with pride how she had started a speech therapy program for stutterers while she was a student at normal school. A new opportunity arose when Clara dropped by to discuss the ongoing problem with sixteen-year-old Tina Courtney after the girl delivered her baby. Clara thought Lily might have some suggestions as to how she could help the girl who had arrived from Port Hope in a float plane.

"Reverend Hives has refused to let Tina return to finish her schooling," Clara said. "He suggested she'd be a bad influence."

Lily listened with interest because all she knew of Native girls was that many in Lethbridge had been forced into prostitution in a seedy area just outside the city limits dubbed "The Point." Lethbridge was the first place where she had heard the demeaning word *squaw* to describe a Native woman. It was this violent, disease-ridden area that caused the mayor of Lethbridge to pass a bylaw creating a segregated area where prostitution could be regulated. Chinese laundries, brothels, immigrants, and young couples searching for low rent populated this part of town. Lily and her first husband, Ed, had rented an apartment above a Chinese laundry.

"Tina was turfed out of the home for unwed mothers on the northern outskirts of the city a week after Little Feather was born," Clara continued.

"What an interesting name," Lily mused. She had her own story, having delivered a son with no one to support her. Ed had died in a mining accident while she was pregnant. Unable to pay her rent at that time, Lily was hired by the wife of the manager of the coal mine where Ed had worked. She struck an agreement with Lily to do light housekeeping in return for food and accommodation. With a crying baby, the arrangement didn't last long. Financially strapped with a child to look after, Lily accepted to manage a brothel where her son was fussed over by the young prostitutes.

After hearing Tina's story, Lily offered the girl room and board in exchange for help with her energetic twelve-year-old daughter, Jane, who was in the local public school and full of opinions. Jane was Lily's daughter with James Barnaby, her second husband. Teddy, Lily's strapping sixteen-year-old son with her late first husband, Edward Parsons, was boarding at Scollard Hall, a boys' private school in North Bay. Ed had been a Roman Catholic, and Lily, who held no particular doctrine, believed her son should be brought up in the faith of his father.

"You'll have your hands full with Little Feather and Jane to look after," Lily said when Tina accepted the live-in job.

Clara thanked her niece for the job offer.

Lily smiled. "I think it's because I lived in my glamorous sister's shadow that I favour the underdog. I suppose I'm sticking up for myself or reliving my childhood."

Clara hadn't known Lily when she was growing up but suspected that was what had shaped her as the advocate of underdogs. Lily was her mother's reminder that she had gotten pregnant before she was married. It had turned out well in the end but not without leaving a mark on Lily. Amelia, Lily's mother and Clara's eldest sister, had become pregnant and was sent from England to Halifax, Nova Scotia, to deliver her baby. She boarded with an Anglican minister and did light housekeeping for a member of the church who was ill and feeble. Amelia fell in love with the parishioner's son, a pharmacist, and they were married before Lily was born. Lily's mother had favoured her younger daughter, Beth, who was quite happy to eclipse Lily. Robert White was more than Lily's father in name. He adored her.

Clara had first met Lily when she was running a brothel and fiercely defending "her" girls when upright ladies in town insulted them. During prohibition, brothels in Lethbridge were often the only place to get an alcoholic drink. The prostitutes gave dancing lessons alongside their more conventional services. Men gravitated to them for the socialization they didn't have at home. Their wives, of course, treated the young entertaining ladies with disdain. Clara was proud to have witnessed Lily's underdog mindset that had allowed her to run a brothel in Lethbridge, teach English to marginalized Italian women in the Soo, and more recently to offer refuge to a Native child.

I've occasionally sparred with Lily, Clara thought, *but never disrespected her.* Her recollections of the past were broken by Lily's enthusiastic outburst.

"I'll get Tina back on her feet and returned to her community in Fort Hope with Little Feather in her arms," she promised. "In the meantime, Jane, who's too old for dolls at twelve, can practise *mothering* a real baby."

Tina settled in well at the Barnabys' house and was teaching Jane to speak Ojibwa. One scorching hot day, Clara arrived to check on Tina, only to find Lily full of excitement about a play chronicling the life of a fictional Ojibwa hero, based on Henry Wadsworth Longfellow's epic poem, *The Song of Hiawatha*. The performance would take place outdoors at the end of July in a small town called Desbarats, thirty-five miles east of the Soo. Lily had heard that rich Americans from Chicago attended the annual performance of *Hiawatha*, including the famous actress Helen Hayes, who had a summer cottage on Lake Huron.

Clara went looking for Longfellow's epic poem and found a tattered handwritten copy in the school library. She speculated that the pages, laboriously written in English, had been a punishment for a language transgression. Discovering Clara poring over the pages, Reverend Hives asked if she was aware of the Garden River performers.

Clara admitted she wasn't, but then said, "I do have a vague recollection that Longfellow's poem was originally published to much acclaim."

"His story of an Indian hero did indeed delight the American public," Reverend Hives said. "And now we have a local performance!" He picked up the well-worn library copy of Longfellow's book-length poem. "This is only a few of the poem's verses."

"Is the production a musical?" Clara asked.

"Natives prefer the oral tradition, but drummers provide a musical background. The production gained international acclaim when a cinematographer, Joe Rosenthal, while visiting friends at Desbarats, filmed the performance. He presented his work in small opera houses across the United States where Americans were ready to pay to have their pictures taken with a 'real Indian.' That was the financial incentive for the impoverished Garden River community to perform annually."

"Such interesting local history," Clara said. "It must be costly to put on."

"It is, but Indian agents with railway interests pay for teepees, headdresses, drums, and other props, justifying the cost because the play increases tourist travel in Algoma."

"I thought Native ceremonies were forbidden," Clara said. "I'm still trying to figure out what is and isn't allowed under the *Indian Act.*"

"The Department of Indian Affairs likes money," the reverend said rather matter-of-factly. "Were it not for their lucrative production, the Garden River Indians would have to succumb to our assimilation policy. Fortunately for the Garden River residents, unlike most Indians, they can hold powwows, sweat lodges, drumming ceremonies, dances, and peace-pipe smoking."

Clara didn't feel she should ask the headmaster his opinion of the policy. *I might not like the answer,* she thought, and thanked Reverend Hives for sharing his knowledge. He admitted he had attended the play in Desbarats many times and had always enjoyed it.

CHAPTER 22

Clara and Lily, with year-old Little Feather strapped on Tina's back, took the train to Desbarats where they planned to stay overnight at the six-bedroom hotel not far from the *Hiawatha* performance. The hotel had a small dining room popular for its home-cooked food and famous for its butter tarts. The ladies had time to eat, and Tina fed Little Feather before they crossed the dirt road to Kensington Point, a spit of land projecting into Lake Huron.

As the sun dropped in the western sky, the Americans, identifiable by their expensive casualwear, secured their mahogany inboards to the dock by heavy metal cleats. Emblazoned in gold on the sterns were names with double meanings such as *Just in Time, Never Again*, and *Too Old?* Already some feather-adorned actors danced and drummed on a torch-lit stage overlooking the lake, waiting for Hiawatha to arrive by canoe. The smartly dressed Americans, bundled in sweaters and shawls against the cool night air, found spots on the crude wooden benches at the edge of the platform. Children sat on the ground cross-legged, swaying to the drum music.

"Let's sit over there," Lily said, heading toward a bench away from the Americans. "I can smell the privilege," she added with a snort. A tall grey-haired man with a red wool sweater draped over his shoulders stood behind the bench with his hands on his wife's shoulders. "That's James Scutter from Lake Forest, Illinois. He has his own squash court."

"How do you know that?" Clara asked.

"My neighbours have a camp on the mainland. Mr. Scutter invited them for a drink. Americans don't hate Canadians. They just think we're boring."

Tina had joined a small band of Garden River Natives not in the pageant, who had huddled under a tarpaulin that served as a tent. She knew a few of them from her time at Shingwauk. The reserve was close to the Soo, and the children from there were able to spend the summer with their families.

Kisses were being planted on Little Feather's bow-like mouth. Clara rose to her feet with a scowl.

"Leave her!" Lily said, grabbing her sleeve. "She's with her own people."

"There's a risk of TB with each kiss."

"Barnaby says it's a problem in the poorest reserves. Garden River's rich by comparison. Let's not argue, Clara. Hiawatha is arriving!"

Natives in elaborate feathered headdresses paddled their birchbark canoes with swift tandem strokes. Hiawatha stood on the shoreline, looking majestically over the water they had just traversed while his men silently and efficiently pulled the canoes onto land. Hiawatha's headdress stood out with its elaborate, colourful beading and abundance of eagle feathers. His waistband held a hatchet and on his back was a quiver of arrows — the tools of a warrior.

Hiawatha leaped onto the stage to join his feather-adorned dancers. They bowed while the seated drummers on the edge of the platform continued their beat.

"We must do this at the school," Clara whispered breathlessly.

Lily arched her eyebrows. "A *Hiawatha* pageant at Shingwauk?"

·"I'm sure Reverend Hives will agree," Clara said, countering Lily's skepticism.

"Let's watch."

Nokomis, Hiawatha's legendary grandmother, sat cross-legged and straight-backed at the door of her wigwam.

"Those are very fancy props," Lily whispered.

Hiawatha strode over to Tina and lifted Little Feather high above his head. He stood before Nokomis, passing Little Feather into the old woman's outstretched hands. Nokomis kissed the baby and placed her in a cradle where Little Feather babbled while the audience chimed, "Isn't she cute."

Making a ceremonial bow, Hiawatha began his lyrical recitation. Lily put her arm around Clara's shoulder. "He's magnificent," she whispered. "If Reverend Hives lets you run the play, I'll help. Maybe Tina could take the part of Nokomis."

They smiled at each other and then shifted their attention to the stage.

Hiawatha turned to the crowd after acknowledging the dancers with a sweep of his arms. The words rolled off his lips.

By the shores of Gitche Gumee,
By the shining Big-Sea-Water,
Stood the wigwam of Nokomis,
Daughter of the Moon, Nokomis.
...
There the wrinkled, old Nokomis
Nursed the little Hiawatha,
Rocked him in his linden cradle,
Bedded soft in moss and rushes,
Safely bound with reindeer sinews;
Stilled his fretful wail by saying,
"Hush! the Naked Bear will hear thee!"
Lulled him into slumber, singing,
"*Ewa-yea!* my little owlet!"

...

Many things Nokomis taught him
Of the stars that shine in heaven;
Showed him Ishkoodah, the comet,
Ishkoodah, with fiery tresses;
Showed the Death-Dance of the spirits,
Warriors with their plumes and war-clubs,
Flaring far away to northward.

Warriors acted out the death dance, writhing, swirling, brandishing tomahawks as they leaped into the air. The audience was too transfixed to clap.

At the door on summer evenings
Sat the little Hiawatha;
Heard the whispering of the pine-trees,
Heard the lapping of the water,
Sounds of music, words of wonder;
"Mirme-wawa!" said the pine-trees,
"Mudway-aushka!" said the water.

Hiawatha cupped his hand to his ear, and the children shouted, *"Mirme-wawa, Mudway-aushka, Mirme-wawa, Mudway-aushka!"*

Saw the fire-fly, Wah-wah-taysee,
Flitting through the dusk of evening ...

The children shouted *"Wah-wah-taysee!"* until Hiawatha raised his hand to shush.

Learned of every bird its language,
Learned their names and all their secrets ...
...
Of all beasts he learned the language,

Learned their names and all their secrets …

…

Forth into the forest straightway
All alone walked Hiawatha
Proudly, with his bow and arrows;
And the birds sang round him, o'er him,
"Do not shoot us, Hiawatha!"

Again, Hiawatha cupped his ear, and the children shouted louder, "Do not shoot us! Do not shoot us, Hiawatha!"

Sang the Opechee, the robin,
Sang the blue-bird, the Owaissa,
"Do not shoot us, Hiawatha!"

There was a mesmerized silence when the performance ended. Hiawatha, surrounded by his dancers and drummers, bowed ceremoniously to the audience.

James Scutter, who was still standing, began the applause. He waved his hat in the air, crying, "Bravo! Magnificent! Touching!"

Hiawatha beckoned the children onstage. Tina retrieved Little Feather, who wrestled in her mother's arms to get down and join the commotion. The baby's mother beamed that her child was part of the applause. Little Feather wriggled to the stage and tottered among the children who were trying on the headdresses the actors had removed, adjusting them to their smaller heads. Parents popped their cameras and then jumped onstage to have their own pictures taken. The band collected more than $100 in James Scutter's hat.

CHAPTER 23

When Lily informed Barnaby that she had rented a cottage at Batchawana Bay, he called it a hare-brained idea.

"Teddy and Jane will be bored to death. Why not send them to a church camp with people their age?" he suggested as an alternative to a wilderness vacation.

"Teddy will have had enough church by the time he comes home," Lily replied wryly. "Church is an everyday occurrence at Scollard Hall."

There was no more discussion of Batchawana until Barnaby entered the house a few days later with a broad smile. "You won't believe this."

"I'd believe *anything* coming from you," Lily retorted as she planted a kiss on his strawberry-blond hair tinged with grey at the temples.

Barnaby's hazel eyes were alight with the news. "Dan MacIntyre's coming to the Soo to visit Clara."

"Dan's a recognized artist in Toronto. The Soo isn't exactly New York City."

"Do you remember how much trouble he had with his prosthetic legs? It was due to Clara, once he was transferred to the Galt hospital and put under her care, that his stumps began to heal."

"You healed his mind," Lily said. "He was so angry."

"I don't think when he enlisted at seventeen he had any idea what to expect. I recall vividly him shouting at me, 'To feel pain in a limb that doesn't exist is unfair.' However, my papers on Dan's phantom limb established my reputation as a medical scholar with the Toronto psychiatrists. Until then, there was little known about shell shock and the painful sensation of phantom limb."

"We have a lot to thank him for," Lily said.

"Clara's going to bring him to Batchawana, and I proposed he stay with us rather than putting her on the sofa."

"I'll be excited to see him."

"Dan will be bringing his wife, Gerda. She's ten years older than him, but I see that as good news for our volatile friend. Clara mentioned his letter sounded quite happy, though phantom limb still plagues him. Apparently, Gerda knows what to do when he has an attack."

"Uh-huh," Lily murmured. "Lucky Dan!"

Dan arrived with Gerda on the same train as the Rossiter girls. K.G. and Jessie were on the platform, beaming as their smartly dressed daughters strode onto the platform. A tall, fine-figured woman stepped off the train before Dan and spoke to the porter, who had been gawking at the Rossiters. The porter quickly stepped forward to assist Dan onto the platform. Gerda thanked him in her Dutch accent.

Clara smiled broadly as she embraced Dan and then shook hands with Gerda. The Rossiters stood back while Dan introduced Gerda to Lily and Barnaby.

"Congratulations, Dan!" Barnaby said, giving him a bear hug. "Your reputation has spread all the way to the Soo." When the

Rossiters remained on the platform, he added, "Dan MacIntyre is a recognized artist in Toronto."

K.G. turned to Clara. "Great War?"

"Double amp from Vimy," Clara replied. "Dr. Barnaby was his doctor in Lethbridge. Dan suffered terribly from phantom limb. Lethbridge was overwhelmed with returning veterans at the end of the war."

Jessie interrupted K.G. and Clara. "No more talk of war. It's not something I want our daughters to know about."

Anne, the eldest Rossiter girl, approached Clara. "My turn to interrupt," she said saucily, smiling at her mother. "Is Ivy home from Montreal? I'd love to see her."

"She arrives next week," Clara said.

"Oh." Anne sighed. "My father's rented a cabin up north to give us an 'Ojibwa experience.'" She rolled her eyes. "I suppose he doesn't want me to become too American."

"Your mother told me you were at the Parsons School of Design," Clara said. "How do you like New York?"

"I *looove* it."

Clara smiled when she detected an acquired New York accent but didn't mention that Ivy would also be holidaying in the woods.

CHAPTER 24

Lily didn't have room in her car for Dan and Gerda after loading the cottage supplies, so the following day they hopped on the train to Batchawana and enjoyed lunch on it while admiring the scenery. When the couple arrived, Lily was busy with Tina Courtney cleaning out the mouse droppings and cobwebs — the annual ritual of opening up a cottage.

Gerda was quick to pick up a broom and help. "I feel I'm back in Holland where the Dutch sweep daily, even if home is a hovel." She whisked the floor with a practised stroke and chuckled, shooing Dan out of the living room area. "We don't want you up a ladder."

Smiling, he joined Jane and Little Feather, who were playing on the screened-in porch.

Lily had invited the Donnelly family for dinner that night along with Clara and Ivy. "I appreciate your extra help to make the cottage spick-and-span," she told Tina as the girl climbed a ladder to dust the curtain rods.

While the ladies purged the cottage of dirt, Barnaby joined Dan on the porch. "Are you up for a walk to the nearby Indian reserve? It's rough ground."

"I'm quite mobile on these legs. I do appreciate you asking. But wouldn't it be dangerous for two white men to arrive on a reserve?"

Barnaby laughed. "Do you think they're going to scalp you, Dan? Truth is, there's not much friction between the white cottagers and the year-round residents on the reserve. At first I worried about Teddy getting into a fight. He can be thorny. But Ed Donnelly heard my concerns and assured me his sons had fished, hunted, and canoed with Indian boys for years. Without trust between the two communities, I imagine Tina Courtney would feel disloyal living with white folks like us."

"Who are we going to visit?" Dan asked.

"Albert Martin, a decorated soldier from the Great War. According to Clara, Albert hobbles around on an old-style peg leg because the government won't purchase a better prosthesis for an Indian."

After hiking for a while, the two men emerged from the woods into a dusty clearing where children chased one another around abandoned rusted cars and machinery.

"Heaven knows what they do with all this junk!" Dan exclaimed.

"Maybe they strip and sell it to the Cohen brothers, who have a scrap metal yard in the Soo."

Albert was sitting on his front stoop, his wooden leg and a crutch beside him. "You the doctor Nurse Durling told me about?" He jerked his chin up in an unfriendly manner, seemingly surprised to have visitors. Then Barnaby's missing forearm caught his attention. "Hard to be a doctor with that."

"I'm the city coroner," Barnaby said. "I was bringing back a stretcher when I got hit. The medics removed the shrapnel but couldn't save the arm."

Albert turned his attention to Dan. "So what's *your* story?" Clearly, the fellow wasn't ready to welcome unannounced strangers.

"They couldn't save my legs, either. Butchering them left me with pretty scarred stumps. I had a hell of a time wearing an artificial leg. Looks like you do, too." Dan picked up Albert's crutch.

"*Whoa now!*" Albert cried. "I need that."

Dan leaned against the stoop railing to unstrap his right prosthesis. Before Albert could react, Dan thrust it at the man. "Give it a whirl."

Albert held up the prosthesis to see how to strap it on. "Much lighter than the peg." He secured it on his stump, walked a few yards, and then turned gingerly.

"You need a better leg," Dan said. "The new ones are half the weight."

Albert took a few more steps. "I can't think what it would be like walking without pain. I could go back to guiding the American hunters in the fall. That's what I did before the war. It was my hunting experience that made me a good soldier." He told them about his time as a sniper and what his war had been like and then shrugged and began unstrapping Dan's leg.

"Hold on," Dan said, raising his hand to halt Albert, who had a suspicious expression. "You've got that prosthetic leg for a week." Before Albert could protest, Dan moved toward the playground awkwardly, supported by Albert's crutch. "Shit!" he yelped. "It's been years since I used crutches."

"Thanks!" Albert shouted as they disappeared into the woods.

Barnaby took up the rear, ready to grab Dan if he stumbled on the uneven ground. When they entered the cottage with a crutch and a missing prosthesis, Dan shot Lily a big grin. She and Tina were perched on round stools husking corn at the kitchen counter while Jane played with Little Feather on the floor.

"From the look on your face, I can see something happened," Lily said, smiling, familiar with Dan's tall tales. "You can be the after-dinner entertainment."

*   *   *

At five o'clock, the appointed hour for guests to arrive, Lily rang the old ship's bell on the back porch.

"I'll head off a bear," Ed Donnelly said confidently, leading the ladies along the path.

Hunched over from his smoking-induced emphysema, Ed didn't reassure Clara, who put a hand over her fast-beating heart. "What would we do if we did encounter a bear?"

"Most likely it would run away," Ed replied, "but a mother with cubs will stand her ground, probably rising on her hind legs to warn us. We would backtrack slowly, avoiding eye contact."

"Red shooed a bear off our porch without raising his voice," Ivy offered. "I was most impressed."

Ellen and Clara exchanged glances.

"It's lap-service tonight," Lily said with a carefree smile directed at the arriving guests. "Plenty of chairs on the porch."

Comments on the beautiful sunny day were interrupted by the arrival of Teddy and Jack, holding either end of a string dangling with rainbow trout.

"We've caught enough for the whole dinner," Jack boasted.

Your bravado is a good match for my son who conserves his words, Lily thought as she gave the boys space in the kitchen to gut and debone the fish. "Dr. Barnaby and I grew up in Cape Breton. Surprisingly, we didn't eat much fish until we moved next door to the Donnellys."

Jack laughed and punched Teddy in the shoulder as if to say "So there!"

Next, Lily put aside a dozen unhusked cobs, ceding to Tina's "crazy" idea to cook them in the fire pit outdoors. She dumped her large pot of boiling water into the sink with a doubtful shrug. Ivy picked up Little Feather and followed Tina to where the young people had gathered around the fire, while Lily stood behind the counter pouring drinks, feeling immensely happy. She pulled off the bandana that had kept her unruly mop of hair off her face as she cooked.

Teddy, who had been full of bravado earlier, followed Lily into the cottage with a downcast face.

"What's wrong, son?" Lily asked.

"Ivy just talks to Red."

"Then talk to Jack. "He's your age."

Teddy kicked open the screen door and went out.

You're moody like Ed, Lily thought, watching her son, who was over six feet tall, descend the porch stairs. *But Ed had reason to be angry.* She suppressed the painful memories of her husband's sad story. His local priest had violated him and his mother denied it.

Her sombre reflection changed as she observed her guests eat their corn, sliding the cobs back and forth across their lips as though they were playing a mouth organ. Barnaby held his cob in his adaptive fork, and a drop of butter ran down his chin. Lily was flooded with affection. *My blessing that he survived the war*, she thought, stepping forward and sopping up the butter with Barnaby's napkin. Everyone else swiped his chin in unison, looking at the hostess for confirmation.

"How was Albert Martin?" Clara asked. "Did he tell you how he earned a citation for his reconnaissance work?"

"He was a sniper," Dan said, "a decorated sharpshooter. He told us he was never promoted beyond a non-commissioned lance corporal because he had no formal education. I suppose that's what accounts for his mistrust."

"It's not much better now that he's home," Clara said. "The government won't upgrade the prosthesis for non-commissioned soldiers." Clara laughed. "Is that how you lost your leg, Dan? I hope not permanently."

"On loan for a week," Dan said. "It sure made me feel good to see Albert walk normally."

"Tell the story," Lily said, pretending extreme patience.

Dan began with the walk through the woods. He kept the story short and ended with Albert's comment that it was his patience, stealth, and marksmanship that had made him such a good soldier.

Ivy entered the cottage, carrying Little Feather as Dan finished his account. She passed the infant to Tina, who had been listening to the conversation about Albert. "Would you mind if I went to the reserve?" the girl asked, apologizing for butting in.

"That's a great idea," Lily said, bouncing up to see if Tina might take leftovers to share with her community. "I'll put Little Feather to bed so you can have fun."

"My friends would like to see her." Tina swung Little Feather onto her hip and slipped out the door where several girls were giggling and waiting.

CHAPTER 25

There was a bit of family fanfare when Jean Donnelly arrived at Batchawana in the last week of Ivy's vacation. She had passed her examinations and was now a nurse, graciously accepting her three brothers' congratulations. Jean and her mother, Ellen, bickered about Jean's upcoming trip to Vancouver to meet the parents of Rupert Nesbitt, the man she had been dating for the past two years. Ivy watched the mother-daughter conflict with a practised eye.

"Time to celebrate," Red said, attempting to interrupt.

"Rupert has a receding chin," Ellen lamented as she arrived at the beach where a picnic outing was being hatched. "You won't want to look at that every day."

"I'm marrying his character, not his jaw," Jean retorted.

Dan and Gerda showed up at the beach in the middle of the argument. They were returning to Toronto and had come to say goodbye.

"As the chin recedes, so does the character," Ellen continued.

"You can alter a jaw," Dan interjected, trying to be helpful. "They used clay models to rebuild many chins that were blown off in the war. I found it interesting as an artist."

Ellen appeared chastised. "I wasn't suggesting Rupert have reconstruction. I just want Jean to be aware that face and character are related."

"Maybe they are," Dan said thoughtfully. "In a war, we're only interested in character."

Red glanced up from his tackle box. "How many rods do we need?" he asked to change the conversation. "Are you ladies fishing or sunbathing?"

Ivy blushed, and Jean's arched eyebrow seemed to ask the question: "Is something going on between my brother and Ivy?"

"Red gave me a lesson on casting." Ivy laughed. "All I hooked was his fishing hat."

"Corbeil Point is a good place to try again, Ivy," Red said, grinning.

Ivy touched her cheek, embarrassed that she might look as hot as she felt. The previous weekend Red had demonstrated casting. Standing on the end of the Donnellys' dock, she hadn't expected an intimate experience. Red had stood behind her, holding the rod and her hand to demonstrate the movement. Ivy's thoughts hadn't been on the extending fishing line. Red's cheek was pressed against her neck, and his warm breath moistened her ear as he gave instructions on flicking back and then snapping forward the rod. It was a graceful movement by Red compared to Ivy's rushed performance.

Clara's facts-of-life approach to sex didn't explain the explosion of feelings Ivy had as Red pulled her into his rod-casting arms. She fixed her eyes on the colourful lure on the line to regain her concentration and was weak in the legs when Red had breathed into her ear, "You've got the hang of it, Ivy."

After a round of goodbye hugs, Dan and Gerda sauntered off to where Lily had parked her blue Rambler. She wanted to check on the Italian mothers and was happy to have an excuse to return to the Soo.

Just then, Albert Martin with his peg leg and crutch came through the woods for the send-off. "Get me a new leg," he pleaded.

Gerda shot Dan a resigned look, familiar with his spontaneous behaviour. Before she opened her mouth to protest, Dan had unbuckled his leg. He was wearing shorts, which made this easier.

Leaning on the car for balance, Dan handed his state-of-the-art prosthesis to Albert. "It fell in Lake Superior by accident. If the government wants to know where, I can show them." He shot Albert the same impish grin that had saved him during his tantrums.

"They'd need ocean divers," Albert said with a smile that broke his normally taciturn face.

Dan grinned. "Get back to guiding, Albert, and take me up the Batchawana River next year."

"You have an open invitation to stay with us," Lily offered.

As the car pulled away, Dan rolled down the passenger window. "All white guys aren't bad! Just the government!"

Albert raised his hand in farewell.

"How well do you know Dan?" Red asked Ivy as they returned to the beach.

"I was quite young when Dan was in the hospital. I remember looking for my mother and finding her kneeling in the corridor comforting him as he howled. He was one of her favourites. Still is."

Ivy helped Red load the fourteen-foot Peterborough runabout with fishing rods and tackle as well as the lunch Ellen had prepared. She had apologized to Jean about the chin, and Jean was now in a mood to enjoy the few days with her family.

"I prefer to sit in the bow to get the wind head on," Jean said.

Ivy donned a life vest so big that her blond head was barely visible above the collar.

"Come back here," Red said as he stood at the transom, ready to pull the cord on the Johnson motor. "Try it."

Ivy, somewhat impeded by the jacket, pulled hard, but the cord didn't budge. Red laughed, and with a quick snap of his arm, the motor began to hum. They headed for the point that protected the northwest corner of the bay.

Philemon Riel, the lighthouse keeper who lived on the point year-round, was at the shore to greet them. She was a small but sturdy woman who had known Ellen Donnelly since childhood, and her cropped brown hair always looked as if she were her own barber. Philemon put the lunch in the icehouse while Red checked the direction of the wind before settling on a fishing spot.

"There's not much sun in Vancouver," Jean said as she wandered off to sunbathe. "Let me know when you stop for lunch."

Ivy, her fine blond hair tumbling over Red's tackle box as she crouched to rummage for an appropriate lure, contemplated Jean glancing back at her. For a moment, it seemed as if Jean was frowning at her. *Does she not like me being with Red?* Ivy thought.

Later, when Ivy caught two small bass, Red threw them back in the lake. "The wind's coming up on this side of the point," he said after an hour of no bites. "We need to move where the water's calmer to catch any fish." Ivy was opening the tackle box to pack up when Red put his hand on hers and leaned forward to kiss her on the mouth. "Can I visit you in Montreal?"

She wondered if her rapid heartbeat showed under her shirt. "I don't have much time off, but I promise to write and let you know when I'm free."

Red seemed disappointed.

"Promise," Ivy added, running her fingers through his thick wavy hair, which had fallen over his forehead. She leaned forward and initiated another kiss. Red pulled her up and put his free arm around her waist as they moved to a calmer location. They settled in a quiet alcove close to the lighthouse. Ivy felt ecstatic.

"Do you mind if I smoke?" Red asked as he hooked a large minnow on the line.

Ivy had objected to touching the squirming bait. "My mother hates cigarettes. I mustn't smell of smoke when I get back to the cottage. Maybe we can have a swim."

Red was wearing a beige cotton vest with multiple pockets. He pulled out a pouch of tobacco and a pipe with a highly polished brier bowl. Then, holding the bowl, he emptied it on a rock and pushed a wad of aromatic tobacco into the cleaned pipe. Striking a match on the zipper of his vest, he sucked until the pipe was lit. "Take a puff and don't inhale," he said, passing the pipe to Ivy.

She could taste his saliva on the stem, and the tingling in her legs returned. Drawing a deep breath, she blew it on Red. "Now you'll smell of smoke." Ivy laughed. "My mother will be mad at both of us!"

Red cupped Ivy's head, pulling her forward for a kiss when the fishing rod suddenly jerked. He jumped up to grab it, began reeling in the fish, and pulled up a six-pound rainbow trout.

Ivy closed her eyes while Red put the fish out with a quick thud of a club. "Jean will be expecting us." She wanted to renew her interrupted kiss but decided returning to the lighthouse would preserve her reputation. *Jean can be a tease*, she thought. *I don't want Mrs. Donnelly thinking I'm one of those girls who make a man quit his education because they get in a family way. I don't want to end up like Tina Courtney!*

They put the fishing gear and the trout in the boat and walked up to the lighthouse where Philemon had spread out their food on a table in her small parlour. Jean was gossiping about her upcoming trip to Vancouver.

Red pulled out a chair for Ivy and then sat opposite. "I want you to have a view of the lake. It changes constantly."

"It's important to know that," Philemon said. "Almost every drowning on Lake Superior was a case of misjudging how rapidly conditions can change. Waves get as high as those in an ocean and can sink a small boat."

"You're wearing Dad's life vest," Red said, seeing Ivy's worried expression.

"Red's grown up on this lake," Philemon assured her. "You're safe in his hands."

"Let's eat," Red said, pleased with the compliment.

Ivy studied Red, though it appeared her eyes were fixed on the turbulent water behind him. His facial features were more refined than his brothers, who had the same red hair and freckles as their father. He had inherited his mother's wavy brown hair and dark brown eyes. At five foot eight, Red was shorter than his brothers but more muscled and agile than the stockier boys. *Red Donnelly, you're as well put together as any young man I've ever met,* Ivy thought, moving her tongue to taste Red's saliva from the pipe.

CHAPTER 26

Ivy had two days to pack and get organized when she returned to the Soo from her vacation at Batchawana. Her trunk had remained at Royal Victoria Hospital. "If they change my room, they'll move it," she told Clara. "Red would like to take me to the train," she added, expecting her mother to look hurt.

"I think that's a fine idea. I'll be less sad seeing you go down Hilltop Crescent in a roadster with Red Donnelly than standing on a platform by myself watching the train pull away."

Ivy hugged Clara. She knew her mother would be lonely at her departure.

Seeing the Donnellys' roadster parked on the street, the eldest resident of Hilltop, Miss Leila Shell, came to say goodbye. She and her spinster sister watched the street's comings and goings from their front porch. Ivy had struck up many conversations with elderly patients at the Galt Hospital and enjoyed speaking with the spinster ladies. They passed on a surprising bit of gossip before she left: "Ed Donnelly has purchased the empty lot across the street."

"Why is it a secret?" Ivy asked.

"Mr. Donnelly doesn't want to be accused of property speculation. There was a feeling that his father, I.J., took advantage of Francis Clergue when he went bankrupt. After all, he was chief of police and privy to private information."

Ivy didn't want to be caught in a web of gossip, so she didn't tell Clara. She wondered if Mr. Donnelly would build or just turn the property over at a higher price when the economy improved.

Leila stood on the street beside Sergeant Stuart, who was admiring Red's car.

Red tossed Ivy's suitcase into the roadster's trunk and held the door for Ivy to get in the passenger seat.

"I'll be back at Christmas!" Ivy cried, waving. Red slipped behind the wheel and put the car in motion. Ivy returned the wave of neighbours working on their gardens as they passed.

It was still August, but fall was in the air. Clara basked in her daughter's happiness and offered Leila and Sergeant Stuart tea. "Company will lessen the loneliness."

Clara was soon occupied at Shingwauk overseeing incoming desks for the smaller students. She had become embroiled in this non-nursing matter before the children left for summer holidays. In June, six-year-old Jimmy Sagebrush had arrived in her office with welts on his knuckles, which had begun to bleed. Clara thoroughly washed the boy's hands and then applied antifungal ointment before confronting the teacher about the severity of her strapping.

"He's disruptive, annoying to other students," the teacher blurted.

"I don't think a thin-skinned little boy deserves corporal punishment," Clara said. "What did he do to make you react so harshly?"

"He swings his legs back and forth until I'm driven to distraction. I keep him up front to stop him."

"So he's bothering *you*."

The same teacher had put a disruptive, short-sighted boy at the back of the classroom where, unable to see the blackboard, he had just created mischief. He spent much of his day in the hallway. Clara asked Jimmy to sit at his desk, and the problem became obvious. His feet were half a foot off the floor. There were no size-suitable desks in the classroom.

Clara had returned to her office and placed a call to D.T. Walker, the school inspector for the Soo. He had held the position for twenty years and was thought to be even-handed by both Protestant and Catholic authorities. Protestant teachers wanted the Union Jack in their classrooms and Catholic teachers a statue of Mary or Jesus, costly in either case to supply. For every cross of Jesus, D.T. ordered a flag. Clara had thought he would understand the problem.

"School supplies, including furniture, are stored in a warehouse on Bruce Street," D.T. had said when Clara called. "Furniture for residential schools is considered a federal matter, but I'll see what I can do. They should be available before the school year begins in late August."

Occupying herself with the desk problem after Ivy left was cathartic, and Clara threw herself into her work.

Most of the children hadn't arrived yet when the dust-laden desks were delivered in a city truck. Noel Thomas brought in the big boys from his workshop to unload the desks and carry them into the classroom. The boys arranged three rows of five on either side of an aisle. Clara returned home that evening, happy she had been able to resolve the desk situation but disheartened by the uphill battle with the custodians. In her mind, they didn't see the problems. She could feel her blood pressure rise much as it had at the Galt Hospital.

A few weeks after Red had returned to the University of Toronto, Clara and Ellen Donnelly spoke about the budding romance. "While they're both in school, they won't jump the gun and get married," Ellen said with a reassuring laugh. "I must say I'd be pleased to have Ivy as my daughter-in-law. She's a good match for my son who's a rough outdoorsman."

"I have little experience as to what makes a good union," Clara said. "My own marriage was fraught with war and illness until George's death. Ivy's had so many complications in her young life. Red would make an ideal partner once she's finished her nursing and has that diploma in hand."

"I'm sure he will," Ellen assured.

While Ivy was at Sault Collegiate and friendly with so many Italians, Clara had expressed her opinion that marriage was tough enough without adding complications like religion, culture, or finances into the mix. Lily would assert that the next generation of Italians would be living in the east end, and Clara would counter with: "They'll still be Catholics!"

She was pleased to see Ivy fit into the Donnelly family where there were no obstacles. Ellen had taken Clara's daughter under her wing, teaching Ivy the culinary tricks she used at the cottage when supplies were limited. Neither mother wanted to be an overbearing chaperone. Clara's ruminations were hopeful, nonetheless. Red, as a budding doctor, seemed a wonderful prospect. He was three years older than Ivy and known to be a little high-strung. Ivy was just the opposite. *This is a good fit*, Clara thought.

CHAPTER 27

Ivy stepped onto the Windsor Station platform and handed her suitcase to the first taxi driver in the queue of cars. His unkempt appearance reflected the hard economic times in Montreal, particularly for French Canadians. The drivers' unshaven faces and rumpled clothes suggested some of them had spent the night in their taxis.

"Royal Victoria Hospital," Ivy said, opening her handbag to check that she had the right change. *The driver might cheat by taking a longer route*, she thought. She had been told that taxi drivers did that in Paris where passengers hadn't a clue where they were going.

"You a nurse?" the driver queried.

"A student," Ivy replied.

The man squinted at Ivy through the rearview mirror. Ivy had walked this downtown route before, and when the driver took a left turn onto an unfamiliar side street and sped up, she was afraid it wasn't the right direction for the hospital. She ran her finger over the lining of her open purse until she felt the hatpin Clara had provided her. Panicking, Ivy moved swiftly. The jab was quick, and the man yelped and braked, jolting Ivy forward before she could exit the car. When she got out, he drove away quickly, no doubt wondering what had happened. Ivy gazed at the receding car and realized she had overreacted. The taxi driver would be familiar with many routes to get to the hospital. She tossed the hatpin in the ditch with an embarrassed chuckle.

Her trudge up McTavish Street through the McGill campus was tiring. Students were milling about with maps in hand, trying to locate their next destinations. Ivy found a shaded place not far from the water reservoir and watched as people hustled past.

She reviewed her last moments with Red. The train to Montreal had been delayed because of an engine problem, so they had returned to the roadster to have a private farewell. There had been few such occasions to talk at Batchawana. Red had lit and drawn deeply on his pipe before passing it to Ivy. She had the same intimate thrill she had experienced at the lighthouse. This time she didn't let an image of an oversized Tina Courtney enter her thoughts.

"Did you want to become a doctor because of your father?" Ivy asked. The question was often directed at her, since people believed Clara had influenced her decision to become a nurse.

Red laughed. "It was my mother who wanted at least one of her boys to wear a suit to work. My father wanted me to follow him into I.J. Donnelly and Sons. I wanted to be a geologist, but geologists rarely wear suits."

The train whistle blew, ending their conversation. He pressed a hurried kiss on Ivy's mouth, and they leaped from the car.

"I don't want to get in your mother's bad books," Red said, grabbing the suitcase and Ivy's arm. He knocked his pipe sharply on the wheel of the roadster and handed it to Ivy. "See you in Montreal."

As the train pulled away, Ivy held the pipe to the window and nodded. Red shot back a satisfied smile, revealing his beautiful teeth.

Ivy's thoughts about their parting were interrupted when a squirrel jumped onto her handbag. She squealed, and the animal scurried off. Most of the students were already in uniform when

Ivy got to the nurses' residence. She stopped by the main desk to ascertain which room she had been assigned and then dashed up the broad staircase to change. Ivy was anxious to share her budding romance with Sass. *Sass's beau will be old hat compared to my news*, she thought.

The two girls didn't have an opportunity to exchange news until Sunday when the nurses had the afternoon off. Ivy was eager to talk about Red when they got together in Sass's room. Pulling a dresser drawer open, Sass let Ivy peek in. A large diamond ring sat on top of a plastic pouch. Sass smirked. "My diaphragm," she said, blushing and crowing at the same time. "I'd be kicked out if Miss Hobbs knew I was engaged. A pregnant student nurse is unheard of, and I'm not trying to make history."

Ivy waited in vain for Sass to ask about her own vacation. When she returned to her room, Ivy let out a self-deprecating laugh as she sat on her bed pressing Red's pipe against her cheek. "What on earth made me think Sass would find a man's spit exciting?" she mumbled with a shrug. The image of the diaphragm on the pouch made her shiver. She erased the fuzzy image of Sass in bed with Robert Mason, replacing it with a sharper image of Red embracing her while she held his fishing rod. Smiling, she then headed off to join the other students in the dining room.

CHAPTER 28

Madame Pelletier, known as Marta to the nursing students, managed their incoming and outgoing mail. Ivy had been back at Royal Victoria for three weeks when her watch showed 4:00 p.m., the time most mail would be sorted by Marta. She hustled to the mailroom, hoping for news from Red. From Ivy's pigeonhole, Madame Pelletier pulled a large packet of letters she had tied with string and placed it on the oak counter. "*Vous êtes comblé des lettres, mademoiselle.*"

Ivy responded, "*Oui, oui, madame,*" understanding "You have a lot of mail." She did a quick scan, noting a return address at Wycliffe College, the university residence where Red boarded. Ivy returned to her room, tossed the packet on her bed, and rushed down the long corridor to the hospital. She relished the thought of having mail at the end of an exhausting day and had a light step and broad smile when she reached her patients. Her second year in nursing school had begun in the maternity ward. She showed the same concern and warmth for mothers with complaints as she had for the elderly patients the previous year.

Dr. Pierre Lavoie arrived on the ward to "check on his moms" while Ivy was administering perineal care to Monique Seguin, a haggard-looking mother from St. Henri, a poor district in the southwest corner of Montreal. This was her ninth birth but only the first time she had delivered in a hospital. Ivy drew up the bedsheet as the doctor approached and then moved aside so the doctor could speak privately with the patient. He spoke in a colloquial French that Ivy didn't understand.

"He's telling her she must say *no!*" Miss Hobbs said with an earthy laugh.

Mademoiselle Seguin made a sign of resignation with her upturned hands before Dr. Lavoie and Miss Hobbs walked on to another patient in a private room.

The director gestured for Ivy to follow, and they remained in the corridor outside the patient's room. "Deirdre MacKay grew up in the Square Mile," Miss Hobbs observed. "She's suffering from the post-baby blues, according to a psychiatrist from Allan Memorial Institute."

Ivy was struck by the skepticism in Miss Hobbs's voice. "For a short time, I lived with a family in Calgary who adopted a baby named Florence. My mother arranged the adoption. I don't know the whole story, but Florence's mother suffered from the baby blues when she lived in England. I was too young to realize exactly what happened, but the mother — her name was Annabel — committed suicide."

"Yes. I remember the little girl lived at the Galt Hospital for a short time until she was taken away," Miss Hobbs interjected. "We probationers were told the mother had died on a ship."

"She jumped overboard," Ivy said quietly. "I don't remember much other than my mother's crying. I do remember seeing Annabel struggling in the water."

"Miss Durling, the patients named you *La Poupée* because you brought them comfort, like their dolls in childhood."

"They must be recalling my blanket blitz," Ivy said modestly. "I have a practical streak," she added with a smile.

"Assigning a student nurse to Deirdre might be practical, as well. You'd be less intimidating, Miss Durling."

Ivy basked inwardly in Miss Hobbs's confidence. "I'll do what I can."

Ward rounds with Dr. Lavoie and Miss Hobbs ended before lunch, and Ivy raced to her room to read her mail. She hadn't noticed earlier that one of her letters was from Mrs. Donnelly, but she tore open Red's first. The handwriting was hurried:

> I was on an excavation site with my geology club north of Toronto when I received a message that my father passed away. I'll be in the Soo by the time this letter arrives. I hope to come to Montreal when I return to Toronto. We're in discussions as to what to do with I.J. Donnelly and Sons, a business my grandfather started and my father expanded. As the eldest son, I feel pressure. I wish you were here, Ivy.
>
> — Red

Ivy sat on her bed, trying to absorb what she had just read. Mrs. Donnelly's letter contained more news of her husband's final days.

Dear Ivy,

I'm sorry to tell you that Mr. Donnelly died of galloping pneumonia last evening. My dear husband hadn't reached his fiftieth year. I'm deeply grateful for your mother's unflagging nursing care. She took a one-week leave of absence from the residential school to stay by my husband's side. Were it not for her war knowledge of lung disease, my husband would have felt he was suffocating until his end. Tending to my husband brought back her terrible memories of nursing the gassed soldiers until their last breaths. We're so happy you're following in your mother's footsteps. I hadn't appreciated her nursing gifts until she tended to my Ed. Sadly, I don't have business experience and have asked Red to return to the Soo. We'll look forward to your visit when you're next home.

— Ellen Donnelly

Ivy had little memory of her own father, who had also died of pneumonia. Poisonous gas unleashed by the Germans had damaged his lungs, she was told. She did remember his dreadful cough. "I'm going to fly you to the moon," he would say between hackings. She had flashes of playing with her brother on their father's sick bed, which smelled of camphor.

Mr. Donnelly had breathed the dust from the I.J. coal business all his life. As a boy, he had swept the dusty floors.

Sass and other students had saved a place for Ivy in the dining room. "What's wrong?" Sass asked.

Ivy sat down and pushed her plate away. "I have a friend from the Soo whose father died. I think he'll have to remain to run the family business. He was in first-year medicine in Toronto."

"Is this a beau?" Sass asked.

All eyes were on Ivy.

"Sort of," Ivy said.

"Why didn't you tell me?"

"You didn't ask."

"Well, I'm asking now!"

"Red Donnelly was already a student at the University of Toronto when I arrived in the Soo. I met him during the summer when my mother rented a cottage next door to his family at a place called Batchawana."

"Sounds Indian to me," another girl interjected. "Is Red an Indian?"

Ivy didn't smile, mindful that she was talking about Red's father's death. "Red has dark brown hair that suits his dark eyes and tanned complexion. We spent most of our time fishing outdoors."

"That doesn't sound romantic," Sass said.

Ivy curtailed the urge to talk about the pipe saliva that had given her shivers down her legs. "Red was mature for his age. Maybe as a businessman he'll be less interested in a student nurse. There will be plenty of young working women in the Soo."

CHAPTER 29

Ivy couldn't shake the feeling that her budding romance with Red might have ended with Ed Donnelly's death. Red had returned to Toronto to gather his belongings and formally drop out of medical school. Ivy had hoped he might sidetrack to Montreal, but instead he headed to Chicago where the American Concrete Institute had organized a conference on industry standards.

"I've inherited a half ownership of I.J. Donnelly and Sons, and I intend to make the business mine," Red wrote from Chicago. "The old-timers are unhappy that I plan to buy machines that will do the mixing of four men. I want to move beyond the bricks and mortar and manual labour of my father's era." Red described the elements of cement as though they were a periodic table. His letters were filled with technical jargon and numbers hard to understand. "The Hoover Dam demonstrates the power of cement," he wrote. "It was built with over four million pounds of concrete to provide energy to millions of Americans." The image of the small dam in the Soo came to Ivy's mind as a poor comparison.

"Nothing romantic in Red's letters," Ivy told Sass.

"I don't believe you. Can I read one?"

Ivy gave one of the letters to her friend.

Sass read it and then put it down with a frown. "Don't you understand what's happening, Ivy?"

"I think he has a new love called 'cement,'" Ivy offered.

"Didn't you ever watch your parents?" Sass asked. Then she apologized for being thoughtless and explained, "My father used my mother as his audience. He never asked her about her day. But he adores her. Robert tells me about his patients, but never asks about mine. That's men, Ivy! Go to the library and read up on cement."

"There's a lot I missed growing up in a hospital."

"You had a unique experience," Sass said, putting her arms around Ivy.

A virulent influenza hit Montreal, and the student nurses had little time off. Ivy had moved to the children's ward, and while she couldn't remember much about her six-year-old brother, she did know Billy had died during the flu pandemic. *I suppose this is part of my "unique experience,"* Ivy thought as she comforted the frantic parents through her face mask. Damping down fevers and soothing sore throats gave her little time to think about Red, but her emotions resurfaced as she packed to go home for the Christmas holiday. Her recollection of Red was at the cottage at Batchawana. Thoughts swirled through her head. *Will Red have changed? His father's passing shouldn't have been a surprise to him. He was studying medicine, and Mr. Donnelly was always short of breath.*

Red's next letter — about aggregates to strengthen cement and methods to speed up the curing process — seemed positive about his road ahead. Ivy accepted Sass's advice and borrowed a book from the main library, comparing the ancient and modern use of concrete. She loved history and was moved that Red, in 1934, was as excited about cement as the Romans thousands of years before him.

Waiting at Windsor Station for the westbound train, Ivy glowed with happiness. *Red delivered me to the station in August, and he'll be there to pick me up.*

Red's fedora was covered with snow as he waited on the Sault Ste. Marie platform to greet Ivy. Ellen and Clara smiled from the station window but stayed put until Red greeted her. She smiled and waved at them, basking in the collective happiness. Red drove the car up Pim Street and turned onto Hilltop Crescent. Neighbours shovelling their sidewalks waved. Lily's blue Rambler was parked in Clara's driveway. *The battlers must be getting along,* Ivy thought.

When they entered Ivy's home, Red put her suitcase in the vestibule with a promise to show her his office in the morning. He seemed older than his twenty-three years. What she had recalled on the long journey home was a bronze-faced, rugged-looking Red Donnelly who smelled of fish. The dapper man who had paled over the season was still handsome, but different than she remembered. She stood at the door until he reached the car.

"Tell us everything," Lily said when Ivy came into the living room where a fire burned energetically.

Ivy knew firewood was costly, so she appreciated her mother's gesture to welcome her home.

Red arrived at ten in the morning in Ed Donnelly's old sedan. He drove to the main office of I.J. Donnelly and Sons on Bruce Street and parked. Ivy was prepared to be what Sass called an "audience."

"Our gravel and sand pits are out of town," he said. "Currently, we transport the cement ingredients to the building site and then mix them by hand. The formula is in the men's heads. Mixing trucks are new to the building industry but much more efficient. One truck can do the mixing of four men."

"Where would you buy the trucks?" Ivy felt cold in her damp wool overcoat when the car cooled.

"Let's go into the building where it's warmer." Red cleaned and lit his pipe as they went into the front office, speaking as though he were justifying his decisions.

"Has there been much resistance to your ideas?" Ivy asked.

"From the men."

"How does your mother feel about these changes to a business she half owns?"

"She asked *me* to come home."

Ivy wondered if there was a note of bitterness that his plans had been changed. "What happens here?" She leaned her elbow on the ten-foot counter in the front office.

"Customers lay out their building plans to determine the amount of concrete needed for the foundation," Ivan Slater said from behind the counter.

"Ivan does the cost estimates," Red said. "He knows a lot more about cement than I do."

Ivan smiled at the compliment.

Ivy followed Red upstairs to a small office with a desk and filing cabinet.

"Dad didn't spend much time in here," Red said. "He liked being out with the men."

"I suspect you will, too, Red. I don't see you as a man sitting in an office."

"I'll do a lot more travelling than my dad. That's the only way to expand. I learned a lot at the cement conference in Chicago. I need to see what's out there as a first step to expanding."

Maybe Sass is right, Ivy thought. *Red didn't ask me about nursing school.*

CHAPTER 30

The Christmas Eve church service was one of the rare times Ivy saw Red in a suit. By New Year's Day he was back in his outdoor attire having convinced her to put on a pair of gut-strung snowshoes and hike through a bitter north wind to a small inlet off the St. Marys River called Still Bay. Ice-fishing shacks dotted the bay, their small chimneys billowing smoke. The bay was about five miles east of I.J. Donnelly's coal docks. Before opening his own shack, Red checked on the old-timers to make sure none of them had been asphyxiated by their gas stoves. The old men, huddled over their rods hoping for a bite, knew the Donnelly family.

"Sorry about your dad."

"How's Ellen doing?"

"How's the business?"

"Thank you and fine," Red answered to the onslaught of queries as he and Ivy went inside Red's shack to fish themselves.

As soon as the coal stove pumped enough heat into the Donnelly shack, Ivy and Red removed their heavy coats. Red broke the ice over the hole with an axe and handed a fishing rod to Ivy. "I'm here if you need me," he said. "The fish will tire before you will, if you let him run occasionally." The only sound was the sizzling of snow from their coats dropping on the stove until the tip of the rod went down and Red grabbed the rod from Ivy. He raised the tip and when the fish was secure, he passed the rod back. Red seemed relaxed away from the prying of the family. He talked about his high school days, his hospitalization, and his passion for geology. It was a pleasant surprise that cement was never mentioned. After three hours and enough fish for two or three meals, Ivy was tired of hunching over the hole and asked to go home. When they reached Donnelly's coal docks where they had parked, the car was buried in a snow drift. Red kissed Ivy's frozen cheeks and put the heat on in the car. Once in the driver's seat he leaned over and kissed her passionately.

Before Ivy returned to Montreal, Red showed her the lot opposite Clara's house that he had inherited. Then he took Ivy back to her mother's place where everybody had gathered in the living room to say goodbye.

"Did you know my father owned the empty lot across the street?" Red asked Clara.

"I heard a rumour."

"Dad loved living on Simpson Street because he could walk to work. If he needed a ride, especially toward the end, he would be picked up in one of the Donnelly trucks. He disapproved of your Hilltop neighbours who had drivers. I think he planned to sell the lot when the value went up with the economy. Now I've inherited I.J. Donnelly and Sons and this property."

"Oh, dear!" Clara said. "And you plan to sell to someone who will build a house and block my view. I can watch the ferry crossings from the ravine. It's a charming property."

There was a prolonged silence while Ivy stood beside her suitcase, waiting for Red to go.

"I plan to build my own home," Red finally announced.

"Unusual for a bachelor," Clara said.

That said, Red and Ivy departed for the train station. When they arrived, the same elderly luggage man was clearing snow from the platform.

"They keep you working in all seasons," Ivy said sympathetically. The old man nodded appreciatively. "Glad you notice, miss."

Red was anxious to get Ivy to himself again. "Ivy, I don't want to be an eligible bachelor," he said above a whisper to return her focus to him and then pulled her away so they could have some privacy. "I want to marry you. If you feel the same way, I'm going back to ask Clara for your hand."

"She wants me to have something to fall back on," Ivy said hurriedly as the whistle made a last blast, insistent she get on the train. "I can't quit."

"You won't need a fallback plan if you marry me."

Ivy entered the passenger car and mouthed from the window, "I love you, Red Donnelly."

"Hallelujah," Red mouthed back. "I'm going to marry you."

Ivy was snapped abruptly from her romantic bliss as soon as she arrived at Royal Victoria Hospital. Sass was throwing up in the utility cupboard her first morning back on the floor. Ivy held her head over the foul-smelling sink, running the water so no one could hear the vomiting.

"Are you … you-know-what?" Ivy asked quietly, frightened someone might hear.

Sass groaned as she sat on a stool waiting for another purge. "I had a party at my parents' house on New Year's Eve while they were skiing in the Laurentians. "I charged the whole affair to their country club," she added, giggling before another gag. "I drank too much champagne, and you know the rest of the story."

Waiting for Sass to throw up again, Ivy reflected on the difference between young Tina Courtney, "who had done it in the washroom," and Sass, who had done it with "too much champagne."

Sass has money and parents. Tina has neither, she noted to herself. In that moment, Ivy appreciated the importance of Clara's down-to-earth approach to sex. *Rich or poor, an unexpected pregnancy is complicated,* thought Ivy.

Sass had a last gag and went to her room. Ivy felt heartsick. Trysts between nursing students and medical residents weren't just discouraged; they were penalized. Sass's fiancé, Robert, was in his last resident year. Ivy's friend hoped that if the chief of staff or his department didn't learn about her condition until spring, Robert would be allowed to finish his year.

Pondering how Robert's and Sass's lives had been upended, Ivy was determined to stay her own course.

CHAPTER 31

Red postponed visiting Clara for several days. She was a much more dominating woman than his own mother. He didn't immediately come up with a reason why Ivy should leave nursing and marry him. She had expressed her dissatisfaction as a nursing student, but Clara wouldn't feel it was his business to advance that argument. It would also be hurtful to repeat what Ivy had said: "I feel I'm reliving my childhood working in a hospital." He could assure Clara that he would always look after her daughter. On the other hand, Clara expressed many times how fortunate she was to have an education to fall back on when her husband died.

Red knocked on Clara's door, expecting the right words would pop out of his mouth at the moment of asking for Ivy's hand. Clara seemed surprised to see him. She stepped back so he could remove his boots. Then she invited him in and offered tea.

He remained at the door, sensing her wariness at what he might say. "I thought you might be interested in the changes I'm making to I.J. Donnelly and Sons. I'm changing the name to Donnelly Building Materials to reflect the expansion of the company into ready-mix concrete."

"Shouldn't you learn the business before expanding it?" Clara asked. "Until your father fell gravely ill, I think he managed the company very well."

"I think it's time for a change. I'm the third generation, Mrs. Durling. I think my father would approve." *Small talk is going nowhere*, he thought, determined to say what was on his mind. "I've come to ask for Ivy's hand. I love your daughter."

"I love her, too, Red. It would be folly for her to drop out of nursing to get married."

"My wife will never have to work."

"Ivy has a year and a half to graduate. Are you willing to wait?"

Red smiled. "I'll leave that to Ivy," he replied, not afraid to challenge Clara.

"I provided a good life for Ivy. You're too young to know what happens during a war."

Red had never seen Clara emotional.

"There will be another war," she told him. "I follow the European news. The German chancellor is building up arms and ignoring the Versailles Treaty. A war creates widows."

"Mrs. Durling, you're too pessimistic. Wouldn't you love to have your daughter living next door?"

"Absolutely — when she has her nursing diploma."

Red knew he was being dismissed. "It will take a year to build the house," he said on his way to the door.

"Then another six months shouldn't matter."

CHAPTER 32

Clara's frugal lifestyle and wise investments put her in a secure financial position. She had taken Barnaby's advice to sell her stocks just before the 1929 crash and could now look forward to retirement with more time to play bridge and enjoy the many friends she had made in the Soo. Clara also looked forward to visiting Ivy in Montreal but had one last responsibility before leaving Shingwauk as the school nurse.

Reverend Hives had asked her to integrate the Wawanosh girls into the new building before she departed. They were currently housed in a rundown home five miles downriver from the new building. Wawanosh was in worse shape than the old Shingwauk. Fitzpatrick Construction was on track and on budget to finish the entire project in the fall of 1935. The new building was designed to accommodate 130 Native children, half of whom would be girls. However, after seeing the ambitious building plans, Clara saw a problem. The plumbing for both genders would be in the same location. She reminded Reverend Hives of Tina Courtney's situation while there was still time to modify the building plans.

"Plumbing should be installed at opposite ends of the school to avoid contact between the boys and girls during an intimate moment."

Reverend Hives chuckled at Clara's delicate use of *intimate* to describe going to the bathroom. "At this point, any change in the building plan will drive up costs. The House of Commons voted to put $450,000 in the budget for three new residential schools. There are a hundred residential schools that need rebuilding."

"Henry Hamilton, our Member of Parliament, belongs to the ruling party," Clara said. "See what *he* can do."

Through a circuitous route, news of Tina Courtney's pregnancy reached Ottawa. Headmaster Hives spoke with Indian Agent Sims, who wrote to the Department of Indian Affairs. Hamilton brought up the plumbing problem in the House of Commons. Despite wry "washroom humour" in the Canadian press, Parliament agreed to an increase in the budget for Shingwauk to have segregated toilets.

The new building plans called for a proper sewage disposal system. However, raw sewage still flowed into the St. Marys River from the old building and would until it was torn down. September being very warm, the boys were allowed to swim. They were asked not to go in the river near the effluent outlet where the water was warmer, but none of the custodians stopped them.

Before long, nine-year-old Denis Plain, from the Chippewa reserve near Sarnia, came down with a high fever and difficulty swallowing. He was quickly transported in the school car to General Hospital with suspected diphtheria. Sister Marie Claire, the director-general of female staff at the hospital, didn't want to admit an unbaptized child to her care.

"This is your chance to bring an uncommitted child into your fold," Dr. McCaig said, knowing full well he wouldn't let a child be baptized a Catholic without the consent of his parents, who were hundreds of miles away. Dr. McCaig diagnosed diphtheria, and to her credit, Sister Marie Claire allowed Denis to remain in an isolation room for two months before the thin, tired boy returned to the school.

When the cook complained about Denis's special diet, Clara, no longer afraid of losing her job, spoke her mind. From then on, Denis was served the same food as the custodians.

Sometime later, Clara was in Dr. McCaig's office on Queen Street on another matter. She asked him how he had become involved with Shingwauk. He opened the middle drawer of his desk and handed her a typed letter he had written, which was addressed to Indian Agent Sims. "The first tender submitted by Fitzpatrick Construction was rejected in 1929 at the time of the stock market crash. However, the Department of Indian Affairs still asked me to report on the condition of the school."

Clara sat opposite Dr. McCaig and read his troubling report:

October 24, 1929

I made an examination of the Shingwauk Indian Home yesterday and find the sanitary conditions there rather unsatisfactory. The boys' bathtubs have never been connected to the sewer, and where they are now placed is very unsatisfactory. The headmaster's quarters, which haven't been occupied for some time, are uninhabitable. The roof leaks, the floors in the lower flat are rotten, the walls are cracked, the plaster is falling off, and the whole place is in a generally dilapidated state. It will require a thorough renovation before it will be fit to live in.

On account of the recent presence of two cases of active tuberculosis in the school, I think it would be advisable to have all the children tuberculin-tested. If the department wishes this done, I'll be glad to do it at any time.

Yours very truly,
Dr. Andrew S. McCaig

"That's how I got involved with the school," Dr. McCaig said. "The Shingwauk children became a very meaningful part of my practice."

CHAPTER 33

Sass quit nursing school and returned to Senneville long before her condition showed. Ivy's own indecision contrasted with her friend's gumption.

"Why did you enroll in the RVH nursing school?" Ivy asked while Sass was packing her suitcase.

"I wanted to be a writer of romance novels, and RVH has a cosmopolitan clientele. I nursed a man wounded in the robbery of a downtown bank and talked to the cops guarding his room. A diseased prostitute working on St. Laurent Street and an unmarried pregnant girl who attempted to hang herself are all great fodder for a romance novelist. My mother can take the stories I don't use for her crime books."

"I wish I had your confidence," Ivy lamented, giving Sass a farewell embrace.

From her dormer window, she watched the Mitchells' car pull away. The large trunk left in Sass's room was the only evidence she had occupied it. The trunk would be on the train to Senneville the next day. Ivy sat on the stripped bed and cried. Sass's parents and her fiancé, Robert, had left Sass's free spirit intact. "I'm a pawn," Ivy whispered, as though her friend were still in the room. She curled up on Sass's bed and slept.

In March 1935, Red booked himself into the Windsor Arms Hotel in Montreal for a three-day seminar on the use of ferro-cement in domestic construction. Ivy, forewarned of his trip, had saved her monthly late-night pass to have dinner with Red. He greeted her in the hotel's large wood-panelled foyer, looking more like a businessman than the outdoorsman she knew him to be. Red ordered cocktails for them, and they sat in the foyer with other diners waiting to be called by the waiter. Ivy was keen to impress Red.

"Is ferrocement a new product?" she asked, recalling Red's letters.

"Ferrocement has been around for a hundred years. It was used to build small ships in the war."

"Wouldn't a cement ship sink?"

Red laughed and patted Ivy's hand. "No!"

"Don't patronize me, Red Donnelly," she said playfully, pull-ing away.

The waiter indicated that their table was ready, and they fol-lowed him into a corner of the dining room about twenty feet from an upright piano. The black jazz pianist glanced in their direction with his finger on his ear. "Got a song?" he asked.

"Later," Red said, matching his white-tooth smile with the black man's friendly grin. Turning to Ivy, he asked, "What have you been up to?"

"My friend Sass Mitchell got pregnant over the holidays and has quit nursing school."

"Hmm, that doesn't seem wise. There are better reasons to quit. Like marriage."

The waiter interrupted to get their order. Red chose venison tenderloin, while Ivy selected chicken in a white wine sauce.

"Do you have wine by the glass?" Red asked.

"Only bottles," the waiter replied.

Red chose a rosé from the wine menu, something suitable for white or dark meat. Then he leaned forward. "My mother informed me that Clara's no longer renting at Batchawana."

"She'll run interference until I graduate," Ivy offered. "Mum will make sure I'm not swept off my feet by you beforehand by keeping us apart. She was single and seventeen when she entered St. George's Hospital in London to train as a nurse. Mum wanted to be Florence Nightingale, dedicated and self-sacrificing. *She* didn't spend her childhood in a hospital."

"Did you have other plans?"

"I wanted to go to New York and take Columbia University's writing course. There just wasn't enough money to do that."

Reaching across the table, Red bumped the bottle of wine that the adept waiter, with a swift catch, stopped from toppling. "Lovers," he crooned as he returned the bottle to the table.

"If Sass can kick over the traces, so should I," Ivy said. "But I'm not Sass."

"You're what I want," Red said, tapping Ivy's foot. They lingered over coffee and then Red asked reluctantly for the bill, adding a good tip.

A young businessman arm in arm with a girl in a fur coat wasn't remarkable on Sherbrooke Street. Passing the Carsley mansion, Ivy told Red about Hugh lugging her blanket-loaded toboggan up the hill.

"Are you dating him?" Red asked, twirling Ivy to face him and backing her up the hill.

"Are you jealous?"

Red frowned. "Just a straight answer will do."

"We went out for coffee before he left for Europe. He's backpacking with his girlfriend for a year before going to McGill."

"I don't want to wait until you finish nursing school," Red said with an intensity that thrilled and pained Ivy.

"Let's not give my mother a heart attack. I shouldn't have brought up Hugh Carsley."

At the front entrance of Royal Victoria, Red handed Ivy a package. "These are the architect's drawings for the house I want to build on Hilltop. Our house." He embraced Ivy and then pulled away. "Look at them and let me know if you want changes. I hope we don't have to delay getting married." He chuckled. "I should threaten to live in sin with you if Clara objects to us getting married."

Ivy watched as he stepped into a waiting taxi, twisting his torso so he could wave goodbye.

When Ivy entered the hospital, she told the curious receptionist, "I had a lovely evening." As soon as she reached her room, she tore open the envelope of plans and spread them on the bed. *The dressing closet, French doors, and fireplace are just what I had asked for.*

CHAPTER 34

In July, before leaving for a summer holiday, Ivy arranged to see Miss Hobbs. The director of nursing had won the gold medal in her graduating class at the Galt Hospital when Clara was the superintendent. Ivy wanted Miss Hobbs to help her mother understand why she wanted to quit nursing school and return to the Soo. She had practised her argument with a fellow student before seeing the director. The day of the appointment, Ivy arrived at Miss Hobbs's office with butterflies in her stomach but still confident that the director, who had intervened when she had previous difficulties, would be helpful.

"Miss Hobbs, I thought growing up in a hospital would make studying to be a nurse a natural choice. I even thought I might have an advantage. It hasn't worked out that way."

"I remember, Ivy, how unhappy you were when your mother retrieved you from Calgary. I seem to remember you were living with the family who adopted Florence. Am I right that you attended a private school?"

"They enrolled me in a school I loved."

"Are you telling me you want to quit, Ivy?" The word sounded so irresponsible coming from Miss Hobbs's mouth.

"My fiancé, Red Donnelly, quit medicine when his father unexpectedly died. He returned to the Soo to run a family business. If he were still in medicine, we wouldn't be thinking of marriage. But he's home now and wants to settle down. He's building a house that we plan to move into once we're married."

"So he had a change of plans and now you'd like to change your plans, as well. Is that what I'm hearing?"

"I suppose I seem selfish after my mother has made so many sacrifices."

"But you have, too, Ivy. Your mother was very busy when you were growing up."

Ivy curled her fingernails into her palms.

"I have a suggestion," Miss Hobbs continued. "Go home for your vacation and enjoy being with your beau. Then come back, and if you're still unhappy, we'll let you go with no hard feelings." Miss Hobbs walked Ivy to the door of her office and stopped. "You deserve a home, Ivy. Your life has indeed been complicated."

Ivy didn't know what to expect when she arrived in the Soo. She did understand from Clara's letters that her mother was busy integrating the Wawanosh girls. Clara had written to Ivy that she and Dr. McCaig had visited Wawanosh to discover the girls did their laundry in the river water. Ivy was aware of the ongoing sewage even after the new school was built. She hated to add to her mother's problems. It was disappointing not to have the cottage, but she was determined to enjoy her vacation. Despite her desire to quit nursing, she had never let those sentiments affect her patient care. After being discharged, the patients on many occasions had left Ivy with grateful notes.

Lily wanted Teddy and Jane to vacation at Batchawana and was pleased when Ivy offered to take over the English classes at the West End Library, which allowed Ivy to become reacquainted with Irma D'Agostina.

Irma had returned to the Soo after spending a year at North Bay Normal School. She was now teaching at McFadden Public School where Anna McCrea was the principal. On Saturdays, Miss McCrea worked at the library that Lily had started. The Italian families, including Irma's mother, revered Miss McCrea. While Sal was in jail, the principal had made sure the D'Agostina children didn't fall behind. A three-month sentence for amateur bootlegging was unheard of in the Soo. Dan Roswell didn't last long as the chief of police, but he had done damage to the D'Agostina family. The school and the whole community had rallied to support Irma, who with her brother, Dominic, had held the fort while their mother was absent. Ivy was pleased to see her high school friend doing well. Irma was confident and full of news.

"Dominic lost his job at Algoma Steel and was hired by Donnelly Building Materials," Irma told Ivy, happy to hear that she was engaged to Red. Irma reached for Ivy's hand.

"Jewellery isn't allowed in nursing school, so we decided to postpone the ring," Ivy explained.

"When are you planning to be married?"

"I'm caught between my mother and Red. Red and I are building a house that will be ready before I graduate. It's complicated."

Dominic drove a mixing truck and offered to take Irma and Ivy to a building site to see how cement was poured. The enormous drums that churned the sloppy mixture before pouring it into the prepared ground fascinated the girls. Ivy asked Dominic to return the truck via Hilltop Crescent so she could show Irma the building site.

"Who are your neighbours?" Irma asked.

"I don't know," Ivy lied. She had never brought Irma home.

Although it wasn't what Clara had intended, by keeping Ivy in town, Ivy saw much more of Red than she would have had he been at Batchawana on weekends. In fact, she saw him every day. The Hilltop house was closed in but much had to be done. Ivy and Red used large canisters of putty or plaster as chairs. Red smoked his pipe, contemplating what was next on the plans, while Ivy dreamed of the house-warming party she would throw.

"I brought up the subject of leaving RVH with Miss Hobbs," Ivy told Red as they sat on their improvised seats.

"All I'll say is don't change your mind."

Clara had battled alongside Dr. McCaig and Reverend Hives for a new school, albeit arriving well after the meetings with the government began in 1929. She no longer expected the children to be enthused. A new school didn't return the youngsters to their communities. Nevertheless, the official opening of the new Shingwauk took place in the afternoon of October 3, 1935. Despite the absence of dignitaries, the Boy Scouts and Girl Guides were in their uniforms, and the children, thanks to Mrs. Aalto, were spanking clean. The only politician to attend was local MP Henry Hamilton, who had been involved in the plumbing modifications to keep the boys and girls apart. Others in attendance included the bishop of Algoma and other clergy. The opening of Shingwauk was Clara's last day. She was exhausted.

CHAPTER 35

Ivy returned to Montreal after her summer vacation at Batchawana with a conflicted heart. Clara had made many sacrifices to ensure she could go to the best nursing school, and Red was offering her the home she had never had. She and Red corresponded regularly, and once a week they talked on the phone. This had to be arranged in advance, since the telephone in the nurses' residence was used for emergencies only. In December, Red made a trip to Montreal to give Ivy an engagement ring, knowing she would have to leave it in her drawer. He wanted to formalize their engagement, though it was too soon to announce while Ivy was still a student at Royal Victoria Hospital.

In February, Miss Hobbs wrote to Clara that Ivy, after much thought, had decided to leave RVH and return home to the Soo. Clara, hoping to convince her daughter otherwise, got on the train to Montreal. Ivy wasn't yet twenty-one and was still considered a minor by the hospital.

As Clara disembarked at Windsor Station, she remembered it was here that she had received the sad news of Alistair Harwood's death. She had been on her way back to Lethbridge after spending three weeks in England with her family. The telephone booth from which she had called the Galt Hospital to inquire about the mayor was still in the same corner of the station. The words *he died in your apartment, Matron* were forever etched in Clara's memory. Ivy's decision to quit nursing school felt like another death.

Climbing into a waiting taxi, Clara headed to the hospital. As the car drove up University Avenue, she recalled her loyal friend, Francis Newbury. He had graduated with honours from McGill and had gone on to train at Royal Victoria Hospital. His first post as a doctor was at the Galt. He moved on after a few years, but a statue of him on horseback stood at the front entrance as a reminder of his medical pioneering. He had removed the first appendix at the Galt. Clara wondered what he would have said about Ivy's leaving. He had once described her as a lovely little girl, in his letter recommending Clara for the position of superintendent of the Galt Hospital — his alma mater, as he put it.

Clara called Miss Hobbs to say she was just leaving Windsor Station. Walking down the corridor to the director's office, Clara breathed in the familiar hospital smells. Her former student still had the same bright blue eyes and warm smile.

"How have you been?" Miss Hobbs asked.

"I retired from the residential school last October. I teach a course to the nursing students as a volunteer." Clara chuckled, and Miss Hobbs did, too, when she quipped, "I haven't been reduced to pushing the auxiliary cart yet." Clara had been known to get impatient with the high-handed volunteer ladies at the Galt.

"Let's talk about Ivy," Miss Hobbs said, motioning Clara to sit down. It seemed the tables were turned, with the director now advising Clara. "Your daughter's been an excellent student, but her heart isn't in the hospital. She seemed quite lonely when Miss Mitchell left. They were opposites but very good friends."

Clara let out a frustrated breath she had been holding. "Ivy's fiancé, Red Donnelly, was spoiled by his family after his kidney was removed when he was sixteen. He's used to getting his own way. Six months isn't too long to wait, to let Ivy qualify."

"You're treating this as a contest, Mrs. Durling, with Ivy as the prize." Miss Hobbs could see in Clara's face how losing her job as superintendent of the Galt Hospital had taken its toll. "Let's bring Ivy into this conversation."

Ivy must have been listening outside the open door because she came right in. Clara was overwhelmed to see her daughter in uniform. Ivy's soft blond hair was rolled into a chignon under her cap.

"Tell your mother how you feel," Miss Hobbs urged.

"I feel I'm reliving my childhood." Ivy avoided her mother's hurt gaze. "Red has built me a home. That's what I missed growing up."

"But you had security," Clara said. "I put you in the best situation I could after the war. I'd lost all but you, Ivy."

"And I've benefited, Mum, from all that you provided. Red calls me his social asset."

Miss Hobbs tried to lighten the atmosphere with a slight laugh at Ivy's comment. No one spoke then until Miss Hobbs broke the silence. "Mrs. Durling, you're a widow, I'm a spurned bride, and your daughter's engaged. Whatever happens to her, she'll manage. I have faith in your daughter, and I don't believe we'll have another war. Ivy will — as they say in the storybooks — live happily ever after."

"Miss Hobbs, thank you for your kindnesses, especially when I reacted so badly in surgical operations," Ivy said, shaking the director's hand.

"You were at your best with patients," Miss Hobbs said. She wished Clara good luck in her retirement and walked them to the door of her office. Clearly, she felt emotional to lose Ivy.

Back in Ivy's room, Clara helped to pack her daughter's trunk, which would be delivered to the train in the hospital truck. She hesitated as she hung Ivy's uniforms in the closet and then started to cry.

Ivy put her arms around Clara. "We're not packing a coffin, Mum."

They were to catch the train the next day, and Clara had booked a double-bedded room at the Windsor Arms.

When they were settled in their hotel room, Ivy said, "Red brought me here a year ago for dinner. We almost knocked over a bottle of wine. What was it like courting in your day?"

"Much the same, except we drank ale."

They stayed up talking, and Clara realized she had spent little time chatting with her daughter. "What are you going to do in the months before the wedding?"

"Understand Red's business. Have you ever heard of ferro-cement?"

Clara sighed. "We can talk about cement tomorrow."

CHAPTER 36

The house on Hilltop was built and ready to move into when Ivy arrived back in the Soo in mid-February 1936. She and Red chose the first Saturday in May as their wedding date. The next twelve weeks were a whirlwind of preparations. Ivy and Clara bustled around, dealing with guest lists, engraved invitations from Henry Birks in Toronto, room reservations at the Windsor Hotel for out-of-town guests, and choosing a dining room for a luncheon reception to follow the ceremony. Clara buried any hard feelings toward Red, and with renewed energy, prepared herself for the wedding of her only daughter.

Percy Paris, the dean of St. Luke's Anglican Church, would perform the marriage ceremony. Ivy attended a round of teas and showers before the wedding, and Jessie Rossiter offered to entertain the out-of-town guests on the eve of the wedding while the family members gathered for the rehearsal dinner. She had already sent a request for hors d'oeuvres to her mother in Toronto.

Jean, now married to Rupert Nesbitt and living in Vancouver, was thrilled to be Ivy's matron of honour. Red asked Max Laird, his classmate at the University of Toronto, to be his best man. Ivy had never met Max but knew he was a member of Red's geology club. Barnaby was touched to the core to give Ivy away.

"You can't wear a pink wedding dress," Clara said, distressed at Ivy's choice from a New York catalogue. "It will bring you bad luck."

"The dress isn't pink," Ivy insisted. "The colour is lilac."

Ivy fussed that the church would be surrounded by dirty, not-yet-melted snow in early May.

"We wanted to be married in May," Red said. "Shall we postpone the date?" When Ivy looked stricken, he added, "I think I have an inelegant solution. I purchased blown insulation equipment in Montreal. It's the first of its kind in Northern Ontario. The men have been trained to use the heavy machinery on cellulose, which is heavier than paper." He suggested they might hide the dirty snow in festive confetti.

"I'm marrying such a smart man," Ivy said during a practice session on the property of Donnelly Building Materials. Shooting confetti got many chuckles from Red's employees.

"We'll be able to insulate houses much faster and with fewer men," Red said as the men laughed.

As more and more wedding guest acceptances came in from Lethbridge and Calgary, Ivy understood that her mother hadn't been disgraced.

Red had ensured the house would be furnished before the wedding day. He had purchased a dining room set, including a sideboard, a carving table, and two settees from an estate auction. "You're the Mistress of the Mansion," he teased as Ivy arranged items from her white shower in the linen cupboard.

She looked forlornly at her empty dressing closet and joked she would have to go on a buying spree.

"Well, we're going to be in Chicago," Red said. He was visibly happy that Ivy had come home.

The night before the wedding, Jean stayed with Ivy. The pre-nuptial dinner had ended early, and Red drove them home.

"Forty-seven Hilltop Crescent," he said proudly as he dropped the girls off at the couple's future home.

Ivy gossiped with Jean late into the evening until Clara crossed the street to say, "Ivy needs her sleep."

The next morning, Clara woke the girls with a tray of Ellen Donnelly's cheese biscuits and coffee made in a fancy double pot that Ivy had received as a wedding gift. Jean served as hairdresser and manicurist.

At ten o'clock, Jack arrived in Red's roadster with the top up. "Can't mess the bride's hair," he said.

Lily came with her blue Rambler to drive Clara and Jean. She had already dropped Barnaby off at the church.

A carpet had been laid on the cleared path from the street to the church entrance. The snowbanks of late-spring snow were covered in a soft blanket of white confetti. Ivy could see Bob Snelling, one of Red's senior workmen, who was crouched on the north side of the church. Bob returned her appreciative smile as she entered.

Ivy was careful not to see Red as she waited in the foyer. That was another of Clara's superstitions. She always tried to jump over sidewalk cracks and had never walked under a ladder. However, she believed the tragedies in her life were God's will and not bad luck.

Ushers had seated Ellen and Clara near the front. Some of Ellen's relatives moved to the bride's side of the church to balance the number of guests. The moment the organ played "The Wedding March," all eyes were on the bride at the back of the sanctuary.

"Thank you," she whispered to Barnaby, taking his gloved hand. He rarely used his prosthesis, but for this occasion he had put it on and purchased a fine cotton glove to cover his artificial hand. Ivy walked down the aisle, smiling and moving at the wedding pace she had practised the night before to Bach's "Arioso."

Red and Max looked handsome in their morning suits. The mothers were beaming and crying. The moment Ivy joined hands with Red, she knew a new life had begun. They said their vows, and a soloist from the church sang Schubert's "Ave Maria," which Clara thought too Catholic but Red loved. The recessional, Mendelssohn's "Wedding March," rang out from the organ. Ivy — now on Red's arm — walked with a livelier step than she had on her way up the aisle.

Once in the car, Red kissed Ivy on the mouth unabashedly while Jack drove them to the hotel.

"I love you, Red Donnelly," Ivy said.

"Mrs. Donnelly, I love you, too."

At the wedding luncheon, the season demanded overcoats, and there was a lull before the receiving line began while guests deposited their outdoor wear with a hatcheck girl. Neither Clara nor Ellen was loquacious, and the queue moved along smoothly. Clara hadn't spared on the food. To satisfy her British roots, she put a hip of beef and Yorkshire pudding on the menu. Her daughter had argued that was too heavy for a noontime meal, but they remained on the menu card. Ivy loved lobster in the Newburg style, and that had seemed to her more appropriate for the time of day. Barnaby had insisted on providing the wine, and Ellen and Jean arranged the table flowers.

Barnaby deferred to Lily for the speech to the bride. While an unconventional choice, she had the guests both laughing and crying. Midway through the speech, she paused, then, for shock value, said her son had been kidnapped while horseback riding with Ivy. She interrupted the resulting table gasps to ask Teddy to stand up.

"We found him," she said to joyful laughter.

Guests from Lethbridge had been placed among the Soo invitees to make for more interesting table conversations. Leading the chatter was Etta Iverson and her daughter, Katherine, Clara and Ivy's closest friends while they were living in Lethbridge. Katherine was at art school and not yet married. She embellished the terrifying tale of Bob Glimp, the American union organizer who had kidnapped Teddy when he was ten years old and riding on horseback with Ivy. Etta then jumped in to describe how Clara had returned the getaway car after knocking Bob Glimp out. "The scoundrel never did get the ransom," Etta said, "thanks to Clara's bravery."

Then Dan MacIntyre, never at a loss for words, entertained the guests from the Soo with his tale of Albert Martin. He went on to make affectionate fun of Clara, who had threatened to wash his mouth with soap if he didn't stop cussing in front of the other patients.

The luncheon ended at three o'clock, and guests were invited to Hilltop to view the presents. Ivy embodied her role as hostess as though she had been entertaining all her life. Growing up in the adult world of a hospital had honed impeccable manners. The perusing guests asked the inevitable question: "Where are you going on your honeymoon?"

"Nowhere for the moment," Ivy replied. "We plan to travel by boat in July to enjoy the blues and jazz clubs in Chicago."

PART THREE

Brief Harmony

CHAPTER 37

Finally alone in their living room, Red stood behind Ivy with his arms around her shoulders as they gazed at the blanket of snow covering the garden. Reflections from the late-afternoon sun had turned the snow orange as far back as the ravine before it disappeared below the horizon.

"As soon as the ground thaws, my men will bring digging machines to stir up the soil," Red said. "Then you can plant your flowers. We should put in a hedge to shield us from the street."

"That will block my mother's view. She loves looking at the city across our property."

Red chuckled. "Once she's seen me naked, she won't be looking this way."

"Mum was a war nurse. She's seen plenty of naked men!"

"None as good-looking as me." Red kissed Ivy on the mouth to stifle her reply, and they both laughed.

Ivy was quite pleased to have many antique pieces of furniture in her new home. "How did you find such lovely items?" she asked Red while putting her wedding dishes into the beautiful burled walnut sideboard.

"I purchased the furniture at an auction of the Plummer estate. William Plummer was a big civic booster here until he moved to Toronto twenty years ago. After his death, much of his estate was found to be in the Soo."

"Is that why there's a Plummer Memorial Hospital?" Ivy asked.

"Yes. The hospital's a legacy of the family's importance in the Soo."

Once the wedding bounty had been unwrapped and put away, Ivy sat at her antique walnut desk from the Plummer estate, situated in front of the French doors, to write the obligatory thank-you letters. "I think I should send a thank-you note to Sir James Dunn," she said thoughtfully.

"What for?" Red asked, settled on the sofa beside Ivy with a book.

"Just as our guests arrived at the Windsor Hotel, Sir James was in the lobby castigating the chef. He was furious that his porridge had been served cold that morning. He threatened to buy the hotel and fire the man he was berating. His tantrum added colour to our solemn ceremony."

"In what way?"

"Our guests thought Sir James was invited to the party. I imagine they'd never encountered a knighted person before."

"Well, that'll be the most interesting 'compliment' Sir James ever receives," Red commented.

"My mother thinks you're a great catch," Ivy said, gazing lovingly at her new husband on the sofa.

"Hmm … makes me sound like a fish!"

In the summer of 1936, an extreme heat wave moved across North America. Ivy and Red were packing for their delayed honeymoon to Chicago when they received some disappointing news. Exacerbated by the intense heat, violence erupted in the entertainment district of the Windy City, and it seemed prudent to cancel their trip. Married for only four months, Red was still trying to understand his bride. They had both agreed to postpone their honeymoon until spring or summer, once the good weather had arrived. He was as disappointed as Ivy at the change in plans. However, he chuckled at how she expressed *her* disappointment.

"I thought it would be so nice to walk into a hotel and sign the guest register Mr. and Mrs. Donnelly," she lamented. "It would make me feel married."

"Well we *are* married," Red said. "We don't have to be in Chicago to have fun. I'm going to lock the door," he added with a grin.

Ivy put her hand on her lips and grimaced. "Oh-oh, I gave Mum a key to check the house while we were away."

"If Clara enters in the next half-hour, I *will* run down the stairs naked to greet her, and she won't come by again."

Ivy started to giggle as Red encouraged her up the stairs to the bedroom.

The disappointment about Chicago was offset when Ellen Donnelly invited the newlyweds to mitigate the heat at Batchawana. Red had suspended all building projects after his foreman was hospitalized with heatstroke. While the heat wave lasted, the cottage was over-run with family members seeking relief.

Ed Donnelly had carved his initials and the date of construction, 1910, into the chimney cement at the back of the house. Red brought Ivy for a brief moment of privacy to show her how Ed had left his mark.

"You're fortunate to have known your father," Ivy said. "I have little memory of mine. I do remember putting flowers on his gravestone and recall being frightened that my brother was buried in the same plot. I thought I might be buried there, too," Ivy added, laughing through her tears. "Silly to be crying over things that happened so long ago."

"Yours was a double tragedy," Red said soberly.

"Mum looked so happy at our gift-showing to see how well we were starting out. She had to auction most of her belongings to pay for our passage."

Red embraced her. "All that's behind you now."

The cottage provided little privacy, and on a windy morning, Red suggested they take the roadster to Gros Cap, a rocky outcropping into Lake Superior where giant waves crashed against the rocks, spewing spray in their faces. Ivy threw some odds and ends into a basket so they could spend the day. They gathered rocks to weigh down the corners of their picnic blanket.

"I hope our marriage won't be as wild as this wind," Ivy said, grabbing Red for balance.

"I don't want it to be dull, either," Red replied. "And I need to get out from under my family."

"We were a family of two," Ivy said. "I love your big family."

"I'm merely suggesting we have our own place — not divorce them."

CHAPTER 38

It was a relief to be out on the water in the blazing heat, the hottest summer ever recorded. Red abandoned his younger brothers, choosing Ivy as his fishing companion. Patiently, he taught her the vagaries of his fishing tackle and let her run the boat once she had learned the simple mechanics of the motor and water safety rules. It was a singular thrill when she drove the boat, and Red shouted from the bow, "Let her rip, Captain!" These outdoor activities, so foreign to Ivy growing up, were feeling more normal.

While at the cottage, Ellen Donnelly gave Ivy a recipe for venison pie with the sage advice that she be prepared to cook whatever Red brought back from the bush during the November deer season.

"Hunting and fishing are Red's first two passions," Ellen said, lending Ivy a well-used cookbook. "You're the third," she added when Ivy pouted.

"What should I expect?" Ivy asked.

"Gruesomeness!" Ellen made a face to match the word. "Fortunately, the hunters dress the animals in the field, so you won't have to see the entrails. They remove the guts where the deer comes down and leave them for wild animals."

"Gruesome things made me sick in nursing school."

"Then you'd better stay inside when the men come home. Skinning the deer is worse than anything you'd see in a hospital."

When the hunters returned to the city, Ivy was too curious to heed her mother-in-law's advice. She ventured into the garage to find Red and his Uncle Geordie grunting as they hoisted a five-hundred-pound buck off the back of the Donnelly Building Materials truck they had backed into the garage. Geordie Plaxon was Ellen's youngest brother, and he ran a farm-supply business. He was only ten years older than Red, and they seemed more like cousins who shared a love of the outdoors.

Ivy remained at the back entrance to the garage, transfixed by the two beautiful carcasses hanging from the ceiling and dripping blood. The men were so engrossed in wielding their sharp knives to peel back the hides that they didn't notice her. Ivy watched Red, who seemed almost like a surgeon as he slid the knife up and under the skin in the direction of the animal's hair. Despite the macabre scene, the skinning of the animal appeared to be a delicate procedure to Ivy. A thought crossed her mind: *It was the hospital odour that made me sick more than the actual surgical procedures.*

She slipped back into the house unnoticed and prepared two mugs of coffee, adding a dollop of brandy to each. When she returned with the steaming mugs, she grimaced at two blood-soaked towels — wedding presents — lying on the garage floor.

"I'll buy you new ones," Red said with a sheepish grin.

"We had to clean out the cavity," Geordie added, jumping in to get his pal off the hook.

"I'll hold you to it," Ivy said.

Moose season followed deer season, and a month later Red was off to hunt with Geordie again.

"What happens to the cuts of the animal you don't want?" Ivy asked before the men left.

"Geordie and I share them with our employees, who are grateful to have any kind of meat during this economic crisis."

Ivy turned twenty-one while Red was away hunting moose farther north of Batchawana on Lake Superior. "Red wouldn't be aware my birthday would fall while he was away unless I told him," Ivy said to her mother.

"He should be here for your milestone," Clara replied.

"I'm not hurt, so you shouldn't be hurt on my behalf."

By January, the St. Marys River was frozen enough to ice-fish, and the Donnelly shack was hauled into Still Bay. It no longer seemed an intimate moment for Ivy now that she and Red were married, but she went along for the companionship.

"I've purchased another cement truck that'll be delivered in May," Red confided. He hadn't revealed his business decision to his mother despite her half ownership of Donnelly Building Materials.

"Isn't this risky with talk of another war?" Ivy asked. "The newspaper reported only last week that Hitler ignored the Versailles Treaty by building up arms and his aggression in nearby territories."

"Houses will still be built, albeit smaller ones," Red countered. "Every house needs a foundation, which we do much faster with our cement trucks. If there's another war, I expect to be sent overseas, so it's better to expand while I can."

CHAPTER 39

A shopping trip to Chicago never did materialize. Ivy had planned to replace her practical outfits from her Royal Victoria days at a fancy American department store. She was making do with her limited wardrobe when Red suggested she take the train to Toronto to shop for clothes with Anne Rossiter, who was now married to Tom Blake and living there. Although Ivy didn't know her well, she called Jessie Rossiter and asked for her daughter's address.

"Anne and Tom live in downtown Toronto not far from Eaton's Department Store," Jessie told her. "I'm sure my spendthrift daughter will be delighted to take you shopping."

"I could certainly use some help. Your daughter's very fashionable."

"Hmm," Jessie murmured. "Anne's negotiated a continuance of her clothing allowance with her father. Tom's a trading clerk in a brokerage firm that managed to stay afloat despite the financial crash. I'm sure he'll rise in the company and keep up with his wife's extravagances. Until then, K.G. is sending his darling daughter a monthly cheque." Jessie laughed amiably. "Ivy, would you like to hand-deliver Anne's allowance?"

"It would be fun to be the delivery girl," Ivy said, smiling broadly and happy this task would facilitate her renewed acquaintance with Anne.

Anne was quick to answer Ivy's letter about her upcoming trip. "We live in a tiny apartment near the streetcar line, so I'd suggest staying at the King Edward Hotel for its convenience," she wrote back.

In Toronto, on her first night in the hotel, Ivy took the elevator to the main dining room and marvelled at the smart-looking guests. She ordered the special of the day, veal in mushroom sauce, and water when the waitress said, "We don't serve wine by the glass." Back in her room, she bathed in the enormous porcelain tub. Snug in the heavy cotton bathrobe provided by the hotel, she then called Red to thank him.

"I feel like a princess," she told her husband, leaning back on the pillows piled on the bed.

"That was my intention," Red said. "Try to find time outside of shopping to call my best man. I'm sure Max will invite you out to dinner. Or maybe Mrs. Laird will ask you over."

Ivy hung up the receiver and wrapped herself in a hug. *I have the best husband in the world*, she thought.

It turned out that Tom Blake knew Max Laird, who wasn't married but had a girlfriend who had been at Havergal College with Anne. Tom bought five tickets to the Fall Musical Revue at the Arts and Letters Club on Elm Street. After the performance, they joined mutual friends in a nearby jazz club. Ivy was pleased to be hobnobbing with such a stylish Toronto crowd and fitting in. She thought of former classmate Sass Mitchell with her unconventional attitude. Ivy didn't think anyone in the jazz club would kick over the traces the way Sass had. She made a mental note to write to Sass on the King Edward notepaper. Her former roommate had given birth to a son five months after quitting her nursing course and had just published her first crime novel. Ivy hoped to pick up a copy in a Toronto bookstore if it was still on the shelves.

Early Saturday morning after the jazz club evening, Anne met Ivy at Eaton's. This was Ivy's last opportunity to shop, and until then she had looked but not bought any clothing. The ladies were serious shoppers that day. Anne led the way to the "weekend wear" floor where Ivy purchased gabardine slacks, coordinating blouses, and a scarf to go with any outfit. Anne, in a good-humoured manner, described her own reality.

"Tom and I are often in formal dress on weekends, thanks to the charitable invitations of my parents' rich friends." Anne laughed. "I don't often get to wear outdoor casual wear."

"You'll think back on your small apartment days and wish you could return there," Ivy said.

Anne leaned forward and embraced Ivy. "We don't know what life will bring, do we?"

In the gown department, both women tried on dresses and paraded in front of the sales clerk to solicit her opinion. Ivy bought a long black dress that was fitted until the bottom where the hem flared out. It had lace overlaying the bodice and off-the-shoulder straps.

"I should probably buy an everyday dress while I'm in Toronto," Ivy said. At the information desk, the lady directed the friends to the third floor for daytime wear.

"Eaton's dining room is a nice place for lunch," Anne suggested.

"Let me thank you for your sartorial advice," Ivy said. "My treat."

"Then let me treat you to the Art Gallery of Toronto before you return to the hotel," Anne countered. "There's an exhibition of Toronto artists who travelled to Northern Ontario to paint the autumn colours. Dad rented a cottage for two weeks each summer near Michipicoten Harbour where Toronto artists gravitated for the exceptional autumn scenery. My father wanted his daughters to experience raw nature before holidaying at our civilized summer home on Lake Simcoe."

"Red's family has a cottage at Batchawana, not far from the harbour," Ivy said. "I can understand why artists would go there in the fall to paint. The colours are spectacular!"

"Lake Superior's a beautiful part of the world," Anne agreed.

Entering the gallery, Anne spoke with the nearest docent and inquired about the exhibit of Northern Ontario art.

"You mean the Group of Seven?" the docent asked.

Anne smiled. "Are they still called that?"

The docent laughed. "By me, yes." She chatted as the women entered the exhibition room, stopping in front of a work entitled *Autumn Leaves, Batchewana, Algoma* by J.E.H MacDonald. "This is a recent gift from the Students' Club of the Ontario College of Art."

"My father was surveying the hydro lines when he encountered the artists living in a boxcar on the Algoma Central rail line," Anne said. "He loaned the artists an Indian guide from his crew to help them navigate the waters. My dad said the artists operated out of the boxcar for four weeks."

"How interesting," the docent said, moving to a work by A.Y. Jackson.

"Jackson rented a cabin not far from ours," Anne said excitedly. "At the time, we didn't realize he was such an important artist."

"He was, indeed!" the docent said. "I'll pass on this added information to other visitors to the gallery who might be familiar with Toronto but ignorant of Northern Ontario. There's a short documentary about the painters. Would you like to see it?"

"Oh, my goodness!" Anne cried. "It's almost five o'clock. I'll bring my husband another day. Some years ago he was on a canoe trip on the Michipicoten River when he got stranded and stopped at our cottage for help. That's how our courtship began in Northern Ontario," Anne confessed with a broad smile.

"You haven't lost your northern roots," Ivy said as they exited the gallery.

"I try not to."

Ivy was leaving on Monday, so Anne invited her for dinner that evening at her apartment. Tom was a serious man, but he possessed a wry and intelligent sense of humour. In the course of the evening, he spoke about his family and the unexpected course of events related to the stock market crash.

"I was at Upper Canada College when my father lost everything. At the time, I was captain of the Cadet Corps, and the headmaster didn't want me to leave the school. He, or someone — I'll never know — provided a scholarship so I could finish my last two years."

"My husband had to leave medical school three years ago to run a family business when his father suddenly died," Ivy said. The unexpected often happens."

"My parents said you have a lovely house on Hilltop," Anne interjected.

"We're in the cheap seats," Ivy said. "Much farther down the street. Not at all like your parents."

"I tried to remain grounded at Havergal, but it wasn't always easy," Anne said. "My classmates had difficulty believing my home was in the Soo. One snide girl suggested I must live in an igloo." They talked well into the evening. Tom and Anne hopped the streetcar to accompany Ivy back to the hotel where they each enjoyed a cocktail in the bar. Before going to bed, Ivy wrote to Sass, who was now living not far from Royal Victoria Hospital where her husband was a doctor. Ivy ended her letter with: "My next trip will be to Montreal!"

Anne had asked Ivy to join them at the Sunday service at Grace Church on-the-Hill to see where she and Tom were married. After the service, the minister shook Ivy's hand on her way out of the church.

"You must be one of Anne's Havergal friends."

"I didn't go to Havergal," Ivy said politely.

"Aha!" the minister exclaimed. "You're a Bishop Strachan girl!"

"I didn't go to a private school. I attended a high school in Sault Ste. Marie."

"I'm so sorry if I embarrassed you," the minister said.

"How long have you been at this beautiful church?" Ivy asked.

"This is my first year. I had the privilege of marrying Anne and Tom."

"And where were you before Grace Church?"

"Smiths Falls."

"We all come from somewhere," Ivy said with an impish grin.

"Touché!" Tom said outside the church.

Ivy and Anne began giggling like schoolgirls.

CHAPTER 40

The cold weather in November 1937 with a brushing of snow didn't deter Red and Geordie from heading to Batchawana to hunt moose. Ivy took advantage of his absence to throw a hen party for the friends she had made at the used clothing depot organized by Kathryn Derrer in the basement of St. Luke's Cathedral. She had gained her knowledge of clothing relief while helping Lily distribute second-hand cocktail dresses to the Italian mothers in the west end. This type of clothing might have seemed impractical at a time when many families were unemployed. However, Italian mothers refashioned the colourful attire into fancy dresses for their daughters. Although Algoma Steel was rehiring again now that a war seemed imminent, many families were still impoverished. Sending their daughters out in nice costumes had been a bright light for many parents during the Depression.

One of the depot volunteers had leaked that the hen party was being held on Ivy's twenty-second birthday.

"I longed for a home when I was growing up," she said emotionally at the party. "And now I have one," she added with an infectious smile as she held up the lounging pajamas the ladies had bought as a group present. Clara was sitting in an armchair next to the fireplace that crackled with heat. Ivy walked across the room and leaned over, kissing her mother's wiry grey hair. "Mum and I are both grateful we discovered the Soo."

"Let's get at the cards," Clara said, giving Ivy a warm smile and avoiding the question: "*What brought you to the Soo?*"

"My mother-in-law sent along a birthday cake," Ivy said. "She doesn't enjoy bridge, though she did play poker with her sons when they were growing up." Ivy chuckled. "Mum's been awarded the title of master player and will be happy to provide bidding tips." There was a murmur of appreciation among the players as they situated themselves across from a partner at the two bridge tables set up near the fire.

When the ladies discovered that Kathryn Derrer had a master's title, as well, they decided the evening was an opportunity to hone bridge skills rather than grand-slam an opponent. Clara advised one table and Kathryn the other. Occasionally, a player, waiting for a bid, interrupted the game with a thought about the possibility of war, given Hitler's aggressive behaviour. "Louis is a retired colonel," Kathryn said, "and he's worried."

Phyllis Crowder was married to Adam, the editor of the daily newspaper, the *Sault Star*. Her father-in-law, James Crowder, was the owner of the newspaper, an outdoors enthusiast, and a hero of Red's. James had published *Wolves Don't Bite*, a wilderness novel. "Adam's last editorial suggested that when the Germans repatriated their coal areas in the Rhineland last year it was for industrial purposes, not war," Phyllis said. "I also think it's quite reasonable for Hitler, an Austrian, to bring the Sudeten Germans back into their homeland. I don't necessarily see that as expansionist."

Eileen Howland, the wife of the local broadcaster, jumped into the conversation with her bit of gossip. "Grant, my husband, allows people to say the most outrageous comments about Germany." She folded her elegant hands over her pregnant belly. "I'm surprised the regulators haven't closed his radio station. We're so far away we don't really know what's happening to the Jews."

Ivy had a tinge of jealousy, wishing she were pregnant herself. Red preferred to wait so he could concentrate on his "new toys," as he called the insulation and ready-mix machines. The ladies were in full-gossip mode and showed no sign of going home. Ivy was enjoying their company and slipped into the kitchen to make more coffee in her new electric machine.

"Let's put the card tables away while we wait for coffee," Clara suggested.

The guests folded up the card tables and put them in the basement where Clara indicated they were stored. Then the ladies settled around the fire to drink coffee and munch on the remains of Ellen's cake.

"What happened to Ruthie Cohen?" Clara asked. "She loves to play bridge."

"She's at a baby-naming ceremony being held above Allen's Ladies Wear," Ivy reported.

"Is that something I should know about?" Eileen asked. "Grant and I can't agree on what we should call our child. Whatever we decide, he'll blast on the radio." She giggled and patted her stomach.

"It's a Jewish custom to name a boy at the time of his circumcision," Clara interjected. "They call the ceremony a bris. There isn't a synagogue in the Soo, and that's why Ruthie's on the second floor of a department store celebrating her nephew's bris."

"This is a terrible time for European Jews," Betty Greensted said. She was a glamorous Toronto girl who had moved to the Soo when she married Beau. Her father, George Frederick Kingston, was the dean of Trinity College at the University of Toronto and had publicly denounced the treatment of German Jews on a radio broadcast. Temple Kingston, Betty's younger brother, was a student at the divinity school at Trinity when Hitler passed the first Nuremberg Law to prevent intermarriage between Germans and Jews. If it hadn't been Ivy's birthday, Betty would have attended the bris.

"Although Louis is the senior engineer at Algoma Steel, there's much he can't say," Kathryn said. "Algoma was heavily committed in the Great War and will be again if Hitler pushes Europe into another conflict." After a pause, she confided, "The government recently accused Sir James Dunn of disloyalty. There are a lot of politics involved in making steel."

"I have a dim view of the government after four years working at a residential school," Clara said. "I'd put my money on Sir James." The ladies laughed.

"During the Great War, Algoma made steel essential to war materials," Kathryn said. "It was a fatal mistake, according to Louis, to dedicate production to tank and shell steel, which would no longer be in demand after the war. Algoma went into a lengthy decline, heading for bankruptcy, until Sir James Dunn took over and directed production to plate steel, which could be used after the war for domestic appliances."

"We'll have to keep our used clothing depot open if bankruptcy happens again," Betty said. "Let's end on a happy note and sing 'Happy Birthday' to Ivy. We forgot to sing it when we served the cake."

"Don't worry," Kathryn said as the ladies pulled on their coats. "Bankruptcy won't happen again under Sir James." Kathryn stayed for a few minutes after everyone else had left. "Let us know when you'd like to visit Gawas Bay at St. Joseph Island," she said. "There's an original log cabin in the bay for sale."

"Red expressed an interest," Ivy said.

"Louis and I would love some young neighbours," Kathryn said. "Louis shares Red's love of boats."

Ivy put the back of her hand across her forehead and groaned. "Is Red thinking of buying a boat as well as the cabin?"

"I hope I haven't spilled the beans," Kathryn apologized

Ivy frowned. "I'll wait for Red to bring the matter up."

"Spend and expand seems to be my son-in-law's motto," Clara said. "I have to trust he knows what he's doing because he married my daughter."

The three ladies laughed, and Ivy offered Clara a nightcap when Kathryn departed.

CHAPTER 41

Red and Ivy were on the car ferry crossing the rough and windy North Channel that connected Lakes Huron and Superior. They climbed the circular metal stairs of the boat to speak with the captain, who had worked for Ed Donnelly before he died.

"I'm sure my old boss would be pleased to see you're married to such a pretty girl," the captain said.

Red grinned at Ivy, who shook with the cold. The crossing took less than ten minutes, so they dashed back to the car where Red switched the heat on.

The couple were on their way to visit Louis and Kathryn Derrer at Gawas Bay on St. Joseph Island and to look at a cabin for sale. When they arrived at the Derrers', Ivy immediately raced to the fire blazing in the living room to warm her hands. "I think I'll skip the boat ride to see the cabin," she said, shivering.

"I'll send the children along with Louis and Red and enjoy having you to myself," Kathryn said jovially. She turned to her children, five-year-old Harry and ten-year-old Audrey, glaring at them with mock severity. "You must behave." Then she bundled them in winter clothes, ignoring their protests that snowsuits were stupid in May. Complaining vocally, the children trudged down the hill to the boat and were drowned out when it sped off.

"They'll thank me when they return," Kathryn said sardonically. She went to the kitchen to prepare tea and returned with a tray and cups to find Ivy sleeping in an armchair. Kathryn covered her with a wool blanket and poured some tea, being careful not to rattle the cup and saucer.

There was only a short, crudely constructed dock in front of the cabin for sale. "We better pull up on shore," Louis advised. Whitecaps rolled in from Lake Huron, rocking the boat. "The bay's calmer once the lake warms up."

The children, arms outstretched for balance, jumped off the bow onto the sandy shore, and with exaggerated grunts, pulled the boat up. Red and Louis finished the job so there was no possibility of it slipping away.

Red laughed as he took a big leap onto the sand. "It would be a cold swim back to your cottage."

Harry and Audrey dashed off to see what critters were in the outhouse.

"Let me tell you something about your Chicago neighbours," Louis said. He pointed at a large cedar cottage painted green perched on a rocky island in the open waters of Lake Huron. Several smaller outbuildings and a large square one surrounded the main house. "That entire complex belongs to James Scutter, a wealthy businessman from Lake Forest, Illinois. The square building is his squash court and the small cottages are for the staff they bring from Chicago.

"Interesting," Red said. "What about the small cabin just across the bay?"

"Betty and Beau Greensted own that one," Louis said. "Her brother, Temple, comes up occasionally and installs his family in a small cabin set back in the woods. Betty rarely comes."

"She's a good pal of Ivy's," Red said. "I've known Big Beau since childhood."

"He's an enormous man," Louis said. "The Greensteds dock their motorboat at our cottage. I cross my fingers each time Beau gets in. He must have divine intervention because he's never capsized."

Red laughed. "Betty's blessed, as well! Her father's the dean of Trinity College at the University of Toronto. When I was at Wycliffe, another Anglican college, Betty would walk around campus smiling at an abundance of admiring men. We were all a little surprised when she married Beau. I don't believe she told Ivy they have a cottage on Gawas Bay. Otherwise my wife would have been more enthusiastic about buying something away from my family."

Louis and Red stepped into the unlocked cabin, which smelled of creosote.

"Nothing to steal here," Louis said. "Would you add on or tear it down?"

"There's history in those logs. What this cabin needs is something I can provide — cement. An addition would brighten it up, though. But how can I convince Ivy? She loves Batchawana."

"Leave that to Kathryn and Betty Greensted," Louis said. "Ivy will appreciate having friends living close by."

As the men inspected the structural soundness, Audrey came screeching into the cabin with a dead squirrel.

"You're not taking that in the boat," Louis said.

She pouted, and with a lasso-like swing, tossed it into the bush.

"It would be nice for our children to have a young couple as neighbours instead of their ancient parents," Louis said.

The boaters were frozen when they arrived back at the Derrers' cottage. Kathryn welcomed the men with drinks. They talked about the cabin and the thirty acres of woods surrounding it. Louis provided more information about the Americans who had summer homes dotting the nearby islands in Lake Huron.

"I learned from Mum that there was an annual enactment of a play about Hiawatha on Kensington Point," Ivy said. "According to her, the American families were so enthused by the production by the Garden River Indians that they put $100 in a passing hat. I remember Mum stayed overnight at a small hotel in Desbarats within walking distance of the performance. Have you seen the play?"

"We saw it when Helen Hayes, the American actress, attended the performance," Kathryn said. "She created quite a stir."

"Charles MacArthur, the playwright, bought a property in 1930 not long after marrying Miss Hayes," Louis interjected. "He purchased it on the mainland near the point, unlike most of the Chicago residents who bought islands. Real estate was relatively cheap compared to the States."

"We're a bit off the main track here in Gawas Bay, but we do get the gossip," Kathryn added. "Apparently, Helen eschews motorboats and rows her small skiff to cocktail parties. It's rumoured she put some money into the Hiawatha performance."

"The Americans hold a sailing regatta each summer in the open waters," Louis said. "We're invited to watch. They fancy themselves an elite group, but one day my son, Harry, will be in that race."

"It'll be exciting to build your own place," Kathryn said. "What a lovely idea to think that our young neighbours on Hilltop will be our young neighbours on Gawas Bay."

Red had offered his own venison for the evening meal, but Kathryn complained it was too cold to cook outside.

"Weather be damned!" Louis cried. The barbecue, embedded in a stone wall, surrounded three sides of a patio with the open side leading to a set of stairs down a steep hill to the lake. "Teamwork," Louis said as he donned an apron and handed Kathryn the meat. "Red shot the buck and I'll throw him on the grill!"

Audrey set the table with some help from Ivy. Louis wasn't a hunter, and the venison was appreciated. At the end of the evening, Audrey played a few songs on a player piano in the living room. Ivy and Red were offered the guest cabin that Harry and Audrey normally occupied.

When they were in the guest cabin, Red said as he slipped Ivy's flannel nightgown over her head, "There's a reason we're here."

"Most women expect to get pregnant in New York or Paris," Ivy said.

"Don't be smart, Mrs. Donnelly." Red bounced up and down on the metal bedsprings and then lowered Ivy onto a braided rug covering the pine-planked floor. "The floor doesn't squeak. If I ravaged you on the bed, the Americans might complain about the noise."

Ivy laughed. "The floor's hard," she said as she swung herself on top of Red.

"Oh, I like that!" Red said.

Ivy was surprised by her own brashness.

In the morning, Audrey found Red and Ivy still on the floor.

"Breakfast's on the barbecue," she said, as though finding houseguests on the floor were perfectly normal. "Don't worry. I've seen my brother naked."

Ivy had slipped back into her pajamas.

"Well, now!" Red replied with an embarrassed grin.

"See you on the patio," Audrey said, scurrying off.

CHAPTER 42

Red bought the Gawas Bay cottage while prices were still depressed, the property was undervalued, and the executor wanted to close the estate file and was happy to take cash. For $1,500, in September 1938, he and Ivy became the owner of the cabin and thirty acres. The money transaction completed, he sent a bulldozer and grader with his men to St. Joseph Island. He anticipated it would take a month to build a half-mile driveable road through the heavily wooded property to the cabin and organized a crew to go to the island. Before leaving the men to their work, he gave them a friendly order: "Stay off the hooch while you're operating heavy equipment. I don't want any accidents. You have four weeks to finish the road before the snow flies."

Red was overjoyed when he learned in September that Ivy was two months pregnant. Their mutual happiness at having their first child had been partly dampened by Ivy's persistent nausea.

"My part in the pregnancy," Red quipped to his brother, Jack, "is to have a ready supply of soda biscuits in my shirt pocket while Ivy retches in the bathroom." During the three months that she felt ill, he dropped in for a meal at his mother's, or occasionally Clara's, for food that Ivy couldn't eat.

In February 1939, Ivy delivered a six-pound daughter who they christened Alice. She was born with a shock of straight black hair that soon fell out to be replaced by a thatch of thick blond curls. Red jokingly questioned Alice's paternity until the curls arrived.

Ivy's caesarean delivery required two weeks in hospital before she could go home. Red came to the hospital in the morning before going to the office and returned in the evening prior to going home. Clara and Ellen visited General Hospital when Ivy was feeding Alice. Ivy didn't do well with breastfeeding after the operation, and when the crowing grandmothers arrived, they took turns at giving Alice the bottle supplied. That would have been forbidden had Clara not relied on Sister Marie Claire to bend the rules. Clara admired the director-general after she bent the Catholic hospital's rules to admit a gravely ill Chippewa boy from the Sarnia reserve who had never been baptized.

When Ivy returned home, she was grateful that Clara had hired a recently graduated Shingwauk girl to be a live-in helper. Ada Kusugak, an Inuit girl from Northern Quebec, had decided to remain in the Soo where there were more chances of finding work. She remembered Ivy from the Christmas party where she had shocked the custodians with her horse performance. Ada was now eighteen, the same age as Ivy when she galloped around the Shingwauk dining room with a small Native boy on her back.

Ada's father was one of the first Inuit to be ordained in the Anglican Church. He conducted services in both his own language and French. The Catholic Church predominated in Quebec, but the Inuit were primarily Anglicans. Ada had already spoken her own language and French when she arrived at Shingwauk, and she was quick to learn English. Reverend Hives had a special fondness for the daughter of a clergyman and let Ada speak Inuktituk with the few students at the school who spoke the same.

Ivy planned to take Alice to Gawas Bay in July, but the cabin still wasn't habitable for a baby. She changed their plans, and Ada accompanied them to Batchawana where she could enjoy visiting friends from Shingwauk on the nearby reserve on her days off.

"I can't speak Ojibwa," she told Ivy, "so I use English to communicate."

"Did you hate your years at Shingwauk?" Ivy asked.

"Reverend Hives made sure I had a good education. I don't think the other students had the same experience. Your mother has arranged for me to start nursing school at General Hospital," Ada added with evident pride, raising her shoulders in a modest shrug, as though Ivy would be surprised.

"I'm happy for you, Ada. But no one will be happier than my mother, who was so disappointed that I quit."

CHAPTER 43

Ivy had enjoyed her time at Batchawana but clearly missed Red. Several new building contracts that had landed on his desk in the spring had kept him in the city on weekends. Ivy agreed he needed someone to run his newly refurbished office more professionally. Ed Donnelly had relied on an office girl with no skills whose main job was to make coffee that she served to the clients and workers at the front counter. Red interviewed several middle-aged women looking for work while their husbands were laid off from the steel plant. When Nancy Stratichuk came into his office, he decided she had the right amount of brashness to deal with his employees, who were all men. Nancy was a graduate of Sault Technical School and could type and take dictation. She had already spent a year as the receptionist in a doctor's office. This was her second job, and she was keen to please Red.

When Ivy returned earlier than expected from Batchawana, she discovered that the new secretary was driving Red's car, a Buick that had replaced the impractical small roadster he'd inherited from his father. She expressed her disapproval to Clara.

"I'm not worried about Red, but it doesn't look good for a secretary to be driving her boss's car," Ivy said.

"I don't think so, either," Clara agreed.

Nancy was driving the Buick on Queen Street when Clara walked out of a grocery store. Nancy had halted at a stop sign, and Clara stepped into the street, blocking the young woman's way. Nancy recognized Clara and got out to ask what the problem was.

"You shouldn't be driving Red Donnelly's car," Clara insisted. She moved quickly to the driver's side, slipped in behind the wheel, and took off before Nancy could stop her.

"I was doing my boss's chores!" Nancy shouted after Clara. "Red told me to use his car!" The windows of the car were rolled down, so Clara could hear Nancy's words. *Mr. Donnelly to you!* she thought.

Never having learned to drive properly, Clara made her way along the street cautiously to Red's office where, once there, she scolded him in front of his employees. "What were you thinking letting your wife push a pram to do the groceries while *that* young woman drives your car?"

Later, after Red drove Clara home, he confronted Ivy and demanded, "What was *your* mother thinking barging into my office and letting loose her opinions of how I run my office?"

"I'm not Clara," Ivy said, upset that her mother had betrayed her confidence.

Red fumed as he returned to the office in the Buick.

The moment Red was gone, Clara trotted across the street. "Tell Red that his secretary should no longer drive his car," she urged her daughter. "Everyone in town recognizes that Buick."

"I'm not confrontational," Ivy retorted, leaving Clara standing in the hall and going to her bedroom to calm down. *I should have told Red myself*, she thought. *Red was very angry when he left. Mum has only made things worse.*

A month after the carjacking, Ivy received a handwritten note from Nancy Stratichuk, congratulating Ivy on getting her man back. Ivy handed the letter, written on Donnelly stationery, to Red.

"I fired Nancy. That's why she wrote that letter. Every secretary wants to sleep with her boss. That doesn't mean she actually does. Nancy misjudged. I love you, Ivy."

"You don't seem like a man having an affair," Ivy admitted.

"Let me prove it," Red said, pulling her up the stairs. "My God, I'm glad we're back in action," he said when they reached their bedroom.

"I'm glad Alice is asleep," Ivy said.

Red smoked his pipe thoughtfully, gazing out his office door at the chair that had been occupied by Nancy Stratichuk. He reflected on whether the carjacking was Clara's first interfering offence, or if there were things he had missed. He frowned, recalling Ivy's words while they were building the house on Hilltop Crescent. *Clara likes to get her own way.* In retrospect, he wished he had dealt with Clara directly rather than unleashing his anger on Ivy. *She doesn't know how to stand up to her mother*, he thought. Red understood his mother-in-law had a virtual following in the neighbourhood. He didn't feel he should pick a fight, and he didn't want to fight with his wife.

Red recalled Clara chiding the grocery boy and reprimanding the taxi driver for charging too much not long ago. Those disagreeable acts contrasted with the time she spent at a sick neighbour's bedside or her daily delivery of edible scraps to Hilltop dogs when she was out for her constitutional. In good weather, Clara kept a bowl of milk on her doorstep for stray cats. She was enjoying her retirement, and Red was happy about that, but he didn't want her meddling in his affairs, so he decided to speak to James Barnaby, who seemed to have a special understanding of Clara.

When Red paid a visit to Barnaby, he invited him in for coffee at his kitchen table. "Clara's a paradox. I first saw her marching around a hospital ward looking as though she were commanding a battalion. I was waiting to see Dr. Newbury about finishing my medical studies in Scotland."

"Clara told me the doctor was a loyal friend," Red said.

"Dr. Newbury was a godsend to both of us. When George Durling died, Clara was left in terrible financial straits. You know the rest."

"Not all of it."

"I was a psychiatrist at the Galt Hospital, so I saw what was happening first-hand."

"Is that how my mother-in-law became a battler?" Red asked.

Barnaby laughed. "I imagine Clara came out of her mother's womb in fighting form. But here's what you need to understand about the paradox. Nurses took care of Ivy while Clara turned a mediocre hospital into an operation fully accredited by the American College of Surgeons. That was remarkable given the chaos in Lethbridge following the war. Lethbridge had the highest per capita enlistment, and thus many more casualties than other towns of that size. It also had the highest per capita rate of venereal disease as a consequence. Alas, now she wants to be a good mother, but Ivy is your wife. She doesn't need Clara's help any longer. That's the conflict."

"Life's filled with paradoxes," Red said, getting up to leave. "I had to stop my medical studies, and you got to finish yours. If there's another war, I'll enlist as a medic."

"Let's hope there isn't another war," Barnaby said, pushing Red affectionately in the chest with his stump.

The Barnabys' house was close to Shingwauk, and Red headed there to hire a few strong lads for the back-breaking brush clearing and renovations to the cabin in Gawas Bay. Clara had informed him that boys who lived far away were stuck at the school and would be glad of a chance to escape. After making an arrangement with Reverend Hives, Red drove the boys to St. Joseph Island in a company truck loaded with the timber to make a forty-foot dock. The headmaster had agreed to release the boys if a Donnelly employee went along to supervise.

The boys from the James Bay area knew how to build rock cribs strong enough to resist winter ice. The St. Joseph Island ferry was soon loaded with bags of cement on a Donnelly truck for the boys to begin the chinking. Red no longer asked the boys what they could or couldn't do. He arrived with materials and said, "Go to it, lads!"

They finished the dock and started chinking the old logs. "If an Indian don't live in a log house, he lives in a shack," one of the boys said, and they all laughed.

Red left them a canoe, so they could have a little fun, then returned to the city to begin drawing up plans for an addition, which he would start the following year. He was happy.

At the end of the summer, the eldest boy about to start in his last year at Shingwauk told Red that being on St. Joseph Island was his best holiday.

CHAPTER 44

"I wish my country had shown some guts," Clara said in conversation with Barnaby.

His eyebrow arched. It was rare for Clara to speak crudely.

"I made my peace with Germans once," she said. "I'm not sure I can do it again."

"Well, you'll have to because we're heading for war. Your prime minister was naive to think Hitler wouldn't continue his land lust. As soon as he united the German people in Sudetenland, he began his world domination. With the stroke of a pen, Neville Chamberlain handed him half of Czechoslovakia. The smaller nations have capitulated, giving Germany a long reach into Eastern Europe."

Clara knew Barnaby to be an eternal optimist. She was now frightened by his dire prediction. "I weep to think Ivy will live through another war."

"Red won't be allowed to enlist with only one kidney," Barnaby said. "Isn't that a good thing?"

Clara sighed as though there were no answer.

The Americans were as pessimistic as Barnaby. On the opposite shore of the St. Marys River, Fort Brady was fast building up its military, anticipating that Germany would continue its expansionism. The four American locks were a strategic location. They managed the twenty-one-foot vertical drop between Lake Superior and Lake Huron, allowing the iron ore ships to reach the steel factories in Michigan, Pennsylvania, and Ohio. The downstream mills operating with few reserves would be crippled if the locks were damaged. The American military buildup was felt on the Canadian side, as well, since uniformed men crossed the river hunting for fun in the much larger Canadian Soo. The Canadian Forty-Ninth Heavy Anti-Aircraft Regiment conducted exercises and practice drills on the Sault Collegiate football field, Belvedere Park on the waterfront, or any other available space. Donnelly Building Materials was busy with contracts to build the infrastructure needed to operate a military base on the U.S. side. The mixer trucks churning the cement took up most of the room on the ferry crossing the river to America.

Business was booming, and Red left his trusted foreman, Clem Giovanni, in charge so he could attend the international boat show in Toronto. Grant Howland was there on broadcasting matters and already booked into the Royal York Hotel. Grant had recently purchased a fancy summer home close to Helen Hayes at Kensington Point. His American neighbours drove Chris-Craft mahogany inboards, and Grant wanted something similar. He had attended Trinity College School in Port Hope on a scholarship given to sons of clergymen. The small, scrappy, and ambitious man was desperate to be "in" with the American Joneses. Eileen, Grant's wife, and Ivy had admonished the boys before they left not to be extravagant. "A runabout will do us both fine," they said.

Red booked a room at the Royal York a few days after Grant, and they connected in the hotel bar to have a few drinks before hailing a taxi to take them across the city to the exhibition grounds. Men in bowlers and fine wool overcoats examined the boats with critical eyes. These were wealthy Torontonians buying them for their summer homes in Muskoka, Haliburton, or Lake Simcoe, closer to the city.

"Do we look like we come from Northern Ontario?" Red asked, chuckling.

"I hope not!" Grant replied. He had his eye on a previously owned mahogany speedboat christened the *Yak Yak*. He laughed. "It must have belonged to his wife. Maybe a separation agreement." A twenty-seven-foot wood cruiser caught Red's eye.

"That's more than a runabout," Grant said.

"Perfect for the Great Lakes, though. It'll handle Lake Superior through the North Channel to Georgian Bay. I'll christen it *Ivy League* to please my wife."

CHAPTER 45

Britain and France declared war on Germany on September 3, 1939, after Hitler invaded Poland. The Canadian government declared war on September 10 after MP Henry Hamilton from the Soo introduced the motion for a declaration of war.

Anne Rossiter came home to the Soo to live with her parents. Her husband, Tom, who had been in a reserve unit of the Twenty-Ninth Royal Regiment in Toronto, enlisted immediately and was soon sent overseas. She was overwhelmed that her son, Daniel, might never see his father again. Ivy did her best to comfort her friend while a nightly gin cocktail deadened Anne's fear of the unknown. Her life, unlike Ivy's, had been predictable until now.

Ivy experienced the onset of war quite differently from her friends. Red was determined to enlist despite his kidney being removed at sixteen. He took the train to Bruce Mines where he was sure he wouldn't be thoroughly examined. The doctor greeted him warmly.

"How's your mother, Red?" he asked in an overly friendly manner, conscious he was going to give Red Donnelly, a boy he had known as a child, news he didn't want. "Ellen must be worried that your brother Jack's already gone overseas."

"Dr. Haslett, one kidney is all I need," Red said. "Please write the attestation order."

"There's a need for men at home, Red," Dr. Haslett said. He apologized for disappointing him and continued with the next recruit in a long queue of young men.

Red didn't return to the Soo but continued on to Toronto and Niagara Falls where the recruitment centres were reputed to be quite lax. The train was loud with young uniformed men singing and shouting as though they were going to a party. Red was filled with despair that an operation while a boy had set him apart as an adult. His intention was to join the Lincoln and Welland Regiment, a reserve infantry unit, and go overseas. Until each medical officer noticed the scar on his side, he was a perfect candidate.

Ivy was frantic when Red didn't return the day after leaving for Bruce Mines. She hated to involve Clara, but Sergeant Stuart had contacts across Ontario and might be able to track Red down. The RCMP relayed what they found. Red Donnelly had tried to enlist in Niagara Falls, and after being rejected again, spent two nights in a hotel in Buffalo where he had previously stayed during a cement conference.

When Red returned to the Soo, Ivy was at the train station with Alice in her arms to greet him. He didn't seem like the confident outdoorsman she had married, or the overjoyed new father she knew when Alice was born. With few men left in their social circle, it became Red's duty, along with men too old to enlist, to dance with the ladies at fundraising galas. Ivy admired her husband's gallantry, but something was amiss.

"You're the beau of the ball," she told him when they returned from an evening of dancing.

"I'd rather be risking my life overseas," Red retorted with a bitter tone Ivy had never heard.

*   *   *

Red's moodiness persisted for several months after being rejected by the military, and Ivy needed an explanation. She crossed the street to see Clara. "Why is Red so rude to Barnaby? They were always such friends."

"Barnaby's wounds are the image of sacrifice," Clara offered. "We need to find a legitimate way for Red to do his part for the war effort. I'm not sure what that could be. Certainly, it won't be mailing off packages."

Louis Derrer was the commanding officer of the Sault Ste. Marie Reservists and made time before being deployed to talk with Red. He wasn't old enough to be Red's father, but he had taken a personal interest in Red, who showed so much promise.

"Cement production is going to be important during and after this war," Louis said. "Ready-mix concrete will be used to build factories for war production, roads, docking platforms, and cement redoubts. I'd recommend you attend the conference on cement in Buffalo next month. See how the speed of production and quality of cement is changing."

With his university education, Red was considered a bright light among the rougher men attending the conference. Many participants represented large companies, yet Red found methods he could scale to his smaller operation. Certainly, hand-mixing batches of cement, except on small projects, was considered obsolete. After the conference, he travelled to Portland, Michigan, where cement-mixing trucks were manufactured. Before returning to the Soo, he stopped in Toronto, booking himself into the Royal York for three days with the hope of seeing some friends from his university days.

Their parents were courteous when he called, but the answer was always the same: "My son's overseas." Red also felt an unintended sting when he went into the main dining room of the hotel. Waitresses doted on the uniformed men sitting at the tables. Red, in a silk suit and tie, was ignored. When he finally got the attention of a waiter, he asked if a big tip would make him important.

"Money always talks," the waiter said. He hovered over Red, opening a bottle of wine with a flourish. The attention continued until the soldiers left. Red cut his visit short and returned to the Soo.

Ivy scoffed when he described the tip to the waiter. "Do you really think a waiter can make you important?" she asked with a disapproving look.

Her words stung Red, who left in his car. When he returned, Ivy was in bed.

"I didn't mean to hurt you," she said as he got into bed, but Red turned on his side with his back to Ivy.

An opportunity for Red to do military training without being overseas came from America. A ski-and-snowshoe patrol consisting of two hundred men arrived in the American Soo, and the commander discovered that the terrain wasn't appropriate to train his men for winter warfare. Louis Derrer, a military man himself, spoke with the commander of the winter-training unit and suggested Red could set them up at Hiawatha Park, which would be an ideal training location because of its varied geography. Many of the recruits from states such as Alabama had never seen snow. Until they met Red, they had no idea of the deadly obstacles winter could bring. Red started with snowshoes. The men thought they were being insulted with such a mindless task until several had frostbitten fingers.

"You have to be quick when your gloves are off," Red said. He spoke like a drill sergeant, making the men run up and down hills until they could do so without tripping and falling face first in the snow.

The men who had never seen a frozen lake were frightened to cross. Red used a hand auger to demonstrate the depth of the ice. "At four inches, you can ski across," he told them. "A little more thickness if you're walking. Remember, an auger is handy if you need drinking water."

"What if we don't have skis?" a young recruit with frozen fingers asked.

"Excellent question. You go on your belly to distribute your weight over a larger area. If you're a group, let the lightest person cross first and keep yourselves tied in case the lead goes down.

"How will we know if a vehicle can cross?" a young lad asked.

"If you don't have a drill, consider how long the lake's been frozen. A truck can cross when the ice is eight inches thick."

The men lined up single file to cross the lake, the snow-novices visibly scared. Red explained the difference between single-file crossing and crossing in tandem. "Has anyone here been ice fishing?" he asked. A few had, and he promised to take them to Still Bay. This brought up the danger of crossing rivers because of the way the underlying current made the ice thin. "You have to know the river outlets and avoid them."

On the final day of the course, Red taught the men various ways to make winter shelters. Alice Donnelly's first birthday was celebrated with fifty parka-clad men building a snow house at Hiawatha.

CHAPTER 46

The winter course ended in March 1941. Training the Americans had been Red's one bright spot. He wanted his team to stop at Still Bay before returning to Fort Brady. There they could experience a practical example of how a frozen lake could support the weight of Belgian horses. It seemed a miracle to the young recruits that the huge beasts didn't go through the quickly melting ice when the daily average temperature hovered around freezing. The horses, with their blond manes flipping back and forth across their thick necks, trotted out onto the ice without a moment's hesitation. They had done this year after year.

"Could ice fishing be on the course next year?" a recruit asked.

"Absolutely," Red said. "Feeding yourself in winter will be part of your survival. Currently, your country's divided on whether to join the war. This course shows the foresight of your leaders."

No one in the course anticipated that the Japanese would attack Pearl Harbor eight months later, bringing the United States into the conflict.

Red's mood was noticeably more cheerful after the course at Hiawatha Park. "If the boys are posted, they will be safer for what I've taught them."

"I'm so happy to hear those words," Ivy said, kissing Red before he could respond. She saw a summer of happiness before her.

In June, the *Ivy League*, the twenty-seven-foot cruiser Red had purchased at the Toronto boat show, arrived and was docked in Gawas Bay. He and Ivy cruised around Lake Huron with Alice in a makeshift crib. The cottage wasn't livable yet, so home was on the boat. They caught fish for dinner and cooked them on a small propane stove. Alice was mobile but had learned what the word *no* meant. She was an easy child. Ivy rinsed her nappies in the lake, and Red revved up the engine and they moved on, leaving the mess behind.

Blueberries were abundant by August. Big Beau had been rejected for his flat feet and hyperextened knee joints. Thus, he and Betty became regular passengers on the *Ivy League*. They had no children and loved to look after Alice while Red and Ivy dived in the lake for a swim. Anne, with a basket of gourmet food, arrived for a weekend driven by her father's chauffeur. Her parents were delighted to have Daniel on their own. After Anne recounted the last letter she had received from Tom, conversation turned to rising numbers of local casualties and the escalation of the war. On the surface, it seemed that Red had accepted his fate, but Ivy still worried.

In October, Red took the *Ivy League* through the locks and put the cruiser in dry dock at Michipicoten Harbour. When he returned, he was soon off hunting with his youngest brother, Ian. His usual partner, Geordie, was overseas. Ivy could feel Red's despair as they skinned their animals in the garage. He didn't have the same camaraderie with young Ian as he'd had with Geordie.

In the fall of 1941, Red received a call from Max Laird's mother. Max had been Red's best man. Mrs. Laird was calling to tell Red that Max's plane had been shot down over Germany in a night raid.

"No one on Max's flight survived," Mrs. Laird said, controlling her voice.

Although Red had seen little of his best man since the wedding, he was as despondent as he had been when he returned from

Niagara Falls after the incident in the dining room at the Royal York. He spent a week in Toronto visiting Max's family and on his return rehired Nancy Stratichuk.

"I thought we'd been through this, Red," Ivy said. "Every day I'll wonder exactly what she's doing in your office."

"She's learned her lesson," Red said.

CHAPTER 47

Every week another friend from Red's Sault Collegiate days or a worker at Donnelly Building Materials would come to say goodbye, dressed in uniform. "We know you tried to enlist," they always said.

"I feel I've been shamed by the military," Red lamented. "The doctor in Niagara Falls said, 'I suppose you feel lucky,' while I feel jinxed."

After the Dunkirk evacuation in the spring of 1940, Red spiralled down emotionally. Ivy found him hunched over, repairing the inboard motor of the *Ivy League*, head in his hands.

"I should've been overseas fixing boats rather than sitting in a comfortable office," he said tearfully.

Ivy was at a loss for words.

Red put on a brave face during the hastily arranged wedding of his friend Jeff Wilkes to Ruth Cohen in the upstairs of Allen's Ladies Wear. Jeff was heading overseas. The presiding rabbi and Anglican priest prayed emotionally, not only for the happiness of the young couple but also for the safety of the Jews in Europe.

Red didn't stay for the reception but returned home to look out at the garden he had excavated for Ivy and weep.

Death tolls increased drastically after the Dieppe Raid in the summer of 1942, and Ivy thanked God the doctors had spotted Red's scar where his kidney had been removed.

Joining Kathryn Derrer's "war machine" mitigated the turmoil Ivy felt about her marriage. Kathryn had organized the young wives whose husbands were overseas into a team for the efficient distribution of packages. The war machine worked from the same place as the clothing depot but expanded to handle more volunteers. Anne Rossiter fitted in comfortably with the well-intentioned ladies. She surprised them by suggesting that Shingwauk boys who went overseas should have letters, too. Reverend Hives gave Anne the names of the former students who had enlisted so she could send notes of encouragement.

"I'm writing these in Oji-Cree," Anne said to the gawking ladies. "They might laugh at my mistakes, but I hope they appreciate my intent."

"Your father will be proud of you, Anne," Ivy said.

Anne laughed. "He expects and never flatters."

Across the city, many imaginative ways to raise funds were emerging. Jessie Rossiter and Clara organized a series of contract bridge tournaments to raise money for the war effort. They had both experienced the Great War. Jessie related memories from her year in Great Windsor Park at the end of the previous war, hobnobbing with minor royals. Clara's experience in London hadn't been so entertaining, since she nursed severely wounded and dying soldiers. The bridge games were intended to raise the spirits of the players as well as money for the soldiers overseas. Clara also possessed an unexpressed gratitude that Red wasn't in the war. At the same time, she worried about his self-destructive choice to spend and spend and spend. *First the Gawas Bay property, then an expensive boat, and finally the mixing trucks*, she thought. Clara worried that Red was expanding the business too fast.

The distribution ladies liked to congregate at Ivy's to play bridge and share their letters from overseas. Red would stay to greet Ivy's friends and then take off. The bridge players were effusive, telling Red how lucky they were to have him around. Ivy was pained to see the cloud spread over Red's handsome face. When he returned late in the evening, he showered and went straight to bed.

"I'll never get pregnant with your snoring," Ivy said.

Red obliged, but Ivy wept in the aftermath of lovemaking that lacked the passion of their early marriage. She lay in bed imagining the loneliness of her friends whose husbands were overseas. Yet she imagined she was lonelier than they were.

CHAPTER 48

Chas and Dot Greer, a few years older than Ivy, moved into the large unoccupied house at the corner of Pim Street and Hilltop Crescent in the fall of 1942. Ivy was delighted to have a friend down the street. Dot grew up in the Soo and left to study nursing at Toronto General Hospital where she met Chas, a post-surgical resident. Sir James Dunn, known as a hypochondriac, hired the newly graduated Chas as his personal physician. Sir James quipped that he needed to be fit for his much younger bride. He enticed Chas to move to Northern Ontario, giving him the Pim Hill house that was listed as an Algoma Steel asset. Chas was immediately appointed chief of staff at General Hospital with a staff of over twenty. The couple had two young children when they arrived, and Dot was expecting a third.

Dot's father, D.T. Walker, was the school inspector in the Soo. Although D.T. wasn't responsible for residential school inspections, Clara remembered when he had circumvented the rules to help her find appropriate desks for smaller students. They had become friends, and it was a nice coincidence for Clara that his daughter would be her neighbour. Chas had fewer patients, given his executive responsibilities at the hospital. However, he did accept to be Clara's personal doctor when she asked.

Free of a house mortgage, Chas was in a position to purchase a hundred-acre farm on St. Joseph Island. It took only one day spent on Red's cruiser circling the island to convince Chas that, despite the inconvenience of the ferry, he wanted to buy the farm. Red and Ivy's renovated log cabin was at the opposite end of the island. Once Dot and Chas had set up the farm, they invited Red and Ivy to come for lunch. The pair travelled by car rather than in the *Ivy League*, since the Greers hadn't put in a dock.

"There's a wooden sign at the entrance to our driveway," Chas had warned. "Watch for it, or you'll end up in Richard's Landing."

Ivy spotted the sign, and Red turned off onto a rough road through a magnificent white birch forest. They drove for about a mile before they reached the open fields where the tractor was parked. After another half mile, they spotted the fieldstone house where the Greers waved from the steps.

Chas had bought the farm at an estate sale, and the purchase had included a Massey-Ferguson tractor with a three-point hitch and another piece of farming equipment. Dot wanted Chas to put the equipment back up for auction, but he refused. According to Chas, the land included sixty acres of woods, forty acres of fields, and a thousand feet on the shoreline.

"Not a typical farm," he loved saying, "with access to a beach."

It was noon when Ivy and Red arrived, and Dot suggested they eat before the men took off to explore the property.

"What are your plans for the house?" Red asked as they ate the cold meats and potato salad Ivy had brought.

"I'd like to build a whole new footprint," Chas said. "And keep the original building as a nostalgic reminder."

"Do you plan to do any farming?" Red asked.

Chas chuckled. "I'm the gentleman sort. I don't have any idea how to run the tractor, but it looks good in the field. There's a round thing behind that looks like a mower."

"That's called a brush hog," Red said. "It does rough cutting. Will you let me have a go?"

Chas nodded enthusiastically. The men hurried through lunch, leaving the ladies to clean up. Dot's helper, a young girl from Richard's Landing, took charge of the children.

"I should check the oil before we start her up," Red said.

"Are tractors feminine?" Chas asked.

"Ships and machines. I've grown up with machines and knowing how they work. And you?"

"My family was in finance."

Red inserted the dipstick to check the level of oil, then levered himself behind the wheel, with Chas climbing up beside him. A few pushes on the starter, and the old tractor sputtered to life. After lurching a few yards, Red got the rhythm and started methodically down the field.

"Why, it's cutting the grass!" Chas said, excited to see the overgrown weeds looking tidy. "Let me have a go!"

The men switched places. Chas went to pull the choke, and Red stopped him. "You'll flood the engine. Just press the starter."

The men brush-hogged the entire field and then headed back to the house to show Dot that Chas was driving. She had been skeptical about keeping a tractor that would never be used on the property. She grinned, and her dark eyes showed how much she adored Chas.

"We're all sweaty," Chas said. "We need to go for a swim."

The ladies went into the house and came back with towels and bathing suits. The four of them headed down the steep hill that led to the water. At the shore, there was a rustic cabin that the men conceded to the girls, while they went behind it. Dot and Ivy came out clad in swimwear and bathing caps to the sight of two barebummed men diving into the water.

CHAPTER 49

Nancy Stratichuk had been working in Red's office when she unexpectedly quit in 1943. Ivy was expecting a second child.

Red arrived home in the middle of the day and again blasted Ivy. "Nancy was a good secretary, and I need her."

Ivy guessed what had happened. *Clara must have interfered in some way again*, she thought. She put her hands on her newly pregnant belly to calm herself. "Alice, go upstairs and play."

Red waited for Alice to get to the top of the stairs before exploding. "Your mother threatened to expose Nancy's past. That's blackmail!"

"Do you want someone in your office with a past?" Ivy was hurt by Red's loyalty to a secretary. "I'm sure my mother has her reasons to threaten Nancy."

"I have to run my own business, Ivy. If she interferes again, she won't be welcome in this house. The next secretary I hire won't speak to Clara."

It was a cold November day, so Ivy bundled four-year-old Alice in a winter jacket and put on her own ill-fitting coat before crossing the street to Clara's. Her mother was playing solitaire at her desk, which overlooked the street, and she seemed to be expecting Ivy.

Clara sighed as though it were her last breath. "Go and look in Granny's trunk," she told Alice. This was a regular routine. Alice would go to Clara's immaculate basement, open the trunk, and come back with a treasure. Her favourite item was a child's woollen coat with a pair of small rubber boots marked "Billy." Each time Clara would tell Alice the same story. "There was a little boy who loved to garden. He especially loved roses." Alice wasn't allowed to remove the preserved pressed rose in the trunk. "The boy's name was Billy, and he wanted to own a nursery one day and be surrounded by flowers. He died when he caught the flu and went to heaven where he's surrounded by toys."

"Can I go to heaven?" Alice would ask with each telling.

"Not for a very long time," Clara would answer.

"Why are you crying, Mommy?" Alice now asked.

"Go back down to the trunk while I talk with your mother," Clara said to her granddaughter.

Ivy sat on a chair opposite her mother.

"Nancy Stratichuk is an extortionist," Clara began. "She was working for a doctor as his receptionist. When she became pregnant, she accused the doctor and threatened to tell his wife unless he paid her. The doctor had never had a relationship with Nancy. He gave Nancy a tidy sum, and she left quietly."

"Why would he do that if he weren't the father?"

"Even an untrue accusation can wreak havoc in a marriage," Clara replied. "Nancy knows everything about Donnelly Building Materials' finances. Who knows what she could extract from Red? That's why I said I'd expose her if she didn't quit voluntarily."

Ivy's moss-green eyes, identical to Clara's, filled again with tears. *Red would keep Nancy despite her bad character*, Ivy thought miserably. "I don't understand Red since the war began. He's wounded without having gone overseas. What does war mean to Red?"

Alice returned to the living room, still gripping the baby outfit, and wiped Ivy's tears.

"It means manliness," Clara said. "An evil person like Nancy knows that."

Clara resigned herself to being *persona non grata* in Red's house. She needed a new focus in order to stop worrying about Ivy. When she discovered William Martin, the Shingwauk boy whose hair she had deloused, was being treated by Chas Greer at General Hospital, she went to see him.

William was in the veterans' ward with much older men. *He must still be in his teens*, Clara thought. *I imagine he lied about his age.*

"Do you remember me?" Clara asked.

William had a grown-up smile. "You're Matron Durling, the lady who told me my hair would grow back."

Clara tugged his braid. "It did. Did your commander yell, 'Follow the braid'?"

"He called it a ponytail." William had the same soft voice and questioning eyes he'd had at the school delousing ceremony.

When Chas came in to check on his patient, he was pleased to see his neighbour. Clara never passed the Greer house without a bag of food scraps for Chas's three English setters.

"William can't remain in the hospital to wait for further surgery," Chas told Clara. "It was hard convincing the nuns to take yet another unbaptized patient. I understand from Sister Marie Claire that you were quite persuasive when you worked at Shingwauk."

Chas had the twinkle in his eye that Clara loved in her doctor. She chuckled. "That's true."

"William wants to go home to Batchawana to be with his grandfather."

"Albert Martin was a decorated soldier, but I can't vouch for his housekeeping," Clara reported. "Why don't I give William a room until the next operation?"

"Excellent, though, of course, he'll have to agree to the arrangement. The dressing must be changed every two days."

"I'll leave you to make the suggestion. If he agrees, I'll have my tenant, Sergeant Stuart, pick him up at the hospital."

Once William assented to the living arrangement, Clara wanted to send Albert Martin a message that his grandson was being well looked after. Red would be hunting near the Batchewana Reserve, but he wasn't inclined to be Clara's postman.

"I would have thought Red could bury the hatchet," Clara told Ivy indignantly. "Albert will be worried about his grandson. I'll deliver the message myself," she huffed. "Such pettiness on Red's part. I'd rather we have our differences out in a good fight."

"While I stand holding the coats," Ivy said, quietly.

CHAPTER 50

It had been rare to see Sir James Dunn out and about in the Soo when he first took over Algoma Steel. However, in 1946, he arrived with his new bride, Marcia, and wanted to celebrate the end of the war. Invitations were sent for an evening celebration at the Windsor Hotel. In his early years running Algoma Steel, Sir James had remained aloof with the locals. He never stayed long in the city and didn't court any friends. But having built a mansion at the extreme east end of Hilltop, he wanted to be more sociable, and the affair was planned for June before families left for their cottages. Dress would be top hat or full-dress uniform, and a train from Montreal would transport much of the food and wine.

The bash was like no other the city had ever seen. It was a party for men, most of them much younger than Sir James. Three gentlemen brought their guitars, and a piano was wheeled into the dining room. The guests sang ribald songs reminiscent of the war, and the merrymaking spilled onto Queen Street, which might have accounted for what happened next.

Sir James stood up and announced that the desk clerk had called for taxis to pull up to the front door of the hotel. He exited out the back with his chauffeur. Chas Greer and Grant Howland were the first to make their way to the street. Red was a few minutes behind them. It was too late to stop the shenanigans.

"I have to take a leak," Grant said, slurring his words.

"Ditto," Chas said, equally fuzzy in his speech.

Grant began to relieve himself noisily on a nearby hydrant. Chas, laughing, unzipped his trousers and joined Grant.

"A pissing contest," Grant said, bowing as he doffed his top hat.

A car pulled up behind the men.

"That's prompt for a taxi," Grant said, adjusting his hat.

Before they could turn to face the street, they were in handcuffs. Two fresh-faced cops stood before them.

"I could hear you partiers all the way to Gore Street," one officer said with a smirk. "You don't got a right to pee in public just cause you're friends of Sir James."

"Good Christ!" Grant shouted at a man snapping a photo. "What the hell are you doing?"

"*Sault Star*," the man said. "You'll see yourselves in the paper tomorrow."

At 3:00 a.m., Red received a call from Dot. "I'm so sorry to bother you, but I don't know who else to call. Chas hasn't returned home, and I'm about to call the police." Dot forgot she had driven Chas with the agreement that he would return home by taxi.

"I'll come right over," Red said reassuringly. When he arrived at the Greers', Dot was on the phone speaking with the police station.

"I'm sorry, Mrs. Greer," the desk officer said over the phone. "Your husband was caught urinating in front of the Windsor Hotel. Mr. Howland's in the adjacent cell."

Dot recognized Grant's hoarse voice cursing in the background. *Serves you right for being up all night*, she thought.

Red took the phone. "Red Donnelly here. I'm helping Mrs. Greer."

"The men will need a lawyer," the desk officer said.

"My business lawyer can handle such a minor case," Red said.

Red's lawyer persuaded Magistrate Bill Langdon, a straitlaced man, to come to the courthouse on a Sunday. The men, in formal attire, top hats under their arms, were led into the courthouse in handcuffs to stand before the cross-looking magistrate.

"I see you've been to an all-night costume party," Langdon said, looking askance at their wrinkled waistcoats. "Do you have anything to say?"

"The men's toilet was locked and we had to relieve ourselves," Grant said cockily.

"Prostate troubles," Chas added gravely, trying to sound like a doctor.

"The officers who picked you up said you used foul language, Mr. Howland."

"Since when was swearing a crime?" Grant replied.

Langdon put down his glasses and suppressed a smile. "The newspaper photo will be punishment enough." He paused. "Another public pee and you'll have more than a night in the slammer. Go home and apologize to your wives."

PART FOUR

Spiralling Down –
Forging Ahead

CHAPTER 51

For reasons more complex than those of her friends whose husbands had been sent overseas, Ivy was glad the war was over. She hoped Red would regain his infectious enthusiasm now that war wasn't the centre of all conversations. People were getting on with rebuilding their lives. The Canadian Soo, by virtue of its proximity to the American locks, had become a de facto military centre during the war. When peace was declared, the Soo didn't immediately return to normal, however. Celebrations across the city were loud and boisterous. Anyone in uniform was offered free coffee in the restaurants and an extra pint of beer in bars. Algoma Steel was at full capacity and the city enjoyed almost full employment.

Ivy felt her life getting back to normal. She had delivered a second daughter, christened Nora at St. Luke's Cathedral, where she and Red had been married. Again a caesarean delivery required a two-week stay in the hospital. It was a coincidence that Nora was born on May 8. Clara wanted the baby to be named Victoria, but Ivy quickly put an end to associating her child with the war, even a victorious one. The name Nora was Red's choice. Unlike Alice's thin black mop at birth that was soon replaced with blond hair,

Nora had thick dark hair and Red's tawny complexion. Alice had arrived in the world with opinions. Nora was a plump, cooing little baby who smiled the moment she noticed a human face. Red was proud and happy when he passed cigars around his office. Nora's birth seemed like a new beginning for her parents.

With the war over, Red spent more time at the cottage, using his cruiser to entertain friends. Cottage life and outings on the Great Lakes seemed to be the affirmation that the Donnellys were a happy family. He had even made peace with Clara and invited her to the cottage. The Greensteds and the Derrers, with cottages so close, were regular guests on the *Ivy League*, as were the Greers, who came over from their farm. Even in a twenty-seven-foot cruiser like the *Ivy League*, Beau Greensted's bulk could tip the vessel to port or starboard side, depending on where he sat. Jeff Wilkes was back, too, and he purchased a cottage on the mainland close to where the ferry took off.

The Americans had brought Grant into their social network in the Kensington Point area, but he never refused an invitation to travel the North Shore islands with Red. He had bought a smaller mahogany inboard in which he would cross the open waters into Gawas Bay. The new chief executive of Algoma Steel was Dave Brewster, an American from Cleveland, Ohio. He and his wife, Patsy, were delighted to discover the Great Lakes geography with Red. Dave and Louis were lifelong fly fishermen and would get out on the upper deck to cast their lines, taking care not to hook Dot's sports cap.

Despite the joy of returning to their families, Red's friends who had been to Europe weren't in perfect physical health. Their wounds were invisible, and the outings on the *Ivy League* were the breath of fresh air they needed. Tom Blake, Anne's husband, had visible shrapnel wounds that had left his legs heavily scarred. His dark hair covered the wounds on his head. A few weeks with Anne's parents would give Tom time to rest before moving back to Toronto. Ivy, having lived through Red's moodiness, was helpful to Anne in understanding Tom's.

Red offered to take Tom on a canoe trip on the Michipicoten River where he had first met Anne. She had told the story of their courtship when K.G. was tutoring her in the Ojibwa language when a handsome stranger paddled up to the dock. Tom had been abandoned by his canoeing partner after an argument and asked if he could stop for a bit to rest. Tom had won his colours in boxing at Upper Canada College. He was an athlete but not as much of a rugged sportsman as Red. Despite their different personalities, Red and Tom got along well, and a trip together seemed a good way to put the latter's past behind him.

"I might not have argued with my canoe partner," Tom said, "if I knew paddling solo would be twice as hard. Seeing where I fell in love will be healing after so many years apart."

Red suggested they bring Alice and Daniel along on the trip and give the ladies a break.

"I feel a bit disconnected from my son," Tom confided.

"Give it time," Red said. "Your boy's been indulged by his devoted grandparents for five years."

The two men set out on the *Ivy League* with a green canvas canoe roped on the roof. When the boat passed out of the Canadian locks into the great expanse of Lake Superior, Tom said, "It feels great to be back in my own country."

Red purchased the supplies for a four-day paddle at the Michipicoten Outfitter's store. Wrapping a bottle of rye whiskey in the groundsheet, the men set out with Tom kneeling as he took up the bow on a cushion to ease his shrapnel-damaged legs.

Dipping a pot into the cold, clear water to make coffee the first morning, Tom said, "There was no clean water in Europe." That was the last comment he made on his war experiences.

Fish was on the menu, and Red collected root plants. "Spuds," he called them, "to replace potatoes." Red had brought his photography equipment, and the men talked about the artists who had captured the same scenery they were admiring.

"Is this your first time up north in the fall?" Red asked.

"My first but not my last as long as my in-laws live in the Soo. You share the outdoor mania like K.G.," Tom said admiringly.

Returning with a four-day growth of beard, Tom heard the news that Anne thought she was pregnant. "I'm upchucking every morning," she declared proudly. With a quick flip, Tom stood on his head on the dining room table, while Anne reached for Red's and Ivy's hands. "Thank you," she said.

Ivy felt the loss of a friendship nurtured during the war years when Anne moved back to Toronto.

In the first postwar months, those Soo veterans well enough to travel had already trickled into the hometown that had sent them off with such pride five years earlier. It wasn't until nearly a year after the war ended that the more severely wounded could return home. They appeared at city events with partially blown-up faces and missing limbs. It wasn't unusual to see a man in uniform being guided by the arm so that he wouldn't trip on the curb. The city paid homage to these heroes. Red would stand beside Ivy in the crowd, hating himself for making money during the war.

With the building boom of small wartime houses in the northern part of the city, Donnelly Building Materials' business increased again. Red purchased two more cement-mixer trucks. It was this purchase that alerted Ivy that Red was in trouble financially. He had tried to borrow from his mother. Over the years, Ellen had lost most of her Donnelly shares by investing in a health food company that went bankrupt. Red was furious that his mother hadn't consulted him about her diminishing funds.

"Neither of us has much money sense," Ellen rebuked. "We relied totally on your father, a man who went to work in coveralls and wore a suit only to church. His men trusted him. I have an offer from a lumber dealer who needs the cement part of Donnelly's to be able to build houses from the ground up. You'll have to take a bank loan to pay for your mixers or cancel the order."

CHAPTER 52

In 1947, Red had to remain in the city to sort out his "self-inflicted" financial problems, leaving Ivy at the cottage with the girls without a car. "You've squandered what most men would love to have," Ivy chastised before they left. She treated his absence as normal in front of the girls, telling them their father was staying behind to work on a large construction project. If the children missed their father, they didn't show it. Alice was a conscientious eight-year-old, and as long as Nora didn't sit on Alice's pillow leaving a "bum smell," they didn't argue. Ivy kept the stress of her marriage to herself. *We're going to the cottage to have fun, and I'm going to make that happen*, she thought.

Since Ivy didn't have a car to drive, Alice's seven-horsepower cedar-strip boat served as transportation between cottages in the bay. However, the outboard wasn't safe to venture into the main waters of Lake Huron. Groceries could be purchased in the general store in the village of Hilton Beach, which was accessible by road or water. Audrey Derrer, now sixteen, could drive her father's mahogany inboard to take Ivy and the girls to buy provisions. Alice loved the roar of the engine when Audrey jerked the gear into reverse to avoid a crash as she sped toward the dock. The Derrers, aware that Ivy was under a lot of strain, found ways to be helpful. Louis popped over on weekends to see if he could get rid of garbage or do any other chores.

It was welcome news that a girl named Harriet Burns had moved into a cabin next to the Derrers'. Harriet was eight, the youngest of four sisters and the same age and tomboy temperament as Alice. Like Alice, she loved to fish, pick blueberries, and eat marshmallows around a bonfire. Audrey and Harriet's older sisters made sure these things happened. Nora couldn't keep up with the older girls and was often left with Kathryn Derrer and Ivy, who enjoyed a summer gin and tonic on the patio while the young people disappeared in Louis's boat.

"I'm so glad Alice has Harriet," Ivy said. "This will be the first summer she hasn't fished alongside her dad. I know she's hurting inside. She adores Red. Alice is a chip off the old block."

"Everyone's hurting, Ivy. We all love Red."

Alice's tonsils were to be removed the Tuesday after Labour Day when the weekend cottagers closed up and children started back to school. Louis Derrer came by with his son, Harry, to see if Ivy needed a hand winterizing the cottage. He had helped Red open the cottage in the spring and was efficient at reversing the process. Until this summer, Red had enjoyed opening and shutting the cottage. A week before closing up, he would put the *Ivy League* in dry dock at the Kensington Point marina. Ivy mustered a grateful smile as Louis whistled while he drained water pipes, dumped antifreeze in the toilet, and unhooked the gas line to the fridge. He then turned off the water, leaving the outhouse as the only place to go to the bathroom. Alice carried a bucket of fireplace ashes to the outhouse to pitch into the hole before they left.

"Thank God I have you as neighbours," Ivy said.

"We're happy to do this," Louis said. "Are you sure Red is coming to pick up you and the girls?"

"Absolutely," she replied, masking her worries.

"Come with us," Louis urged. "We can call Red once we're on the mainland."

Ivy refused, unwilling to believe Red might not arrive. She held back tears as she watched Louis's boat disappear from sight, shuddering at the overcast sky. Lake Huron could get rough, and Gawas Bay, normally calm, churned with whitecaps.

She distracted herself by finishing the work of winterizing the cottage with her annual anti-mouse campaign. Mice were always a problem in the spring. In search of water, they drowned in the toilet after eating seeds. Mice couldn't tell the difference between antifreeze and water. It was a messy job to remove them at the beginning of each summer. To prevent mice burrowing into mattresses, the girls wrapped plastic around the beds.

Red had taught Alice how to make an ingenious mousetrap that caught several mice at one time. After filling a metal bucket with water, she threaded the straight part of a metal clothes hanger through a can, resting each end of the wire on the edge of the metal bucket. Nora was quite happy to dig into the peanut butter jar and smear a handful of the gooey mixture onto the can. Alice then rested a yardstick on the edge of the can — the plank that led the mice to the delicious-smelling peanut butter. Ivy called this the Bridge of Sighs. The moment a mouse stepped on the can, it spun and the rodent dropped into the pail.

"Don't lick your fingers," Ivy scolded Nora.

Finally, the fireplace was blocked with plywood to prevent animals larger than mice coming into the cottage and wreaking havoc. The winterizing complete, Ivy realized they were in trouble if they missed the last ferry. It only operated on weekends after Labour Day.

"We're going to start walking," Ivy said. "Maybe Daddy had car trouble. We must get to the Derrers' before they leave for the ferry."

"What about our suitcases?" Alice asked.

"We'll have to leave them and Daddy will pick them up next weekend," Ivy said.

It was dark going through the woods until they reached Gawas Bay Road. But the light was fading fast. There were piles of bear droppings, and Ivy motioned with her hand to talk quietly when Nora let out a scream. "The bears will move away if they hear voices. They'll be feasting on roadside berries before hibernating, so keep your eyes open," she warned. Ivy had never liked bears because of their unpredictable nature. Doubt now crept into her mind as she watched the girls troop along the dirt road, expecting to see their daddy's Buick. *Please, Red, don't disappoint them*, she thought.

They had been walking for an hour when car lights shone in the dim light.

"It's Daddy!" Alice shouted. "I knew he'd come."

The car slowed, and Ivy couldn't hold back her tears. It was Louis and Kathryn.

"Just checking before we left," Kathryn said.

Ivy and Alice climbed in the back of the car. Nora sat up front on Kathryn's knee. Not a word was spoken as their eyes focused on the road, certain they would intercept Red. Louis drove onto the ferry, and the boatman slammed down the gate.

"Take the girls up to see the captain," Louis suggested to Kathryn. Once they were alone in the car, Louis glanced back at Ivy. "You're as thin as a rake."

"Hurt eats away like a cancer," Ivy said. "I still love Red." *Louis knows I must make a decision*, Ivy thought. *Yet neither of us knows what that should be.*

When the ferry reached the mainland, Red was standing by his car. "I missed the last ferry to the island," he said, tucking in his shirt as he spoke.

"And what did you expect your family to do then?" Louis growled harshly.

Red said nothing.

"Red, you're squandering the best asset you have," Louis said.

"Louis, take the girls home," Ivy said. "I'll go with Red." They drove in tandem to Hilltop Crescent, and Louis dropped off the girls.

Red crossed the street to Clara's to borrow some milk. When he returned, Ivy had locked the door.

Through the window, she said: "It's over, Red."

Alice wailed and begged Ivy to unlock the door. Nora looked frightened and followed her mother up the stairs.

Sitting in the vestibule, Alice clutched a pair of her father's old spats. "Please don't leave, Daddy."

Red returned to Clara's and asked her to intervene. Dressed in a navy wool dressing gown, Clara crossed the street and banged on Ivy's door, but she didn't answer. Clara returned to her house and telephoned, but Ivy let the phone ring.

Alice's tonsils were removed the next day. The operation was simple enough, and Ivy waited for her to come out of the anaesthesia. Dot came into the hospital room, expecting to see a chipper eight-year-old.

"The anaesthetic should have worn off," Chas said. "Nothing has roused her, Ivy. Call Red and tell him to get down here right now. Dot told me what happened last night. Alice needs to see her father."

Frightened by Alice's lack of response, Ivy called Red. He arrived at the hospital dressed casually in a crimson viyella shirt.

Alice lifted an arm that minutes before had seemingly been paralyzed. "Daddy!" she cried. "I caught a big fish while you were away."

Red had been a good father, Ivy thought. Barely able to swallow, she turned away.

CHAPTER 53

Barnaby found Ivy in the front pew in the General Hospital chapel. The strong smell of incense suggested there had already been Mass that morning. He slid in beside her. Ivy turned with a wan smile, receiving his unique hug. Her eyes were puffy from crying.

"Alice seems fine," he told her, his face quivering with emotion.

Barnaby had been like a father to Ivy during her lonely years as a schoolgirl in Lethbridge. She knew it pained him to see her so unhappy. "You wouldn't have expected this when you walked me down the aisle to join Red. We were so happy until the war."

"Red's an enigma. I've been trying to figure him out for seven years."

"We all have," Ivy said. "We looked on helplessly as a man who had the world by the tail was destroying himself."

"In my years as a psychiatrist, I did treat some veterans with self-loathing, but they had visible and limiting handicaps like Dan MacIntyre. I remember Dan speaking at a public meeting in the Lethbridge Legion Hall. The officer of public health for the city called the community together to address the problem of venereal disease being spread by returning soldiers. You would've been too young to know what was happening. Your mother was instrumental in the city-wide effort to control that debilitating disease."

"Tell me about Dan," Ivy said. "I can't imagine the man I met at Batchawana — the man who gave up his artificial leg to a Native veteran — was ever unhappy."

"Dan hated himself and everyone around him when he returned to Lethbridge, at least until he met a prostitute who made him feel important. I'll never forget his moving testimony."

Ivy could barely understand Barnaby's words because his voice was so filled with emotion.

"Dan stood in front of the crowd that day and tearfully spoke about a young prostitute. 'Betty Sanchez,' he said, 'found the person within me who had been crushed or distorted during the war. She made this disfigured soldier feel attractive.'"

"Have I done the opposite with Red?" Ivy asked. "First it was Nancy Stratichuk, and then while I was alone at the cottage with the girls, he took up with a waitress he met at the Windsor Hotel. Apparently, she moved to the Savoury Café. And who knows how many more there will be? Are these women *his* Betty Sanchez?"

"War has a long reach. It crushes those who fight and crushes those who can't."

"What can I do, Barnaby? Red's already taken an apartment above the Savoury Café. He had breakfast in the restaurant this morning before coming to see Alice."

"I'm sure this girlfriend won't last long. Let the girls visit him. They won't be the first children to see a paramour. It will go over their heads if you let it."

"I'm frightened, Barnaby. My mother-in-law has sold what was left of her share of the business to Wentworth Lumber. I expect the Wentworths will want the other half."

"Don't fret about money. But I do advise getting a lawyer. We have no idea what Red might do. But don't burden the girls."

Alice had to remain at home for a week after being discharged from the hospital. Clara walked Nora over the "spooky ravine" to her first day at King George School. She had implored Ivy to wait it out with Red as had Barnaby. Both suggested she would need a lawyer for a separation agreement so that she and the girls would have enough income to stay in the Hilltop house.

CHAPTER 54

Adam Wright, the lawyer handling Ivy's case, lived next door to the Rossiters. Ivy didn't want to meet Adam in his office, since she knew the other members of his law firm, so their first meeting began on a bench in the courthouse where Adam had arranged to use the Crown attorney's office. Normally, the benches were for criminals waiting their turns in court, and Ivy's navy tailored suit seemed incongruous. She was sound asleep with her head on her handbag when Adam approached.

He shook her shoulder gently. "Ivy, you've become so thin." Leading her into the office, he motioned for her to sit, then took a seat beside her. "I kept a second chair for the supporting parent," he told her.

As a neighbour, Ivy thought, *Adam is probably aware of the sentiment on Hilltop Crescent that Clara's been an overbearing mother-in-law.* She figured he likely understood why her mother wasn't with her.

Adam smiled encouragingly. "So how can I help you?"

It took Ivy a minute before she could say, "My husband's become a serial cheater. He had an affair with his secretary, and when she quit, he took up with a waitress in town. I'm humiliated, Adam. But much worse, I'm afraid."

"Take some slow, deep breaths," Adam said, reaching for Ivy's hand. "Cry if you need to."

With a stoic steadiness, Ivy described the gradual disintegration of what had started as a happy marriage.

"We'll need proof of infidelity to obtain a divorce under our laws," Adam said. "I can arrange for a Pinkerton detective to obtain that discreetly."

"Could I begin with a separation agreement to establish support before I sue for divorce?"

"Of course, you can. A divorce is final. Maybe you and Red can still work things out."

"What am I going to live on, though?" She hated recalling Clara's words when she quit nursing school: *You'll have nothing to fall back on.* At the time, Ivy had thought her mother was referring to death, not divorce.

"Spousal support is less binding than divorce alimony," Adam explained.

"Divorce is too final. Let me leave Red in stages."

"You'll need to establish what it costs to live before we can tackle Red. Most wives don't keep a budget. But don't worry. You're going to be fine, Ivy."

When Ivy met with Adam again, he had news from the Pinkerton detective he had hired. Spying was offensive to Ivy until she was told the detective had found Red at the Royal York with a female friend he'd registered as "Mrs. Donnelly."

Ivy shook her head in disgust. "It's no consolation to discover Red's cheating on the waitress. It's ironic that he paid a Royal York waiter to make him seem important years ago. How did a man with everything come to lack such confidence? That's when I should have made him talk to Dr. Barnaby, his friend and a psychiatrist."

"I'm sorry to have shown you the proof," Adam said, closing the manila envelope and returning it to his briefcase.

*   *   *

Red's support payments fell far short of what Ivy and the girls would need to remain at 43 Hilltop Crescent. Ivy suspected he was now in his own financial trouble after expanding too fast. However, though it was less than she needed, she was relieved to have a legally binding agreement of support.

Ivy began scanning advertisements in the local newspaper for job openings. There was nothing advertised for a person with no skills. When Adam called to tell Ivy the Algoma District welfare department was opening a local office in the Soo, it felt like serendipity.

Russ Thompson, a man of about sixty, was the regional manager and an acquaintance of Adam. The lawyer called Russ to arrange a face-to-face interview for Ivy. She went to the meeting determined to get the job.

"You've never worked, Mrs. Donnelly, yet you trained as a nurse," Russ Thompson said when she was seated in his office. "Welfare work is quite different. We offer a crash course for new recruits to learn the rules, regulations, and benefits that make up our system of welfare. It will require you to live for two months in Toronto, and you must have your own car."

"I'll need to take a bank loan for the car," Ivy said, trying to smile, though she didn't feel the least bit cocky.

"The government will reimburse your mileage."

Ivy didn't hide her disappointment. "That would be helpful, though gasoline is very expensive these days."

"I'll need you more often on the road seeing your clients than in an office," Russ told her to justify the car. "I believe it's in the modest homes and shacks where the real social problems play out. You need to see people in their own environment to help them."

"I have two young daughters at school. I'll ask my mother to take care of them for two months. She's over sixty, and a five- and eight-year-old can be quite a handful, but my mother managed a hundred-bed hospital, so I'm sure she can manage them."

The interview ended with Russ talking about his own daughter. "She moved to Australia with her soldier-husband at the end of the war," he said wistfully. "It'll be nice having someone her age in my office." He stood up and shook Ivy's hand. "I'll do everything I can to help you do your work, but you have to take the course."

"Let me get back to you tomorrow after speaking with my mother."

"Your mother's very capable. I knew her when she was nurse-matron at Shingwauk. She was a vocal advocate for the new building. Shingwauk has a lot to thank her for. Please give her my best." Russ then saw her out the door.

CHAPTER 55

The day after her meeting with Russ Thompson, Ivy sat in the lobby of the Bank of Montreal waiting to see the manager, Reginald Monteith. Clara had readily agreed to care for Alice and Nora for two months while Ivy took her course in Toronto. She advised Ivy that she might find Monteith tight but not heartless. Clara knew him through his wife, with whom she played bridge. "It's three years since the war ended," Clara said. "I think banks are used to helping families remake their lives." The stress on Clara's face had aged her beyond her sixty-one years.

Monteith opened his office door and invited Ivy in. "Come in. I hope I haven't kept you waiting."

A tall, slim man with a trimmed grey moustache and neatly combed grey hair, he wore a dark blue pinstripe suit that seemed to be the uniform of all bankers. She followed the manager into his office and waited to be asked to sit down. He smiled and gestured toward a chair in front of his desk.

"I'm surprised, Ivy, that you want to be a social worker rather than a nurse. What was the point of spending three years in Montreal training at Royal Victoria Hospital? This must disappoint Mrs. Durling." Monteith raised his eyebrows. "Why, your mother *ran* a hospital!"

Ivy resented the implied comparison. She took a deep breath and released it slowly before replying. "Mr. Monteith, I'm trying to stand on my own two feet, and I need your help. My support payments from Red won't be enough to buy a car." She held back tears, recalling how isolated she'd felt from her own mother while growing up in the hospital. *My children will have a normal home despite missing a father*, she thought, tightening her fists so that she wouldn't cry in the banker's office.

The manager pushed back his chair and stood up. "Ivy, I *can't* lend you $800 unless your husband signs this document." He held up the loan form in exasperation.

"The courts have recognized my separation," Ivy retorted. "Why can't the bank?"

"A loan must be guaranteed by someone with liquefiable assets."

Ivy shrugged and sighed audibly. "I haven't seen my husband since he sold his half of Donnelly Building Materials. I was told he moved to Michipicoten Harbour and apparently takes tourists out on Lake Superior in the *Ivy League*."

Monteith seemed confused.

"Red's boat is named the *Ivy League*. It's a twenty-seven-foot cruiser he uses to earn money, I suppose. No one in the family understands Red's behaviour, Mr. Monteith."

"Well, Red must have assets from the sale of his company. Your *only* asset is your house," he added, raising an eyebrow. "Banks would go out of business, though, if loan repayment depended on a person selling his house. Just have your husband sign this paper and then we'll lend you the money to buy a car."

"I'll have to think this over and get back to you. I believe your bank has a misguided policy. How can any woman be set free with such humiliating practices?"

He didn't attempt to answer.

Ivy left the bank and walked west along the main street, searching for a place to have coffee. The Savoury Café was on the south side about four blocks from the bank. For a moment, she thought about crossing the street to the Savoury to commiserate with the waitress who had also lost Red. It seemed bizarre that he had left so suddenly for Michipicoten Harbour. *Maybe they had a disagreement,* she thought as she continued to the Tea and Talk Café owned by Carl and Mildred Grey, who were her neighbours. She entered the café and ordered a blueberry muffin and large coffee, then settled back in the corner of a booth to figure out how to buy a car. Her reflections were interrupted when Carl slid into the booth beside her.

"How are you doing, Ivy?" he asked. "I know what's happening with Red across the street." Carl was referring to her husband and the waitress at the Savoury.

"That's not happening any longer. Red's escaped to Michipicoten Harbour. I think he's had a breakdown."

"Normally, we ignore gossip, but Red's blatant infidelity angered us," Carl said. "We are *your* friend and see Red as the guilty party."

Those words made Ivy feel guilty herself and caused her to wonder what she might have done to cause the breakup of her marriage. To Carl, she said, "You know, that was the best part of my marriage — the many friends Red and I shared."

"I doubt if any of them will be going to Michipicoten Harbour anytime soon. Red's isolating himself up there." Carl's face brightened. "I hear you're looking for a job. You're a gutsy lady." He made the *V* sign.

His congratulatory tone caused Ivy to spell out her troubles with the bank. By the time she finished her second coffee, which Carl insisted she enjoy on the house, she had agreed to swallow her pride and ask her mother to guarantee the bank loan.

CHAPTER 56

Ivy donned a cheerful face, despite her heartache at leaving, as she waved at Clara and Ellen, whose arms were around Alice and Nora. Initially, the children were to be split up between the two grandmothers. Clara was close to their school and it was decided they could visit Ellen on weekends to give Clara a rest. The grandmothers and the girls were happy with this arrangement. As the train pulled away, Ivy realized her mother-in-law's shame at her son's behaviour had been turned into loyalty for the girls.

Anne and Tom greeted Ivy at Union Station in Toronto to take her to the new house they had bought on an upscale street near Havergal where their daughter, Beth, was in junior school. Daniel was enrolled at Upper Canada College, a twenty-block drive from their home. It took a week before Ivy found a one-room bachelor apartment on Avenue Road, a mile south of the Blakes'.

A large room at Queen's Park had been seconded for the course to accommodate fifty students. They, like Ivy, would return to work in welfare offices in their home communities. There were men enrolled who were younger versions of Russ Thompson.

At first, Ivy spent her spare time with Anne and Tom, if he was home. He had risen in the investment firm and would soon become a partner. Anne was involved with Daniel's and Beth's schools and volunteered one day a week for the Junior League, an upper-crust ladies' organization. The Soo had a more modest sister league called the May Court Club. Anne was her usual clever and witty self. Her wit rivalled Tom's well-honed sardonic humour. Anne enjoyed the cocktail hour, and on at least one evening consumed too much. Tom enjoyed performing his head trick for Ivy, flipping himself upside down on the formal mahogany dining table. They were happy.

Ivy soon discovered that her classmates had led varied and interesting lives. She was the only one in the course who was divorced, a fact that sparked an interesting conversation in a nearby restaurant where the students congregated one evening.

"Why didn't you just divorce your philandering husband?" one female student asked.

Ivy took a moment or two to answer. "I loved and hated Red at the same time, so I chose to start with a separation agreement."

"I suppose divorce is permanent," the inquiring student said thoughtfully. "You're the first divorcee I've met." The word *divorcee* seemed awkward on the young woman's tongue.

"Marriage with Red was very confusing. Looking back, I think he wanted me to fight to stop his philandering. Despite his business success, he never felt confident after being rejected for enlistment. Going to war was the definition of manhood."

"You show real understanding," the student said admiringly.

"Not without counselling. Womanizing, I've concluded, made Red feel manly."

Clara guaranteed the bank loan, and Ivy purchased a green Morris Mini in Toronto, which allowed her to drive back to the Soo rather than pay for the car's delivery. She made the trip in two days, staying in Sudbury overnight. When she arrived back in the Soo, she was ready to begin her life as a single mother of two with a job. Now, turning left off Pim Street onto Hilltop Crescent, she stepped on the gas pedal. She knew the girls would be thrilled to see the new car. As soon as she was in front of her house, Ivy honked, aware that Clara would chide her, and the girls rushed out. Clara had kept them home from school to be at the house when Ivy arrived.

Before they even inspected the car, Alice delivered an urgent message that their neighbour across the street, Milton Redman, had spanked Nora for showing his son, Marvin, her bum.

"Well," Clara said, "Mr. White did come here indignantly to justify his actions." She rolled her eyes. "'Mr. White,'" I said, "'the first time children expose themselves, I call it science. If they do it again, I'll tell them it's bad. You shouldn't have spanked my granddaughter.'"

"Let's inspect the new car with Granny," Ivy said. "If a bum inspection is all that went wrong, you've had a good time while I was in Toronto."

CHAPTER 57

Armed with the practical knowledge she had gained in her welfare course, Ivy settled into her tiny office on the second floor of the courthouse with twelve hundred files on her desk.

"Get familiar with the cases before going on the road," Russ said. "Old-age allowance, disability pension, and single mothers' benefits make up most of your case files."

As she ploughed through case after case, Ivy found that *desertion, alcoholism*, and *physical violence* were the words that stood out. In each scenario, the person or family had to "qualify" to get any benefit. This troubled Ivy.

"Wouldn't 'benefit from,' rather than 'qualify for,' be a better way to express the need for social assistance?" Ivy asked Russ. "Means tests are degrading."

"I'm of the old school and believe recipients of welfare must prove their cases," Russ replied.

The Morris Mini was economical on gas but stylish enough to please her girls. Ivy also needed warm clothes if she was to be on the road in winter. The local weatherman predicted an Arctic winter. Most people ignored his warnings, but Ivy went to Friedman's Department Store to buy practical outdoor clothes. Previously, she had dressed in Montreal chic. She joked with the saleslady after choosing a burnt orange car coat with a beaver collar, lined leather gloves, and brown wool hat with leather trim. "Will I look too stylish for my clients?" she asked, gazing at the dressing room mirror.

"You look like a woman who can help them," the saleslady responded with an admiring grin.

Once Ivy's divorce came through, the difficulties of a divorced parent began. Alice arrived home from school in tears one day. She didn't want to fill in the mandatory form that asked: "What is your father's occupation?"

Ivy wrote "non-applicable" in the allotted space, but the teacher sent Alice back home with a note: "Put anything you want, Mrs. Donnelly, but you must fill in that space."

Frustrated but not wanting to make a fuss that would further humiliate Alice, Ivy wrote "boat captain" in the allotted space. "The question is to find out if a father has lost his job so the school can react accordingly," Ivy said, disguising her indignation. She was facing her own challenges. The minister who had married her in the Anglican Church had passed her by at the Communion rail, never offering her the cup.

Soon after Nora started school, she, too, arrived home crying. "The teacher strapped me," she blurted through her sobs.

Ivy arranged a meeting with Fanny Pace, Nora's teacher.

"Your daughter's been swallowing her classmates' goiter pills," Miss Pace said indignantly as soon as Ivy took a seat in her classroom. "I found Nora standing at the fountain with her hand out. The pills taste like chocolate to ensure each child takes a pill."

"Well, I guess that's why Nora liked swallowing them," Ivy replied.

"She's showing off because she misses her father," Miss Pace countered with a defiant cock of her head.

"Strapping Nora won't help. I told my daughter that every child has a gland that needs the iodine in the pill or a big bump will grow on the neck. I showed her a picture of a goiter. Nora will swallow only one pill from now on."

Ivy left Miss Pace's chalk-smelling classroom with the cruel reality that her girls were the only children in the school to have divorced parents. It was an unexpected benefit that Clara, who had been a distant mother, was now throwing herself into enjoying her granddaughters. She had become a vital presence, permitting Ivy to do her job without worrying.

The courthouse was a stimulating environment. Lawyers, criminals, reporters, police officers, witnesses, and couples waiting to be married paced back and forth in the hallway. Some fell asleep on the same bench where Ivy had waited to see Adam Wright. If Adam was in the courthouse on a case, he never failed to stick his head in to see how she was doing. Ivy knew some of the corridor-pacing characters from her welfare work. It wasn't unusual for Magistrate Langdon or one of the lawyers to ask her questions "off the record" about family circumstances that might mitigate a committed offence. She offered information concerning sickness, unemployment, desertion, abuse, and death, which might influence the outcome of a case. The lives of her clients mattered.

Many of Ivy's clients were Native families. They lived on reserves east or north of the Soo, where some houses resembled temporary shelters. She had come to know more about the hurdles facing Native people when William Martin had recuperated at Clara's. He never talked about his years at the residential school. However, like Albert, his grandfather, he loved to talk, and Ivy was a good listener.

It was the intervention of Dr. Chas Greer that insured William would have the modern artificial limb that had been denied his grandfather. Alcohol abuse plagued some of the reserves, and Ivy was often involved when these issues resulted in problems for the families. Clara would accompany Ivy on these calls for safety. In an effort to understand the law surrounding Natives and alcohol, Ivy sat in on a court proceeding. The owner of a bar was being fined for posting a sign: NO INDIANS.

Magistrate Langdon clarified the law for the courtroom audience. "Natives have the right to purchase alcohol in a bar but not in a government outlet."

Ivy had heard of the "Indian List." The only person she knew on this list was a doctor's wife. She left the hearing with a better understanding of the issue. The government believed alcohol was the problem and ignored the pitiful housing conditions and many other hardships on reserves. She could see that the opportunities she had for re-education wouldn't be given to a Native person.

"I condemn government prejudice as much as Clara does," she muttered back in her office.

CHAPTER 58

Among the hard-nosed lawyers in the courthouse, Ivy had a special place, since she was the only woman they considered educated. Marc Russo was a softer sort of person than the other counsellors. He was a shy man and a confirmed bachelor, which suited Ivy, and they became friends. Her outgoing nature complemented his more restrained personality. He was quiet with a dry sense of humour that Ivy appreciated. Alice and Nora thought Marc was marvellous. He could pull napkins out of his ear and perform many other magic tricks. Entertaining the girls, he made up stories, mostly about heroic Italians. He was the celebrated native son of the Soo's west end community.

Ivy hadn't realized how much going through a divorce and finding a job had changed her until a lawyer, waiting for his turn in court, came into her office with a coffee. "My wife admires you for staying active in the May Court Club. She thought you'd find the ladies boring. She did say she found you a bit flighty when you came back from Montreal."

Ivy smiled. "That's a backhanded compliment, but I'll take it."

"I think that's how my wife meant it."

Marc entered the office just as his colleague was leaving. "You're looking a bit downhearted." He grinned. "Are you up for some Italian food?"

"Just a little thoughtful today. Do I have time to make a quick call on the way to lunch? I have a client who has to sign a form to get the government to send her old-age allowance. It'll only take a minute. She lives on John Street on the way to the restaurant."

Marc agreed, and they left the office. After driving to the client's place, Marc waited in the car while Ivy popped in to complete her errand. As soon as she returned, they drove on to Cleto's Restaurant, which was packed with corpulent Italian men enjoying wine and pasta.

The waiter knew Marc and led them to a quieter table near a window overlooking Gore Street. Ivy watched as the patrons twisted their forks and shoved spaghetti in their mouths. She did the same, checking with her napkin that she hadn't dribbled sauce on her chin.

"Do I seem flighty?" Ivy asked Marc, tilting her head. She expected an honest answer.

"What on earth makes you ask that?"

Ivy related the lawyer's comments about his wife's opinion of her.

"I think you're fun, not flighty." Marc kicked Ivy's shoe under the table. "What's up?"

"Looking back at my life with Red, I think what I thought was funny was actually inappropriate. I believe it hurt Red."

"So get it off your chest, Ivy. It's not like you to be so morose."

"There was talk in 1941 that Red might run as the Liberal Member of Parliament. Lester Pearson was in the Soo to check out the situation. Red was financially secure, a father of one child, and had a family that went back three generations. People still remembered his grandfather, I.J., the oversized chief of police. Red seemed an ideal candidate."

"As a philanderer," Marc said quietly.

"That wasn't well known back then. I was to entertain Pearson in the evening. Red took him out on Lake Superior during the day. Pearson returned to the Windsor Hotel to change and then arrived with two colleagues for dinner. He had visited the Soo earlier in 1935 as part of a royal commission on price spreads. Pearson was an important man in the federal public service. I organized a lovely dinner with venison pie as the main dish and chocolate éclairs for dessert. In retrospect, what I did wasn't funny."

"So what was so terrible that it's still bothering you so many years later?"

"It was the comment about my flightiness that brought back the memory."

"So what did you do, Ivy?"

"I put shaving cream in everyone's dessert. I had proper desserts in the kitchen to serve once the joke was over."

Marc laughed. "So what happened? You were playing a prank to lighten the atmosphere."

"I thought a successful man like Pearson would enjoy the joke. And he seemed to. 'I wouldn't be much of a statesman if I didn't know the difference between shaving and whipping cream,' he said, handing back his dessert. But Red never got the nomination. I think subconsciously I was angry about his philandering. I never confronted him. Maybe that was my way of getting back. It was a flighty moment, and I wouldn't do something like that again."

"Then that would be a shame," Marc said. "Your éclair ruse had nothing to do with Red not being nominated, and it sounds like you had a fun evening."

CHAPTER 59

Ivy's frequent road trips on business had made her an excellent winter driver. Despite occasional encounters with wildlife, snow-drifts, and glare ice on the highway, she felt safe on the road. Ivy wasn't as confident, however, about her trip by air to Wawa. It was mid-February, and as the weatherman had predicted, very cold. She was to travel north with Keith Messenger, an experienced bush pilot. This was Ivy's fourth month as a welfare officer but her third trip to Wawa — her first by air. Previously, she had taken the Algoma Central Railway train. She had six files in her briefcase and had reviewed them all before leaving to make sure there were no missing government forms to be signed.

Keith was a man's man, and weather rarely provided him with a reason not to fly. That morning, while it was still dark, Sergeant Stuart accompanied Ivy as she left her house. The provincial police officer normally on call for northern trips was unavailable, so the ser-geant filled in. Keith greeted them at the airport, leaning against his ski-equipped Norseman. He asked Ivy to sit with him in the cockpit.

"Don't worry. I'll get you home to sleep in your own bed," he reassured her as he revved the plane.

There was nothing to see but blue sky, white snow, and forest. Two hours later, they landed on Wawa Lake in the middle of a raging snowstorm. A car with chains on the wheels clanged across the frozen lake to meet them. Drifting snow made it hard to see the shoreline, but the experienced driver managed to get them off the lake and into town where Keith had business. Ivy went on with Sergeant Stuart and Stan Nahdee, a local Cree, who was to drive her to the homes of her numerous clients. Stan lived outside Wawa and was familiar with the area.

Her last call was to Stella Brownlee, a Cree woman whose file Ivy had inherited from Russ Thompson. The wind had picked up, leaving drifts that narrowed the navigable roadway. Every road sign was buried in the six-foot snowbanks.

"My notes show Mrs. Brownlee lives in that house coming up," Ivy said.

Stan stopped the car, rolled down the window, and leaned out to brush snow off a mailbox. "It says Brownlee."

Sergeant Stuart shifted to speak to Ivy in the back seat. "Are you sure you don't want me to come with you?"

"Stella trusts me," Ivy said. "She's been to my office in the Soo on several matters. It's a complicated family situation, and I have to deliver some bad news."

"How long will you be?" the sergeant asked.

"As long as it takes."

Stan laughed. "We'll wait on the road buried in snow."

Sergeant Stuart jumped out into the blizzard and used his foot to lever the back door open, which gave way with a crunch of scraping metal. Then Ivy passed the sergeant her briefcase and scrambled out.

"If you fall in a snowbank, we'll know where to find you in that orange coat," the sergeant quipped.

Ivy pulled the brown fur collar up and the hat down over her ears and trudged through the snow of the unshovelled walkway. *I shall buy taller boots*, she thought as snow packed in against her ankles. Plastic sheets stapled over the windows billowed and flapped with each gust of wind. Ivy hesitated before stepping into the plywood porch that leaned away from the blowing. She rapped hard, and Stella, wearing a brown jersey wool skirt and pink sweater, came to the door in her deerskin slippers. A mongrel dog growled in the doorway.

"Does he bite?" Ivy asked, separating herself from the dog with her briefcase.

"Come in, Mrs. D. The dog's fine. I didn't expect you'd come in weather like this." Stella took Ivy's coat and hung it on the tip of an antler that served as a coat rack. "Put your boots by the stove to dry." She moved away from the door. "You'd be comfortable on the sofa. It's the back seat of a Studebaker. We're lucky to have any furniture at all." She sat on an iron cot piled with blankets, then motioned that her daughter, Cindy, and her boyfriend were asleep in the bedroom.

The flimsy hollow door had a hole in it that Ivy assumed was a kick from a boot. "Stella, you're in a tough situation that I hope to mitigate."

Heat radiated from a wood stove where a bucket of melting snow caused small drips to sizzle on the stove. Stella leaned over and tossed in a log.

"Is the pump frozen again?" Ivy asked, contemplating the piles of dishes, laundry, and liquor bottles.

Stella shrugged. "I pack that bucket to the top with snow and half an hour later I got nothing but two inches of water, hardly enough to make tea." She cocked her head toward the bedroom. "They wouldn't have hangovers if they'd been drinking tea. Her boyfriend just laughs when I suggest that."

"That's why I'm here, Stella. The courts are worried about sending your granddaughter back. Sylvie's in a nice home with kids her own age. And she's doing well in school."

"What right do the courts have to decide what's best for my family?"

Ivy slid sideways on the green vinyl sofa to get off the spring pushing into her buttocks. "It's a wonder this place hasn't burned down." She stuck a finger into a cigarette burn on the sofa. "Alcohol and wood houses are a bad mix."

"Mrs. D., I'm a good *kokum*."

Ivy came over to sit beside Stella on the bed. "I know you're a good grandmother."

"It's the boyfriend who's the problem. Every time they get drinking, he gets angry." She took in a large breath and let it out with an audible sigh.

"Listen, Stella, each punch has been recorded at the hospital. Do you want your granddaughter to grow up seeing her mother being hit?"

"I don't see no good coming of a Cree child growing up in a white family."

"I've seen Sylvie and she's happy," Ivy said. "I can get Cindy into a rehab program. She needs to be sober for at least three months before the courts will let Sylvie return. Stella, you have to kick the boyfriend out. Since you have legal custody of your granddaughter, you must sign the form to allow the foster parents to keep Sylvie for another three months so she doesn't go into a government home. Trust me, Stella."

"It's not you I don't trust, Mrs. D. It's the damn system that's so stacked against us."

Ivy stood up. "Do you want me to haul that man out of bed and send him packing?"

Stella looked frightened. "He'd hit you, Mrs. D."

"The police can remove him, then."

Stella put her hand on Ivy's arm. "We need to settle our own problems." She signed the form Ivy had taken from her briefcase, then shook Ivy's hand. "I know you mean well."

"Send him packing," Ivy repeated, "then we'll get Sylvie back to her *kokum*."

Stan and Sergeant Stuart were standing beside the car when Ivy came out of Stella's. Their worried looks disappeared.

When they arrived in town, Keith was in the bar chatting with a group of miners from the Helen Mines.

"Is it safe to fly?" Ivy asked.

"I wouldn't fly if it wasn't."

"Keith will fly above the turbulence," Sergeant Stuart assured.

"I've got family, too," Keith said. "And I intend to get back to them." Keith's confidence was backed up by well-chronicled heroism.

Ivy stood quietly, trying not to worry while Keith knocked back his drink.

"Thanks for the round!" one of the men shouted as they left.

Keith glanced back with a grin. "Next time the chit's on you." He made a thumbs-up sign and put his arm around Ivy as he ushered her out the door and into the snowstorm. "You're a plucky gal."

Once in the plane, Ivy began to think about her pluck. "Pluck didn't come easily, Keith!" she shouted across the engine noise. "My mother was confrontational. She didn't know how to compromise. I didn't want to be the same."

"It was your mother's pluck that turned the Galt Hospital around," Sergeant Stuart said. "But it's her integrity that I admire most."

Keith laughed. "Hey, Sergeant Stuart, you sound smitten."

"At sixty I don't talk about love, but I do appreciate living in Mrs. Durling's upper duplex," the sergeant replied.

Silence prevailed as Keith dealt with an increase in turbulence.

CHAPTER 60

The flight from Wawa had been much shorter than travelling by train would have been. When they arrived in the Soo, the streets still hadn't been cleared. So when Sergeant Stuart eased his car away from the airstrip, he drove slowly despite Ivy's urging to go faster to get home to her girls.

"I hope Alice and Nora weren't too much for Clara," Ivy said as they neared Clara's duplex.

"Your mother can cope with anything," the sergeant said.

His further comments were cut short as they turned onto Hilltop. Clara's duplex and Ivy's house were entirely lit up, but it was Chas Greer's car in Clara's driveway that signalled to Ivy and the sergeant that something dreadful had happened.

They pulled up behind the doctor's car, and Ivy dashed in. Still in her winter coat, Clara was lying on the front hall floor covered with a blanket.

"Granny was shovelling the walk," Alice said, sobbing. "She said she wouldn't wait for Sergeant Stuart. She wanted you to have a clear path."

"It was her heart," Chas said. "She wouldn't have suffered."

Dot was sitting on the stairs, trying to calm Nora.

Ivy pulled the cover back, choking as she spoke. "How could you do this, Mum? I had something I needed to say — that I love you."

Sergeant Stuart knelt and put his arm around Ivy. "You didn't have to. You showed it every day."

Ivy stood and put her arms around Alice. "What happened, darling?"

"I was getting dressed to go out and help Granny when she fell. I tried to pull her by her coat into the house, but I couldn't. I ran to Dr. Chas's house, and he helped me bring her in." Alice heaved through her sobbing.

"We'll all mourn Clara," Chas said. "She kept us on our toes."

Lily and Barnaby came out of the kitchen where they had been preparing coffee.

"It'll be a long night," Lily said. They had both been crying.

"Our friendship started thirty years ago," Barnaby said emotionally.

"Well," Lily said, tears streaming down her face, "I guess I'll be the battler now that Clara's gone."

Lily's humour was a reminder that Clara was sometimes mad but never sad. "You don't have time for that," Clara would say to a moping friend.

"The coroner will be here soon," Chas said. "Are you up to choosing an outfit?"

"Maybe tomorrow," Ivy said. "I'll speak with the girls. I don't want them to watch the coroner remove Clara."

Dot tucked Alice and Nora into Ivy's bed, and Lily served coffee. It was too soon to reminisce. When it was two in the morning, Ivy said she wanted to be alone. Chas asked if she needed any medication, but Ivy refused.

After everyone was gone, Ivy stood at the French windows and looked at the blanket of snow illuminated by a full moon. She could feel Red's arms around her waist as he talked about the garden they would plant in their new home. She could smell his pipe breath. Then she turned to see if Clara was in the chair where she normally sat. Loneliness felt like a second skin.

Alice was determined that Clara should be buried in the dress she'd worn to Ivy's wedding. A mauve dress overlaid with lace didn't seem appropriate, but Ivy respected the choice because the girls had spent so much time with Clara.

"I know this is what Granny would want to wear," Alice said, as though Clara were still alive.

Ivy didn't take Alice to the funeral home. She wanted to see her mother's preparation herself. To her horror, the funeral director had put a considerable amount of makeup on Clara.

"My mother's never worn makeup," Ivy said to the person who had applied the stuff.

"Oh, then I'll remove it," the man said apologetically.

"I should do that myself," Ivy said quietly. Alone in the room with Clara, she etched in her head the wholesome English face she would never see again. "I did love you, Mum, and I'm sorry I didn't say that enough."

She began to cry and moved away from the casket, which would remain open at the funeral. Seeing her mother motionless in her mother-of-the-bride dress, she recalled Clara's pride at putting on such a grand wedding for her only daughter. At that moment, the funeral director came into the room to see if he could help.

"I'll go home now and plan the funeral," Ivy said simply.

CHAPTER 61

Clara's fatal heart attack had occurred late on a Friday afternoon in 1952. By Saturday morning, a dozen casseroles and desserts had been delivered to the house with notes expressing heartfelt condolences. The road without Clara was frightening for Ivy. *Who will look after the girls while I'm travelling?* she thought with panic. Clara's stolid presence had been Ivy's insurance that Red could never take the girls if anything happened to her, but Ivy settled her fears with the realization that Hilltop neighbours had embraced Alice and Nora when Red left. They would run interference if he tried to take them away.

Despite her dark thoughts and grief, Ivy made arrangements for a visitation at the Mather Funeral Home from four to six on Sunday evening and the funeral at St. Luke's Cathedral the following day. In the midst of people flowing in and out of the house offering help or just doing what they thought was needed, Ivy went looking for Alice and Nora. She started her search in the upstairs bedrooms, descended to the basement playroom, and finally checked the garage where in happier times Red had skinned the deer. They were nowhere.

"They weren't dressed very warmly," Lily said. "I saw them cross the street to Clara's. Would you like me to bring them back?"

"No, I'll go myself," Ivy answered. There was a catch in her voice. "I think I know where I'll find them."

The door to Clara's apartment was open, and Sergeant Stuart stood in the living room with a finger on his lips. Ivy entered quietly and tiptoed to the top of the basement stairs. The shelf adjacent to the stairs provided storage for Clara's canned goods and cleaning supplies. A jar of Marmite and a can of Lyle's Golden Syrup were the symbols that Clara remained British to the end. Alice and Nora were sitting on their coats, leaning against Clara's steamer trunk. Alice was holding the forbidden rose and telling Nora the story of the little boy who wanted to be a gardener. Nora was wearing the boots marked "Billy" that had only occasionally been removed from the trunk. Ivy was overcome with love, noticing they were on the wrong feet.

Alice glanced up, her face stained with tears, as Ivy descended the stairs. "Can we put the rose in Granny's coffin? She can take it to Billy."

"Billy's in heaven surrounded by flowers, but I'm sure he'd love to see his rose," Ivy said. "Shall we put the rose in one of Granny's lavender-smelling handkerchiefs? The flower's very delicate."

Sergeant Stuart drove Ivy and the girls to the funeral home in advance of the visitation. Ivy had expected they would have a few minutes alone with Clara. She was surprised that so many visitors were standing in the foyer, waiting for the affair to begin. Lily and Barnaby acted as hosts, and Alice and Nora stood beside them after seeing Clara. She seemed peaceful in an open casket, arms folded on her lap and unadorned with makeup. The most extravagant flower arrangement had come from the Pim Hill Children, each having signed his own name. There was a drawing of a dog paw on the corner of the card signed "Nipper" — Clara's favourite of the Greer dogs.

Messages sent from out-of-towners unable to get to the funeral were reminders of Clara's long life and varied paths. Di Shaw's telegram recounted waving at Clara and young Ivy from the quay as their ship pulled away. Etta Iverson and her daughter, Katherine, Ivy's best friend in Lethbridge, wired flowers with a note that made Ivy cry. "Your mother was the kindest person I've ever known," she wrote. Miss Hobbs, the director of nurses at Royal Victoria Hospital, sent a humorous reminder of the probationer's military-like regime under Clara. "Matron Durling was always one step ahead of our shenanigans," she recounted. "I recall our indignation when she cut off the lower rung of the fire escape ladder."

Ivy had pinned the notes to a corkboard so visitors could see the many hats Clara had worn. Condolences from the new headmaster at Shingwauk were the evidence that Clara had never severed her connection with the residential school. Dr. McCaig, who had retired, expressed high praise for Clara's work integrating the Wawanosh girls.

As the visitors flowed past, most with anecdotes about Clara, Ivy was struck, as she was with the personal notes, at how diverse Clara's life had been. Her mother's bridge cronies, including the Rossiters, the new headmaster of Shingwauk, and three new doctors who had moved onto Hilltop while Ivy was at her welfare course in Toronto, expressed their admiration for Clara. The new neighbours hadn't been on the street long before they discovered Clara — the "dog whisperer." Ivy was touched that Irma D'Agostina, married now and living in the east end with her husband, who was a dentist, came to the funeral home. She spoke warmly of Clara, and Ivy realized that somehow Clara must have made peace with Italians.

William Martin, looking steady on his artificial leg, told Ivy he was now the caretaker of the Greers' farm on St. Joseph Island. Ivy asked about William's grandfather, Albert, and learned he had passed away. "Matron Durling was the only white woman Granddad liked. She was very kind to me while I stayed in her home until my leg healed."

Ivy's friends, who had spent so many happy hours touring the Great Lakes on the *Ivy League*, lingered after they went through the formal condolence line. They were planning to have a drink at the end of the visitation, which went on longer than the allotted two hours. The director of the funeral home assured Ivy there was no need to rush.

Before going to the Greers', Ivy asked to have a few minutes alone with Clara. The Barnabys took Alice and Nora and went to wait in the parking lot. When they were gone, Ivy placed a hand on Clara's forehead and lightly brushed back her wiry grey hair. "I'll remember your sacrifices when I make my own," she whispered.

ACKNOWLEDGEMENTS

I want to thank my husband, who read endless drafts only to find I disagreed with his comments. The encouragement from friends and family is what kept me writing when I wished to throw in the towel. Roberta Jamieson, a Mohawk of the Six Nations Grand River Territory and an extraordinary Canadian, read the entire manuscript to ensure it was neither racist nor appropriating a culture that wasn't mine. David Staines, writer, literary critic, and editor, has faithfully read and commented on various iterations of *Patchwork Society*. I didn't argue with David. Joe Kertes, former dean of creative arts at Humber College in Toronto, is how my writing career began, and I'll always be grateful for his ongoing encouragement.

There are many people I can't acknowledge because they're no longer alive. I'm grateful for the personal letters of K.G. Ross given to me by his grandchildren. His personal accounts of life in the bush surveying hydro lines working alongside local Indigenous people was culturally informative. The cruel truth of the assimilation policy and what it did to our First Nations communities was gleaned from many public archives. Medical records, government records, truth-and-reconciliation statements, and documents from the Shingwauk project at Algoma University provided a trove of information for writing this novel.

Italians have a long history in Sault Ste. Marie, and Judge Ray Stortini supplied a rich source of cultural and social history in his two-volume personal account of Little Italy and its inhabitants. Personal interviews gave insight into the bootlegging industry that was often the only way families survived through the Great Depression years.

I'm especially grateful to Kirk Howard and Dundurn Press, who took a chance on my first book, *Matrons and Madams*.

Finally, I must thank my mother and grandmother post-humously for the brave lives they lived, which I have faithfully tried to record in my novel.